# BENEATH
## THE DARK ICE

# BENEATH
## THE DARK ICE

Greig Beck

St. Martin's Paperbacks

This is a work of fiction. All of the characters, organizations, and events portrayed in this novel are either products of the author's imagination or are used fictitiously.

First published in 2009 by Pan Macmillan Australia Pty Limited

BENEATH THE DARK ICE

For information address St. Martin's Press, 175 Fifth Avenue, New York, NY 10010.

ISBN: 978-0-312-59979-9

Printed in the United States of America

Pan Macmillan Australia trade paperback edition published in 2009
St. Martin's Paperbacks edition / September 2010

St. Martin's Paperbacks are published by St. Martin's Press, 175 Fifth Avenue, New York, NY 10010.

10  9  8  7  6  5  4  3  2  1

*For Barbara, who still makes it fun.*

# Acknowledgements

I want to thank my wife, Barbara Weir, whose eye for detail is second to none, my son Alexander for making me laugh every day, and Cate Paterson, Joel Naoum, and Nicola O'Shea for their editorial skill, patience, and good humour, and for showing me how to turn a story into a book. Thank you.

In 1996, Russian and British scientists discovered a warm-water lake two and half miles beneath the Antarctic ice. "Lake Vostok" as it has been named, is the size of Lake Ontario and biologists suspect that it may contain life forms that have been unseen on the surface for millions of years.

Hundreds of these hidden bodies of water are thought to exist all around the world.

# Prologue

The Colony of Roanoke Island, 1587

Eleanor cradled baby Virginia in her arms and smiled at the little pink sleeping face. She was the first baby born on the island and the colonists were delighted by her arrival, seeing it as a good omen for the new outpost.

Roanoke's late spring sunshine bathed the new mother and baby in a warm comforting blanket as Eleanor sang a soft lullaby to her snuffling infant.

John White, Eleanor's father and the island's Governor, was proud of what he'd achieved. This was the golden age of colonisation for England and it looked to be another year where his homeland flexed its muscles and attempted to further expand its global domain. Earlier that decade, in 1583, Sir Humphrey Gilbert had claimed Newfoundland as England's first overseas colony and now Roanoke was set to be the first English colony in the New World.

Governor White was making sure all was well before he reluctantly returned to England to collect more provisions. Roanoke Island was long and narrow, and lay just off the coast between the mainland and the treacherous Outer Banks of the Atlantic Ocean. White knew the surrounding waters were cold and an uninviting grey-green, as the freezing currents of the Atlantic encircled the twelve miles of land. But thankfully the island itself was an oasis of dense marshes, low-grassed meadows and tall oak forests teeming with game.

The local Indians were on the whole a friendly but strange bunch, sometimes timid and at other times aggressive, shouting loudly at the colonists to warn them away from particular tracts of the forest. White found that as long as they stayed within certain areas of the island there was never any trouble. A sporadic but uneasy trading relationship developed and overall White was satisfied the indigenous population posed no threat to the group.

White's main concern had been that the site of the settlement was not as secure as he would like from the heavy sea storms that kicked up out of the Atlantic. Their site was too close to the shoreline, and now that babies were being born, he was determined to ensure that no unplanned-for risks would endanger his new colony, particularly as he would be absent for months.

White had organised a small party of men to search the surrounding areas for naturally sheltered areas that could be retreated to in times of harsh weather. Within a week the men had reported back that they had found a large cave opening, and though there seemed to be an odd smell emanating from its depths it seemed well protected, dry and large enough for all one hundred colonists. White had ordered that water barrels be placed inside the cavern. Looking at the provisions, he hoped that he'd done all that was necessary to secure the colony and he turned to board his ship for the return to England.

Eleanor made her way down to a soft grassy spot beside the clear stream just outside of the settlement. She came to this part of the riverbank to wash Virginia's tiny clothes and let them dry on the flat rocks beside the water. When she met the young Indian girl, it seemed natural that they would become friends.

Incara, as Eleanor had learned was her name, came to the bank to do her daily chores around the same time, and it wasn't long before a wave and a smile became an opportunity to sit together and show off their first-borns. Though neither could speak the other's language they managed to communicate and connect as young, new mothers.

Eleanor pulled her shawl closer and looked up to the sky; dark clouds were racing across from the west and rain looked to be imminent. She rose to her feet with Virginia in her arms and made her farewell to Incara who smiled up at her and tried to mimic both the wave and the words. Eleanor giggled at the attempt; perhaps she would make Incara a dress, depending on how much fabric her father returned with.

The wind was rising quickly so Eleanor picked up her pace for the walk back to the colony. The horizon was now heavy with enormous purple clouds that threatened to burst like boils over the island. Just as she was entering the clearing at the very edge of the colony, Eleanor's husband, Ananias, met her and pulled her into a quick embrace. He was out of breath and already his blond hair was plastered down from the large drops of rain that were beginning to fall. He shouted over the top of the screaming wind that she should gather as much food and clothing as she could carry as the colony was going to take shelter in the caves to the south of the island.

Already, the ferocious wind was picking away some of the thatch and wooden shingles from the cabins and flinging them like knives throughout the camp. The rain, catapulted by the strong wind gusts, was now stinging their faces as they made their way to the centre of the camp. Eleanor spotted Incara in the tree line looking extremely agitated and motioned for her to come closer. Incara ran to her and tried to pull her away while vigorously shaking her head and gesticulating wildly in the direction of the caves. Over and over she repeated a word that sounded like "croatoan" with wide, imploring eyes. She made waving motions with her arms and hugged herself tightly. Oddly, this gesture did not seem to be an attempt to give an impression of trying to stay warm, but to impart a feeling of struggling or crushing.

Eleanor's father had said that the local natives believed everything was the work of spirits, good and bad, and the weather was no exception. Eleanor gave her a quick hug and headed off to the cave with the last few colonists.

Incara had repeated the word *croatoan* so many times that Eleanor took it to mean the name of the caves they were heading to, and just in case they were still there when her father returned, she asked Ananias to carve the word into the large tree at the edge of the camp so her father or anyone wishing to know their whereabouts would only need to ask the Indians for directions.

Incara hurried back to her father, Manteo, the chief of the Roanoke tribe. He was consulting with his holy men around the fire in the centre of their hut and she fell to her knees in front of him, gasping out where the colonists were heading. Though the Roanoke were mostly indifferent to the settlers, they knew the dangers of the caverns. Generations ago the ground had shaken and opened the cavern to the light of the surface. Incara had heard the legends of the hungry caves and it had been many years since any young hunter had been foolish enough to venture into them. Those who had were never seen again.

The weather was now quite violent and tribal taboos forbade all Roanoke from venturing into or even near the caves. However, Manteo knew of the bond that had formed between Incara and the white "Eleanor," and Incara was greatly relieved when her father announced he would send his strongest warriors to try and stop the colonists. Against her father's wishes, Incara went with them.

The small party of Indians made it to the cave just as the last of the colonists were disappearing inside and beginning to seal the entrance against the elements. Incara called out and was rewarded by both Eleanor and Ananias appearing briefly at the cave mouth. The image Incara and the warriors saw was one that would stay with them forever: Eleanor standing in the rain, cradling her baby daughter. As she smiled and waved goodbye to Incara, Ananias's head snapped around as though he had been called and he raced back into the cave. Eleanor turned to look over her shoulder as shouts started to echo from the depths and then she too hurried into the darkness.

It was only a few short minutes before the screaming started and the moaning began. The sounds of pure animal fear and distress emanating from the cave made Incara sink to her knees and wail loudly. She grabbed handfuls of wet leaves and earth and covered her head and face in anguish. Even the brave Roanoke warriors were ashen-faced with fear as the screams rang out then were cut off one by one. Manteo stared into the cave for many minutes, remembering the ancient legends, knowing what they would mean to his people. He turned away from the cave, he had decided; they would leave the island immediately.

John White had not intended to be away for as long as he was but well before he landed he knew there was trouble. There were no small fishing boats on the water, no smoke from fires. At the site of the camp there were no signs of life—no people, only the remains of collapsed huts; already the forest had started to reclaim the site back from his clearing. The single clue was the word *CROATOAN* carved on a tree in ragged capitals.

Weeks of searching refused to reveal any trace of his beautiful daughter, her baby, or any of the other colonists. In fact, the local Indians had also departed and the distressed Governor's only hope was that Eleanor was safe with them, wherever that might be.

# One

In the final seconds before impact, John "Buck" Banyon, arguably one of the wealthiest hotel owners in North America, released the U-shaped steering column. He folded his large arms over his chest, obscuring the hand-stitched, gold lettering across a bomber jacket that simply read "Buck." He knew he was as good as dead as soon as the engine restart had failed and all the other backup systems which had at first gone crazy winked out one by one. There was no time now for another restart and bailing out was a joke in this weather. He snorted at the white-filled cockpit screen and whispered a final "fuck it," as the altimeter told him the ground was just about in his face.

Banyon had invited his senior executive team and their wives or lovers on a reward-for-service flight in his private jet, the *Perseus*—a one-day flight out of southern Australia over the Antarctic. He had made the trip several times alone and this time he hoped to show his young Turks that there was more to Buck Banyon than making money and eighteen-hour days. There was such rare and exotic beauty here; you could keep your wildlife colonies—he could see a fucking penguin at the zoo any day. But down here he had seen things only a handful of people on earth had witnessed: rare green sunsets where the sun hovered at the

horizon for hours and a band of emerald flashed out between ice and sky; floating ice mountains caused by the
stillness of the air creating the mirage of an ice peak which
seemed to lift off and hover hundreds of feet above the
ground.

He should have known better; you fall in love with the
Antarctic and she'll hurt you. Buck had forgotten one thing;
she was as beautiful as she was unpredictable. Even though
he had checked the meteorology service before leaving, the
icy continent had surprised him with a monstrous katabatic
flow jump. She hid them behind mountains and deep crevices; and then when you were close enough she revealed
them in all their ferocious power—mile-high walls of snow
and wind and fury that climbed rapidly over a rise in the
landscape.

Light that was once so clean and clear you could see
for hundreds of miles in all directions suddenly became
confused and scattered by rushing snow and ice. The result was a freezing whiteout where the sky and the ground
became one and there was no more horizon. In seconds,
temperatures dropped by a hundred degrees and winds
jumped by that amount again. A rule book didn't exist for
what to do when you were caught within one; you just
avoided them—and once inside them, a plane just ceased
to exist.

Buck's ten passengers were not as calm as he was; the
cacophony from the main cabin resembled something from
one of Dante's stories on the torments of hell. Martinis and
cocktails were voided onto the plush velvet seats which the
passengers were crushed back into as they felt the combi-
nation of velocity and steep descent.

The seventy-foot white dart fell at roughly 500 miles
per hour towards the Antarctic ice on a terminal pitch; its
small but powerful turbofan jets had ceased to function in
the blasting icy air above the blinding white landscape.

As it plummeted towards the desolate ice plains below it was all but silent, save for a high-pitched whistling that could have been mistaken for a lost snow petrel calling to its fellow wanderers. This too vanished in the louder scream of the ferocious katabatic storm pummelling the skin of the sleek metal bird.

The initial impact, when it came, was more like the sound of a giant pillow striking an unmade bed than the metallic explosive noise of 30,000 pounds of metal impacting on a hard surface. A funnel-shaped plume of snow and ice was blown a hundred feet into the air, followed by a secondary spout of rock, debris and a hollow boom as the once sleek Challenger jet at last struck solid stone. The plane penetrated the ice surface like a bullet through glass, opening a ragged black hole into a cavern hundreds of feet below. The echoes of the impact reverberated down into the tunnels for miles, bouncing off walls and ceilings as the silent stone caught and then transferred the terrible sounds of the collision.

Silence once more returned to this subterranean world—but only briefly.

The creature lifted itself from the water and sampled the air. The vibrations from the high caverns drew forth a race memory dormant for generations as it dragged itself from its primordial lair in confusion. In its darkened world it had long learned to be silent, but the noises and vibrations from the ceiling caverns excited it and it rushed towards the high caves, making a sound like a river of boiling mud.

It would take hours for it to reach the crash site, but already it could detect the faint smell of molten alloy, fuel and something else—something none of its kind had sensed in many millennia. It moved its great mucous-covered bulk forward quickly, hunger now driving it onwards.

# Two

A band of warm Connecticut sunshine bathed Aimee Weir as she sipped her drink and looked up from her latest project results to stare evenly at her co-worker. With jet black hair and soft blue eyes, Aimee lived up to her Scottish bloodline. She was the first of her family of shop-keepers and boat builders to become a scientist, and her brilliance in the field of fossil fuel synthesis made her a sought-after commodity by resource-hungry corporations around the world. She was a tall woman of twenty-nine, with a way of setting her jaw and making her eyes go from soft to piercing that her friends referred to as the "Weir lasers." She was able to stare down the most fearsome university faculty or boardroom member and when push came to shove, she usually got her way. She finished her soda and directed that stare at Tom now.

"It won't do any good, Aimee; I'm not even going to look at you. I don't need to be blinded so early in the morning." Tom chuckled and continued to pour himself a coffee. Aimee could tell he knew she was looking at him and guessed he was playing it cool, hoping she would just blow off some steam for a while before giving him her blessing to go on the field trip. Tom stirred his cup noisily and continued, "Besides, I know you hate heights and we have to ropesail or something down into a frozen cave on, or rather I should say under, the Antarctic ice."

"Ha! It's called 'abseiling' or 'rappelling.' There is no such word as 'ropesailing.' And that heights thing happened a long time ago. It's not a phobia, Tom."

Tom sipped his coffee, making an exaggerated slurping sound. Aimee mouthed *OK then*, to his back. She tore a small fragment of paper from her computer printout and rolled it into a ball which she popped into her mouth, working it around a little more with her tongue. She lifted the straw from the small bottle and placed it in her mouth, took aim and fired the wet projectile at the back of Tom's head. Satisfyingly, it stuck to his neck.

"Yee-uck. I hate it when you do that." Tom wiped his neck with his hand and turned around. Aimee sat smiling with her left eyebrow raised and the straw dangling from her bottom lip.

She had known Tom for ten years, ever since he had been at her university spotting on behalf of his company. Even as a gangly, or as her father said "coltish," nineteen-year-old, her grades and natural scientific talent in the areas of biology and biogenic decomposition made her stand out from a crowded and impressive field. Her potential was a magnet to companies looking for the most valuable of corporate assets: intelligence. Tom had made her laugh till tears ran down her cheeks and humanised science more than any dry professor ever had. He was like an older brother and could still make her laugh today like that kid at university a decade ago, yet over the years he had looked out for her and guided her career and now she was one of the most respected petrobiologists in the world.

Tom Hendsen was the lead scientist working for GBR, a small research company that specialised in geological and biological research into fossil fuels, their discovery, use, synthesis and hopefully one day, replacement. He was

forty, slim and tall, with an easy laugh. Though they all had
an informal working relationship within GBR he was the
natural leader due to his maturity and encyclopedic knowledge of deep earth petrobiology.

Aimee loved Tom, but as with all sibling relationships
there were flare-ups—rare, but they happened; just like
now. Tom had been urgently requested by the government
to accompany a rescue mission to the Antarctic. A private
jet had gone down on the ice, or rather, through the ice. A
large cavern had been opened up and initial data received
indicated a large body of mid-crust liquid that could be
surface petroleum and natural gas. It was probably nothing more than screwy data or some illegal dumping ground
used by the numerous nations that visited the Antarctic for
everything from research to mining—nations that eyed
the continent hungrily as the last great unexplored, or rather
unravaged, continent on earth. However, it could also be
something significant; the Antarctic wasn't always covered in snow and ice and about 150 million years before,
when Gondwana began to break up, what was now the
Antarctic coalesced around the South Pole. A number of
species of dinosaur were known to have existed and the
lush plant life became dominated by fern-like plants which
grew in swamps. Over time these swamps became deposits
of coal in the Transantarctic Mountains and could have de-
composed into reservoirs of oil below them.

"But you hate the cold, and you don't like field work.
I'm more than qualified to at least assist you down there."
Aimee hated the whining tone creeping into her voice.
She knew Tom was the best person to go, but she had been
working on her current project now for eighteen months
and was looking for any sort of interesting diversion—and
this sounded like just the sort of thing that she'd like to do.

"Aimee, someone has got to front the board on Wednesday and discuss our results on the viability models for syn-

thetic fuel production or we won't get the additional funding," Tom responded in his most patient tone. "You know you're better than I am at twisting those board members around your little finger." Aimee could tell Tom was deliberately flattering her and she gave him a fake "gosh, thanks" smile.

"I'll be back in a week, probably with little more than a cold to show for it," he said without looking up from his packing. "I'll take some electromagnetic readings and map the near-surface alteration effects of any hydrocarbon migration and then we can turn the results into some nice 3D models for our friends in the boardroom."

"Well, make sure you use plenty of colour and description and lose all the jargon or you might as well show them pictures of your auntie's knitting for all those board members will understand," Aimee responded half-jokingly, knowing Tom was the best in the business at making complex subjects easy to understand and accessible to even the dullest bureaucrat. "And bring me back some snow."

"I'll bring you a penguin, no two, to make a pair of slippers," he said, both of them now laughing at their silliness.

Her eyes had once more returned to the soft Aimee blue. As usual he had managed to disarm her with a sense of humour that was more at home in a schoolyard than a laboratory. Knowing Tom, he'd spend his time in the tent hunched over his computer and be cold and bored by the end of the first day.

Next time, she thought, it would be her turn, no question about it.

# Three

Alex Hunter walked from the warm seawater after his dawn swim; it was his favourite time of the day—with the screeching of the gulls as they circled overhead and the shushing of the surf as it crashed onto the golden beach. The sea mist blew gently across his face as his grey-green eyes scanned the horizon. He closed them briefly and drew in a large breath to totally absorb the smells of his world.

After an hour of hard swimming he wasn't even breathing hard. At thirty-six years old and just over six feet tall his body was lean but strongly muscled across the arms and chest, representative of someone who trained vigorously and often. However, numerous scars attested to the fact this was no frame created in a gymnasium, but one that was hewn in and for battle. Alex shook his head from side to side and then dragged his hand through his short black hair. His square jaw and angular cheeks ensured there was no shortage of female attention, however, a complex and dangerous lifestyle meant there could never be any permanence to his relationships. Alex had been trained to win, to fight and succeed no matter what the odds, but there were some things that he felt were beyond even his capabilities. He could never settle down, could never describe his work, and could never share his success and failures with anyone other than his military peers. And now, following his field accident, he was more alone than ever.

Like a bronze statue Alex stood motionless on the sand, hands tightly gripping a faded beach towel; his eyes became lifeless chips of glass as he travelled in his head back to a life that now seemed to belong to someone else. Angie was gone, she was already leaving him before his last mission but had promised she would wait and be there to talk to him when he returned; he never made it. He didn't think she had stopped loving him—just couldn't stop the worrying, he guessed. In the time they had together they had loved and laughed like teenagers, and even now little things about her still haunted him: her thick brown hair that always smelled of fresh green apples, the line of perspiration on her top lip after they had made love, her enormous brown eyes. She said he could make her blush and go tingly just by talking to her. They were going to be married, and now he couldn't even call her, he had ceased to exist. He had heard she was seeing some suit from Boston; she'd be OK.

His mother had been told he was dead, heaven knew when he would ever be authorised to tell her the truth. Since his father had been taken by a heart attack ten years ago she had quit her job and slowed right down; she swapped a job in advertising for flowers, vegetables, and games of bridge two nights a week. He could still see her on the front porch in late spring with her spoilt Alsatian, Jess, asleep at her feet, her paws twitching in a dream where snooty overweight Siamese cats tripped over right in front of her. Until he learned to control and conceal his new abilities, it wasn't safe for anybody to know he was alive.

Life had made Alex a strange trade, one where he had both gained and lost. The thick towel Alex was gripping tore in half; he hadn't realised that the pressure had been building within him.

His rehabilitation, if you could call it that, was complete. Two years ago on a clandestine search and rescue mission in northern Chechnya, Alex Hunter had been ambushed and shot in the head—a trauma that should have killed him. He had been in a death-like coma for two weeks and when he had emerged from hospital after another month he was different, somehow altered. The bullet was lodged deep within his cerebellum in the junction between his hypothalamus and thalamus, a position that made removal more manslaughter than surgery. However, instead of causing irreparable damage as it should have done, it had ignited a storm of both physical and mental changes that had astounded his doctors.

Alex remembered them trying to explain what had happened to him and their assumptions when some of his abilities had started to emerge. Even among the gathered specialists in his room there was debate on how the human midbrain functioned. Some argued that humans make use of less than half of their total brain functions, with the other significant portion locked away for evolution to make use of when environmental or chronological factors dictate they are ready. Others were just as adamant that the unused portions were an evolutionary remnant of no more use than the appendix or tonsils.

What the bullet had done was force a significant re-routing of blood to his midbrain, the area largely responsible for selecting, mapping and cataloguing information. Alex had also been told that it was the primary powerhouse of endocrine functions, where control of pain, adrenaline and natural steroids are monitored and distributed. What had disturbed Alex the most was that the midbrain was the part of the human brain that contained the largest areas with an "unknown uses" classification. The flush of extra blood into these areas of his brain triggered massive electrical activity as a new engine room powered up and switched on, waking new or long dormant abilities.

Alex's agility, speed, strength and mental acuity had increased off the scale, and now in high intensity activities, the world around him seemed to slow to a crawl as he out-thought or out-moved reality. His doctors had been left in amazement that he could complete agility or strength tests at a speed that could sometimes only be further analysed with reduced motion camera equipment. It wasn't all good news though; Alex had been left with bouts of rage that were sometimes barely controllable. During these outbursts his strength and speed peaked. To date he had been able to channel that aggression back into his exercises—but God help those around him if ever that control slipped.

After the first few rages, and the realisation that they looked to be part of the package that had come with the physical upgrade, he had been happy that Angie wasn't in his life anymore. If he had ever hurt her, even while thrashing in his sleep, he may have been driven to turn that murderous fury back on himself.

Alex's superiors had quickly shut down any further testing by the hospital and allowed him to complete his recovery at a private house owned by the United States military on the northeast coast of Australia. The brass were keen to ensure Alex's psychological rehabilitation was as complete as the physical improvements as soon as possible. No psycho-suppressant drugs had worked with Alex; his body would overwhelm any chemical with more natural stimulants of its own; that battle could only end in one of two ways—Alex's heart exploding in his chest or a massive embolism in his midbrain. The military psychologists had managed to provide him with some tailored sensory techniques that allowed him to gain control of his furies and at least keep him out of the hands of the chemists. Alex smiled to himself. He was living one of the techniques right now; salt, sea and sand always helped him to unwind. He only had to mention it to the doctors and here he was—his simple task was to upload the sensory experiences and play them back in his mind to inject a wave of calm into his consciousness. However, he also had a secret safeguard, a smell, a redolence, one that immediately soothed him even during the most lethal of rages; he simply imagined the fragrance of fresh green apples.

It was working for him. The military had their first super soldier by accident, and as long as he was available for further testing, he would be allowed to stay on the active duty list. But Alex Hunter was now like a caged lion—training up to six hours a day and still not fatiguing, he needed something more than further exercise or drills. He judged himself fit for duty and was looking forward to the promised call from his superior and mentor, Major Jack Hammerson. As he drew in one last breath, he smiled. "Holidays are over," he said quietly to himself.

Major Jack Hammerson's face advertised all his years of active service like a billboard. Deep lines etched his forehead and cheeks and where the elements hadn't carved his features, combat scarring had. In his fifties, he was still a man of iron who kept up the daily training that had taught him how to incapacitate a foe in less than seven seconds, a skill he had needed to call on in active service many times. A Greek military history buff, "the Hammer" had refused promotions so he could maintain an active role with his beloved special services unit and ensure his lads were the best trained and the most lethal soldiers on earth. He made sure they always came back home from battle like the Spartans— with their shields upon them.

Hammerson sat with one fist clasped in his other hand

and looked at the information spread out on the desk before him. SOCOM, the Special Operations Command, had been tasked with directing a covert rescue and research mission down to the Antarctic. They'd all disappeared. Science personnel and a supporting team of Green Berets had all fallen off the grid. No radio contact, no satellite images, and nothing showing up from the VELA thermal imaging satellites—they were just gone. Hammerson reached down and picked up one of the photographs sent before the party had stepped off the earth. His eyes narrowed as if he were trying to will himself down into the ice so he could make sense of the images. He knew General Malcolm of SOCOM and the guys he sent down to be the mission shield wouldn't have been slouches. With their hostile-environment training and thick clothing, even in a freezing environment, their bodies would have taken several hours to cool; VELA should have picked up something.

Now it was his turn. Politically, command couldn't send a larger force, but they still wanted more military potency. There would not be a third team deployed; this was it. They needed maximum defensive and attack capabilities. Jack Hammerson dropped the photograph; he already knew who he was going to send.

Hammerson had known Alex Hunter since his first days in the squad and had initially thought of him as an enthusiastic and talented but average member of the team—if anyone could be just average in his specialised unit. However, in the eighteen months since Alex's mission accident, he had become vastly different. Now, no one could touch him in the strategy and tactic exercises, and in hand-to-hand combat training he had lifted another man weighing over 200 pounds above his head and thrown him fifteen feet as though he was no more than a hollow, store-built mannequin. Alex's doctors thought it was some form of beneficial side effect of the bullet lodging so close to his endocrine engine room; Hammerson saw it as a gift to be fully honed to its ultimate potential.

Hammerson took personal command of Alex and provided the extra training he needed to mould him into the special service's first super weapon—codenamed "Arcadian." Like Zeus, born of Arcadia and destroyer of the Titans, the new Alex had been created by war—he would go in fast, hard and with maximum lethality.

Alex was again primed for red duty and the current situation in the Antarctic was just the set of circumstances that required a special resource. Jack Hammerson reached for the phone; it was time Arcadian came in.

# Four

Wednesday morning Aimee checked her presentation for the last time to ensure she had the relevant information bullet-pointed and just enough feel-good blue sky built in to entice the most hard-boiled petroleum investor. Her handouts were printed up and bound professionally and she thought they looked pretty damn good. More than anything else she wanted to walk out of that boardroom in two hours (or less if lucky), and have good news for Tom when he returned on the weekend.

Aimee hoped that the progress of their project would give the board enough confidence in them to continue further funding. She drew a breath and smoothed the front of her only blue power suit. She knocked on the door and entered without waiting to be invited.

Instead of the seven members of the board she was expecting, she only recognised one, Alfred Beadman the chairman, who greeted her warmly just inside the door. Seated at the table were four people she had never met before. She assessed them all quickly—two sporty student types, a middle-aged nerd and a military man. She turned her attention back to Alfred, a fatherly figure to her and someone she knew she could always trust. He led her to a seat without letting go of her hand and asked her to sit down.

Her immediate thoughts were that they were going to

be shut down and that she had somehow already let Tom down by failing in her funding request and further, getting them bounced right out the door of GBR. Aimee closed her eyes and imagined Tom walking back in at the weekend and saying in his boyish manner "I've got a surprise for you," while holding a box behind his back, and Aimee responding with "and have I ever got one for you."

After a few moments Alfred spoke softly. "Aimee, we've lost contact with Tom—with all of them."

It was as if the entire atmosphere had been sucked out of the room; no one moved or spoke, no one even breathed. They just sat and stared.

"What do you mean you've lost contact?" Aimee was on her feet radiating a mix of disbelief and red hot anger.

"It may not be serious, but exactly what I said, Aimee. I think it might be best if we give you all the facts, bring you in from the cold so to speak, and then we can determine what the first and best course of action is to be. Please sit down, Aimee dear, so we can begin." Knowing how volatile Aimee could be, it was clear that Alfred was speaking as calmly and evenly as he could. He watched her retake her seat, then turned to his left and introduced the fearsome looking man that couldn't have been more military looking if he were wearing a uniform cut from the stars and stripes.

"Aimee, this is Major Jack Hammerson. Major, would you like to, umm . . ."

Hammerson met Aimee's laser-like stare with his own, and held it—this time it was Aimee who dropped her eyes. The Major waited a few more seconds and then began speaking.

"I'll get right to it. At O-eight hundred hours, Eastern Standard Time Tuesday, we received a final communication from our initial insertion team. The Hendsen team's brief was to check in every three hours due to the potentially hazardous nature of their mission and the hostile environment." Hammerson turned to Alfred and nodded, and the chairman pushed a button on the table to raise the far wall panelling. As the room darkened a blank white wall was revealed. Immediately, images flickered onto the screen. Major Hammerson went on, "Every three hours from touchdown at ten hundred hours Monday, until Tuesday eight hundred we received a packet of encrypted image and voice data. Before you now on the screen are some of those images. I don't need to remind you that everything you see is highly classified, however, until your security ratings have been increased you will need to all sign a non-disclosure prior to leaving the room."

Aimee felt both nauseous and restless; the knot in her stomach was making its way up into her rib cage and she placed her hand against her chest in an attempt to quieten the thumping of her heart. Tom was missing in a vast continent at the end of the earth where temperatures could drop to less than a hundred below zero and any rescue attempt would be measured in hours not days and all "General Patton" was worried about was their security ratings. She knew Tom was no Grizzly Adams and outdoors for him meant a stroll across the office courtyard to bring back some donuts. The thought of her honorary big brother being trapped—or worse—in some frozen hell almost made her want to throw up; she reacted the only way she knew how.

"Security rating? Listen Major, I don't give a damn about forms, security ratings or your entire shit-kicking army right now. I just want to know what happened to Tom and what you're doing to get him back." Arms folded across her chest, Aimee glared at Major Hammerson, hoping he wouldn't see that her hands were shaking. Alfred rolled his eyes and, as if conducting an orchestra, tried to make "calm down" motions to her from across the table.

The Major regarded Aimee coolly for a full twenty seconds before responding. "Dr. Weir, I work for the government, that's no secret. I also work for the United States military machine, that's also no secret. But we have a lot more in common than you realise." Hammerson paused, pinning Aimee with his unblinking stare. "You see, Dr. Weir, we own GBR. We fund your research. If we like what we see we extend your grants. We give you what you need; we even put the choc chip cookies in your little blue jar at work."

Hammerson's voice went up a level. "We own GBR, we own you, and we own over fifty companies similar to yours across the country and some in other countries as well. Like it or not, Dr. Weir, you also work for the shit-kicking army. And while you've lost contact with Dr. Hensen, I've lost contact with almost thirty good men and women, some with families, goddammit."

Aimee opened and closed her mouth, anger morphing back into fear and confusion; she wanted to respond but didn't know how.

"The known worldwide reserves of gas and oil are estimated at about one hundred and forty-two billion tons, and with current rates of usage will last only another fifty years. But with China and India's thirst for oil growing exponentially, our prediction is we have reserves for just twenty-five more years," Hammerson continued. "The fact is your additional funding request is a foregone conclusion. We are thirsty creatures, Dr. Weir, and even if you'd walked into the room with all your clothes on backwards and asked to use the NASA space shuttle for the next round of electromagnetic mapping, we probably would have funded it."

Aimee felt the Major let her off the hook as his penetrative stare relaxed and his voice lost its hard edge. "We need your help, Dr. Weir, to find out what happened to Dr. Hendsen, and to the other civilian scientists and medical team members that vanished down there with him."

Aimee sank down in her chair. Not trusting her voice she simply nodded. Hammerson slid the non-disclosure forms across the table and continued with his briefing.

"To continue, the first image you are seeing is the collision point. The plane that struck the ground was a seventy-foot turbofan Challenger jet. Its maintenance records showed it had been fully serviced and was only a few months out of the box. Owned and flown by Mr. John Banyon, who was accompanied by several members of his corporate executive team on a business team-building and sightseeing flight over the Antarctic. For reasons undetermined, it dropped out of the air and collided with the ground at approximately 1907 hours Eastern Standard Time Saturday." The image displayed on the screen was an aerial shot of a giant hole in the white ice—no debris or engine oil, just a black gash against the blinding white.

"You can see from the entry point that this is no collision crater, what seems to have occurred is the impact has punched straight through the ice and rock crust and opened access to an underground cavern. Next slide please, Mr. Beadman." Hammerson continued his clinical briefing. "This image shows initial cavern insertion by the Hendsen party and the wreckage of the Challenger jet." The picture this time showed a large team of men and women inside the mouth of an enormous cave system. Using them as scale this must have been a gigantic hole—it had to be over a hundred feet from where the people were standing to the roof of the cavern. Several members of the rescue team were working among fragments of a completely destroyed plane and holding up pieces of torn and empty clothing. In the background, Aimee could see Tom standing there in his favourite bright orange cold weather parka examining something intently, as was his usual style. Tears sprang into her eyes and she became angry, with both Tom and herself. With Tom for getting himself caught up in this mystery—she wanted to grab him by the collar of that stupid big parka and drag him home like a schoolboy who was late home from the ballpark. But she was even more angry with herself for letting him go alone; she should have pushed harder to go with him. She balled her hand into a fist and punched her thigh under the table.

Major Hammerson picked up the narration once again. "The debris was closely centred with a slightly eastward elliptical spread indicating that the plane came in at an approximate eighty-five degree angle at more than five hundred miles per hour. This accounts for the small fragment sizes. No survivors were expected; what *was* expected was bodies, body parts, at least significant blood patterning."

The next slide appeared, showing some of the rescue team heading further down into one darkened end of the cave. Hammerson continued. "Nothing was found other than several strange semi-liquid residues. This is where you and Dr. Silex come in, Dr. Weir."

Hearing her name brought Aimee back from the Antarctic ice and once again into the boardroom.

"Sorry, 'Dr. Silex'?" Aimee asked.

Alfred once more spoke up in his warm and authoritative voice. "I apologise Aimee, we were so rushed and determined to bring you up to speed we failed to provide full and proper introductions. Let me begin with someone you have already met. Going around the table, from my left starting with Major Jack Hammerson, who will be in charge of support, security, medical teams and logistics." Alfred turned to Jack Hammerson and enquired, "Major, I never asked what your areas of specialisation are?"

Hammerson ignored the chairman and turned to Aimee

and smiled. "My specialisation is keeping people alive and safe. My friends call me Jack." Hammerson smiled and held out his hand across the table. "It's a pleasure to meet you, and hopefully work with you, Dr. Weir."

At first Aimee was determined to dislike him but was quickly disarmed by his strong and easygoing nature. She liked him, but in the way you liked an enormous attack dog that was always friendly with you but threatened to rip the throat out of anyone else who looked sideways at you.

"Nice to meet you, Jack, and please, call me Aimee." With that Aimee turned to look at the next man in line just in time to catch him staring at her breasts.

Dr. Adrian Silex licked his already wet lips and swallowed. "How do you do? I'm Dr. Adrian Silex. I'm disappointed you haven't heard of me, Dr. Weir. Tom Hendsen and I go way back."

Adrian Silex was a tall thin man of about forty. His most unusual feature was a long head with a circle of fine hair fringing his ears. It looked like the crown of his skull had actually outgrown his hairdo. His ovoid head had an unpleasant way of bobbing and jerking, giving the impression of some sort of large bird. Most likely a vulture, Aimee thought.

Now it was coming back; Aimee remembered that Tom had mentioned Dr. "Sinex," naming his colleague after a brand of nasal decongestant spray because he always got up Tom's nose. Tom and "Sinex" often competed for papers published in the geological or petrobiological scientific community. The problem Tom had with Silex was that he was a sore loser. If Tom published a new paper, rather than publish his own work, Silex would put his energy into trying to discredit Tom's research. He rarely found fault with any of Tom's procedures or results, but he was clever enough to hold up the paper's acceptance and therefore Tom's credit for the work for years.

"I head up PBRI, or Petrobiological Research Incorporated. I am, I mean we are, the developers of an advanced electromagnetic geological scanning device, or AEM, which the military is very interested in. I'm looking forward to working on you, err sorry . . . with you on this."

Aimee turned her head from Dr. Silex and looked down at the notes in front of her on the desk; she exhaled through compressed lips and suppressed a small shudder of revulsion.

Alfred interjected smoothly. "This is a critically important project, Aimee. We need scientists with a mix of chemical, geological and petrobiological expertise. In addition, your work on organic-petrochemical interrelationships and Dr. Silex's research into stratigraphic imaging techniques makes you two the best qualified candidates."

Alfred looked at Aimee sympathetically and went on. "The ionosphere down there suffers from a lot of magnetic disturbance, so we might just have total communications failure. Or maybe they've gone deeper into the caves and can't get a message out. Of course, our objective is to bring them back, Aimee, but until we know for sure they have come to any harm, the project expedition remains scientific. Therefore, as the senior scientist, it will be headed by Adrian."

"I like to think I'm more working with you rather than being assisted by you," Silex said. "But I'll pass the introduction baton on, and we can talk more later on."

The young woman next to him broke into a wide smile. She had an open face and Aimee couldn't help warming to her. "Hi, Dr. Weir, my name is Monica Jennings. It's nice to meet you." With her hair tied back and a spray of small freckles on her face she looked like a hundred other healthy young women Aimee saw playing volleyball or on the athletic track in campuses across America. Aimee smiled back and asked Monica to call her Aimee, then nodded for her to continue. "I'm here to get you down in the hole and navigate the belly of the beast. My specialty is twofold; I've climbed just about every significant mountain there is to climb, and there's not much I don't know about going up or coming down ice. But my real love is caving—I'm a spelunker."

The young grad-student type next to Monica was looking at her admiringly. "Very cool," he said. Aimee could tell he was already smitten by the rock climber. The young man cleared his throat, obviously nervous and introduced himself. "I'm Matt Kerns, Professor of Archaeological Studies at Harvard University. I specialise in ancient civilisations and protolinguistics, and ahh . . ." Matt looked around at his table companions. "And if this is just a plane crash into a hole in Antarctica, I don't know why I'm here."

"Thank you, Dr. Kerns, a perfect time for me to pick up the threads from where I last left off. Mr. Beadman, please." Once again the lights dimmed and Major Hammerson continued to describe and explain the detail of the new images filling the screen. These showed the crash site and the different teams, now further into the caverns, sorting the collision information. Aimee leaned forward; in the background of the current image she could see Tom giving a peace sign and holding what looked like a test tube. The next few shots showed the cavern from different angles and it became clear that this was no simple hole in the ground but a vast network of caves leading deep into the impenetrable darkness.

The next slide had Matt Kerns on his feet and scurrying towards the screen. "What is that? Is that a structure?" Matt asked to no one in particular.

"And now you know why you are here, Dr. Kerns," said Hammerson. To the rest of the group the screen showed a jumble of eroded, carved boulders, with just the hint of some facial features on one of the walls. To Matt Kerns, it was his calling.

Matt was now inwardly focused, muttering to himself. "Large modelled stucco mask decorating both sides of a stairway on a former pyramidal platform. Very similar to Uaxactun, El Mirador, I'd say. Masonry is crude and roughly cut, thick layer of stucco evening out surface imperfections, corbelled archways built on stepped slabs. Looks a little like early Peten, about 150 BC, but with plenty of unique variations. No, the corbels are wrong. Must be earlier, I think; much, much earlier."

Matt Kerns paused for a few seconds and then, nodding vigorously at Jack Hammerson said, "OK, yep, I'm in."

Adrian Silex cleared his throat. "OK, our turn, please tell Dr. Weir and myself about the liquid residue you found in the caves."

"I'll do my best, Dr. Silex, but be patient as I'm no expert." Major Hammerson opened a slim folder and drew out half a dozen sheets of tightly typed paper. He flipped over the first sheet, and ran his finger down the page. "This was in the last data packet we received from Dr. Hendsen— talks about various chemical compositions in subsurface hydrocarbons and the results of some propensity modelling for Antarctic potential; OK, here we are, this is where it gets interesting. There were two items in the report that made us both sit up straight and scratch our heads—two items that we believe require your unique talents in petrobiology and stratigraphic mapping."

Hammerson put the papers down and looked from Dr. Silex to Aimee. "The first item of interest is the result of Dr. Hendsen's ground-level EM mapping of the stratigraphy associated with the potential oil and gas traps. Initial images show a massive body of liquid below the surface which if it is oil, could hold reserves of between one hundred and one hundred and fifty billion barrels of oil."

Major Hammerson paused and then went on slowly and softly, almost as if he were speaking to himself. "That's a lot of oil, enough to start a war over."

At this point Alfred Beadman spoke up, "The United States, like eleven other countries, is a signatory to the Antarctic Treaty. If I'm not mistaken, it was the first ever arms control agreement signed during the Cold War at the end of the fifties, isn't that right, Major?"

Hammerson nodded and picked up from Beadman. "That's correct, Mr. Beadman, presented in 1959 to be exact, and there are even more signatories now. We'll continue to respect that treaty. Problem is, there are dozens of countries who haven't signed, or have no reason to even acknowledge the 'hands off' approach we are taking to this continent. We believe if one of the other large resource-hungry countries detects what we have found they will stake a formal claim of sovereignty over Antarctica, it could take several decades to unravel the mess through the United Nations, and by that time they would have digested the lot."

"What about China?" asked Silex.

Beadman went on smoothly. "China was a late signatory and our feelings are we will be able to trust them provided the fair commercials stack up. Frankly, America doesn't care if it has to pay for its share; it just wants to make sure that it is made available evenly to the world. We'll bring China and all the other signatories in when we have some more concrete information." Aimee frowned. Alfred Beadman was clearly no ordinary chairman of the board.

Major Hammerson brought their focus back to him again. "Now to the second item, and a little puzzle for our petrobiologists." Hammerson looked directly at Aimee. "Why is the only chemical trace we can find in those caverns a type of organic ammonia—biology and source unknown?" Hammerson raised his eyebrows and went on. "And why did Dr. Hendsen write one word, a question, next to his results—secretion?"

Silex jumped in. "Contamination. Tom's results were always a bit flaky." Aimee's head snapped around and she gave Silex a look that immediately had him backpedalling. He shrugged, "I mean, whose results wouldn't get contaminated in those conditions?"

Hammerson interjected quickly; there were bigger and stranger issues to deal with. "Contamination? Possibly, but that's not the only problem with the data we received."

He nodded at Beadman who brought up the last image. It was indistinct and watery, but showed a young girl dressed in old-fashioned clothing, certainly not warm enough for the freezing temperatures of the Antarctic. She was holding a baby.

Aimee felt a chill up her spine and leaned towards the screen. "Who's that?" she said.

"We don't know. There was no woman with a baby on the original crashed flight, and it wasn't one of the rescue team members." He shook his head slowly. "Frankly, we just don't know," he repeated, "who she is or where she came from, and more importantly where she and everyone else went."

The meeting had broken up quickly after Alfred and the Major had given brief details of the trip logistics and now Aimee just wanted to rush home and start packing. She saw Matt and Monica sipping coffee together, and Silex looking over the top of their heads while holding up a cup and pointing at it. She didn't feel up to small talk, so as Hammerson shook Alfred's hand and then headed for the door she went with him.

"Major, err sorry, Jack, have you been down to the Antarctic before?"

"Yes I have, Aimee. We have a number of research stations down there, and I spent a few weeks at our McMurdo base one spring. Beautiful country; cold, but beautiful, so pack your woollies." He smiled at her and his cheek creased along an old scar.

She smiled back and realised she was still a little unsettled about Tom and nervous about the trip. She was thankful that he would be down there; he made her feel safe.

"Jack, I wasn't clear on whether we'd all go together or you'll meet us down there."

"Ahh, these old bones feel the cold too easily now. I won't be there, but you will be met on route when you arrive down in Australia. I'll be sending my best man and a few HAWCs." They got to the stairs and Hammerson turned to shake her hand. "Don't worry, Aimee; they'll look after you. Good luck and see you in a week."

A week, no problem, Aimee thought. She glanced at the elevator, changed her mind and followed Hammerson down the stairs.

# Five

"*Chyort vozmi*; now I get my information!" Viktor Petrov, Resources and Energy Minister for the Russian Federation, read the security squawk from one of the dozens of their American sleeper agents with frustration and growing anger; he had just left a surprise meeting with President Volkov where he had been severely ambushed. He knew there was going to be trouble when the President had refused to shake his offered hand and had come around his desk to stand mere inches from Petrov's face—a sign this was to be more a confrontation than a meeting.

President Vladimir Volkov was ex-KGB and had earned the name "Little Wolf" on account of both his small stature and terrifying presence. What he lacked in height he more than made up for with a blood-chilling ferocity; the Little Wolf was a predator whose bite was much worse than his bark.

Petrov wiped his brow and took several deep breaths. He still felt sickened by his own feebleness but had been pinned by the President's mesmerising gaze. Those eyes—almost colourless and unblinking. He just knew his legs had been shaking. Damn him for having better information sources than he did. Petrov remembered the chilling exchange and again felt a wave of nausea pass over him.

"Russia is a giant hungry bear, Petrov. It must be fed constantly so it slumbers and remains docile. If it is not it will grow weak and get eaten by another hungry bear, or it will rear up and tear its masters to pieces before devouring them." The President stood close and looked at different points on Petrov's face, watching the beads of perspiration fatten and then slide down his cheeks and neck to disappear into his tight, yellowing shirt collar. Petrov stood mute, not knowing whether he should respond to the cryptic little analogy or simply nod. He decided to do neither.

"Do you know what we must feed our hungry bear, comrade Petrov? What the Americans feed theirs, or the Chinese or the Europeans . . . Oil, lots of oil; the very blood of the earth. Tell me, how much oil do we have locked away in the soil beneath our feet, Petrov?"

Petrov didn't like where this was going. "About sixty billion barrels, President Volkov."

"And how much do the Americans have?"

Petrov stood a little straighter, "Less than a third of that of Mother Russia, comrade President."

"And if the Americans run out of oil before us, that is a good thing, da? But what will happen if Russia runs out before America? What will our giant bear do to us, dear friend Petrov?"

"Impossible, with their rate of consumption and volatile relationship with the Middle East, they will be using horse-drawn carts within twelve years."

"I see. How much oil do you think they will find down in Antarctica, comrade?"

"What? They would never touch it; they are signatories to—"

"*Svoloch!* They are already on their way now!"

Petrov, bludgeoned by the ferocity of the Russian curse, had an urgent need to use the bathroom. He suddenly felt very small before this man who only came up to his nose and he wanted to be out of this room and his presence immediately. The President brought his face even closer to

Petrov's until he was no more than an inch from his nose. The cold grey eyes bored deep into Petrov's very core.

"When we next speak you will tell me what you are doing about the American secret mission in Antarctica and why you should remain my Energy Minister, da? *Do svidanja*, comrade Petrov."

The Energy Minister's name was spat out like an obscenity and the President turned away from Viktor Petrov, signalling the meeting was over. On shaky legs Petrov wobbled towards the door and as he put his hand out to open it, he heard a final chilling warning from the President. "The bear feeds on incompetent ministers first, comrade Petrov."

Petrov went out through the door quickly for a large man, only just managing to close it and get his hand over his mouth before the bile hit the back of his teeth.

In the soft burgundy leather chair Viktor Petrov finally felt his heart rate returning to normal. The small bottle of Stolichnaya Elit was half empty on his desk and he felt he could finally think clearly enough to organise his plans. The first thing he would do was find the agent who had delivered his information to the President before he had given it to him and see he spent his next assignment on the Afghani border; perhaps that would teach the little *koshka* to recognise his priorities.

Petrov read the security paper again. The Americans were preparing a research team to investigate a possible sub-strata oil find in the Antarctic; no wonder the President had been so explosive.

He knew that if they could in any way secure and exploit the find it would destroy the carefully crafted plans that Russia had been building slowly over the last decade. Russia was once a contender to be the supreme superpower in the world and jostled with the United States over dominance in armaments and the space race. It had an army that shook the ground when it paraded its military might through Red Square. Now it had descended into a corrupt and bloated pretend-capitalist nation that had watched its soldiers boil cabbage to eat from their helmets. But as Energy Minister, Petrov was well aware that Russia was sleeping on gold. Locked beneath its soil were an estimated sixty billion barrels of oil and twenty-one trillion cubic feet of natural gas. As the world around them became ever hungrier for oil and the Middle Eastern countries became more fractious with the West, the price of the black gold went through the roof.

Russia was the second largest oil producer and largest natural gas producer in the world. It had more than it could use domestically so could sell millions of barrels. Petrov didn't have to negotiate better prices for the oil; he merely had to threaten to withhold supply and Russia's customers came back magically with more to spend. This booming resource revenue once again allowed a Russian leader to square his shoulders and look the United States in the eye.

Petrov had been at the radio interview when President Volkov had gone so far as to hint that they would price their oil in Euros and move away from using dollars—the Americans could only grind their teeth. They knew that the dollar-based global oil trade gave the United States carte blanche to print dollars without sparking inflation—to fund huge expenses on wars, military build-ups, as well as cut taxes. This suggestion was immediately seized upon by Iran, the world's number five oil producer and even by the United States' traditional ally Saudi Arabia. And of course the Europeans would like nothing better than to see another needle in the eye of the United States.

Eventually the American President would have to knock

on Vladimir Volkov's door and the terms of trade would be all Russian. Petrov took another sip of the expensive vodka and leaned back into the leather of his chair. Everything would go to plan, unless the United States could somehow secure an unclaimed source of petroleum or natural gas reserve, then all their careful machinations could be destroyed.

He sipped again and swirled the alcohol around in his mouth. On face value, the Antarctic was off limits to all nations. It was earth's last uninhabited continent; nearly six million square miles with more than ninety-eight per cent of them ice covered. Every Energy Minister around the world looked hungrily at the continent but was held in check by an agreement signed decades ago that prohibited military activity and mining but allowed scientific research. This treaty was largely policed by Australia, being the closest nation.

Petrov knew that when push came to shove, the Americans had a way of bending the interpretation of the rules to allow them to act and get what they needed. With the United States' huge resource requirements and the oil-producing nations of the world becoming increasingly hostile towards them, they would find a way. Added to this, Australia, one of their strongest allies, was monitoring activity in the Antarctic; no one would hear a thing until somehow they had secured some form of beneficial access to any new reserves.

Petrov could not allow the Americans to gain any sort of self-sufficiency from a large, unexploited oil reserve. He had to stop them or at least slow them down so he could formulate a longer-term plan. He could share the information with the Chinese who were just as hungry for oil as the Americans; however, they had a tendency to act in their own interest and were more likely to stake their own claim or cut a deal with the Americans. Besides, they were Russia's biggest customer. Going public with so few facts or presenting the information to the United Nations was a waste of time; either the UN would take six months to come up with an angry letter or the Americans would simply state they were doing research just the same as the 4,000 other scientists that worked down in their nationally marked-out zones. It would be much better for Russia if no one obtained the oil in the Antarctic or even knew about it.

This job needed something a little more arm's length; something that didn't involve the Russians directly. Until they were publicly exposed the Americans would deny all knowledge of the secret mission in the Antarctic; "plausible deniability" the Americans called it. Well, if the Americans could deny all knowledge of the existence of their secret team, then Petrov would ensure it really didn't exist. He knew a man who was very good at making things cease to exist—and knew exactly what to tell him to ensure he got results immediately.

Chechnya, Outskirts of Grozny

Uli Borshov walked from the little hut, wiping his bloody hands on a piece of torn Chechen dress fabric. As expected, it hadn't taken him long to learn everything he needed to know from his victim and he was preparing to rejoin his Special Forces team so he could upload the rebel base information.

Borshov was an imposing sight, standing more than six and a half feet tall, with a flat Slavic face that betrayed no emotion. He and his entire squad were made up of handpicked ex-Spetsnaz personnel who had displayed some form of special skill or ruthlessness that made them ideal for jobs that were either extremely dangerous or distasteful to the Russian public or sometimes for roles that broke the very laws of humanity.

His unit, known as the Krofskoya, or blood people, were not necessarily the first into combat, but they always infiltrated behind enemy lines. More assassins than soldiers, they were selected for the worst of the worst assignments. There were six of them—none were friends and all knew they were expendable. The pay was non-existent, food terrible and unless on special assignment, weapons were only upgraded from the bodies of their enemies. However, the main attraction was that they were allowed to kill, and torture, and do it often. Never could a more suitable job be found for a psychopathic profile.

Borshov's GSM communication unit pinged once softly; he frowned, there was less than a handful of people worldwide who had this number and all knew only to call in extreme emergencies. The global system for mobile communications meant he could be contacted anywhere in the world via satellite; it also meant he could be pinpointed via the same technology, and there were a dozen nations who would like to see Borshov obliterated. He hunkered down beside a ruined car, plugged in the earpiece and spoke one word: *"Da."*

On the other end of the line, Viktor Petrov did not bother with a greeting. Borshov listened as the Russian politician briefly outlined his new assignment, his rules of engagement, and gave him one final piece of information. "You may be interested to know, comrade Borshov, that Captain Alex Hunter, the ghost you said you killed, is not only walking around, but leading the American team on this mission." Borshov tightened his grip on the small communication device and a low rumbling could be heard from deep within his chest.

Petrov continued the needling. "Doesn't he have something of yours? Something in his head, I believe. What are you shooting these days, Borshov, peas?"

Alex Hunter still alive was an insult to Borshov's skills and reputation as an efficient killer and assassin. It had been nearly three years since they had faced off not far from where he was now. Borshov had beaten Hunter senseless and when he wouldn't give away any information, had shot him in the head and walked away. He saw the bullet hole; how could he have survived?

Borshov hung up on Petrov and stood motionless in the cold Chechen air for several seconds, before pressing more buttons on his phone and holding it to his ear. There was another who needed to be kept informed. One who paid even better than Petrov.

Borshov hurried back to the camp and drove straight to the airfield where he would be kitted out and flown directly down to the Antarctic. He selected two of his best team members to accompany him.

His rules of engagement were simple as usual—leave no one alive, leave nothing in one piece. To his men there was one extra rule—Alex Hunter was to be his.

# Six

Aimee stretched her back after the uncomfortable flight in the bulky transport plane and slowly paced around the huge hangar while waiting for the entire team to assemble. The sun was just peeking over the horizon as they arrived somewhere in the Southern Hemisphere. Hammerson had said it was Australia, but it could have been southern New Zealand, or perhaps even Tasmania—it was certainly much cooler here, but not uncomfortably so. The base they were at was obviously military, old and largely deserted on the outside, but inside someone was evidently paying the bills. The floor space was immaculate and lights flared across the hangar floor and even in the small empty offices. The only identification markings were of a large circular shield high up on the rear wall; it was of a fisted steel gauntlet holding red lightning bolts. Aimee had never seen the insignia before, but the imagery was powerful—defensive strength and lethal attack.

Aimee couldn't help feeling impatient; it was all taking too long and they still had to get down to the Antarctic ice. Thinking about Tom in the cold gave her a knot in her stomach and it turned another twist when she thought how they were only sending a small team—and only half of that science and medical. She had agreed with Alfred when he had said there was a need to balance speed and secrecy, and Major Hammerson had convinced her that they needed to stay below the radar on this one or else the UN could demand to monitor their expedition. With the pace of their decision-making and organisational skills it would take months just to decide which nations would even participate. Still, she had expected several hovering helicopters and multiple teams on bobsleds whizzing over the snow and ice, never resting until they had found their missing countrymen.

She put her hands on her slim hips and turned back to the floor of the hangar. In the corner, Adrian Silex was checking his equipment and towards the back Matt Kerns was making light conversation with Monica Jennings. The sound of Monica's laughter could be heard tumbling across the hangar floor like light music. Aimee smiled to herself; looked like Matt was making some headway there. She turned away, in time to catch Dr. Silex checking her body out again. He quickly licked his lips and gave a small wave. She nodded back, but couldn't help groaning in distaste. Silex was already shaping up to be a pompous windbag; now it seemed she might have to deal with some very unwelcome advances. She wished Tom was with her; the knot in her stomach gave another twist.

Jack Hammerson had said he would send his best "hawks" to assist them and as Aimee started to pace nervously, the small steel double doors at the rear of the hangar slid open silently. In filed six of the most lethal-looking men she had ever seen. All conversation stopped and everyone stared; Aimee even found herself taking a step backwards. The soldiers walked to the middle of the hangar floor and slowly examined the assembled group. The man in their centre was just over six feet tall, attractive and gave off an aura of authority and danger that was almost tangible. His eyes scanned the room and took in everything about the people he was to take care of; they stopped on Aimee.

Aimee felt blood rush into her cheeks but returned the steady examination. *Brutally handsome and confident, OK, I like that.* His hands were gloved so she couldn't see if there was a ring on his finger, but she bet he had a little army wife at home somewhere. Aimee folded her arms and stared at the tall soldier.

Alex Hunter slowly looked over his charges. For the most part they seemed physically fit and moderately capable. His eyes were drawn to the tall woman in front of him—it had to be Dr. Aimee Weir. Her eyes bored into his with an unwavering stare; perhaps a little hostility. *Good,* he thought— *I'll take spirit over nice any day.* As far as he was concerned, the mission started now.

"Good morning, ladies and gentlemen. My name is Captain Alex Hunter. The time is O-seven forty-five; at O-eight hundred hours we will begin briefings and final preparations—that will be for one hour only. We will then board our choppers at O-nine hundred hours for immediate dust off. It is imperative we move quickly."

He looked around the room and asked loudly, "Is Ms. Monica Jennings present?" Monica raised her hand and shouted a hearty "Yo," which caused Matt to snigger.

"Have the caving suits arrived?" Alex asked.

"Have they ever," replied Monica, unzipping the front of her bulky snow overalls and displaying what appeared to be a type of wetsuit. "Where did you get these, they're unbel—"

Alex cut her off, and spoke again in a loud and clear voice. "Everyone, please see Ms. Jennings who will distribute the caving suits. Each one has your name tag on the front and is tailored to your exact measurements. Ms. Jennings will be able to answer any questions about them in her briefing, occurring in twelve minutes. For now, carry on."

Alex wasn't going to tell them too much until they were in the air or at the insertion point. The thing about civilians was that they had a tendency to want to pull out if things sounded like they were going to get a bit hot or complex, and at this point in the mission every one of their special skills was going to be needed.

Alex had read all of their bios and the detailed mission notes from the Hammer; he already knew a lot about the team members before he had met them. Some were going take more watching than others, but for the most part they seemed physically and psychologically ready for a day under the ice.

When Alex was a boy he remembered his father telling him that you started to feel old when policemen and teachers began to look young. Alex was still in his mid-thirties, but looking at the youthful archaeology professor, he suddenly knew what his dad had meant. Alex saw that Matt Kerns had managed to be first into his high-tech caving suit and was doing a little clowning for Monica Jenning's benefit. Matt stood with his hands on his hips, turned and did an exaggerated walk across the hangar in a mincing, catwalk style. He looked back over his shoulder at Monica and Alex used his hypersensitive hearing to draw out the young archaeologist's words. "Does it make my bum look big?"

"Your bum, no. Your head, very," Monica retorted, laughing. She walked over to him and helped tighten some loose strapping on his suit.

Alex envied them—free to do what they wanted when they wanted. No demons of the id to hold them back. Before turning back to rejoin his men, he looked once more at Aimee Weir. He caught her looking at him before she quickly turned away.

At O-eight hundred on the dot, Alex Hunter strode once again to the centre of the hangar. "Ladies and gentlemen, can I have your full attention please. In less than sixty minutes we will be boarding the chopper out on the airfield. Our objectives are speed and invisibility; therefore we have to trade some of the comforts of flying you may be used to. The trip will be in two hops, the first to Macquarie Island, nine hundred and sixty miles to our south-south-east. It will take us approximately six hours. The island is little more than a cold dry rock, so we get to stretch our legs while refuelling and then we immediately dust off for the final hop. This last one will take us directly to our insertion point on the ice, some eighteen hundred miles further south. Provided we get favourable weather, it should take us just under twelve hours." He smiled inwardly as he heard the audible groans from most of the group. All except Dr. Aimee Weir, she just nodded and kept the look of determination on her face.

"You will now be briefed on our primary objectives, security operations, and some basic safety and caving techniques by Ms. Jennings. We will have a final equipment check at O-eight fifty and be in the air by O-nine hundred hours. There will be an opportunity for further questions on the chopper, and briefly again on arrival."

Matt Kerns started to ask a question, but Captain Hunter held up his hand and shook his head. "Be patient, time is critically short. Dr. Silex, if you please."

"Thank you, Captain. You and your men may stand at ease."

Alex didn't budge; he had worked with civilians before, and it was rarely a pleasant experience unless their roles were purely advisory. Giving them anything like authority always ended poorly for the civilians. Alex thought he could play along for just a few days, especially if they were both headed in the same general direction.

Alex Hunter's men never moved or acknowledged Silex in any way; as far as they were concerned Captain Hunter gave the orders, end of transmission.

Dr. Silex cleared his throat, "Our objective is twofold. Firstly, to verify the existence of surficial sub-shale deposits of liquid petroleum, their size, depth and viability for extraction. Dr. Weir and I will be deploying ground-based electromagnetic imaging devices to allow us to 'see' exactly what is below the surface. At this stage it could be a vast petroleum bed or nothing more than a contaminated water cave. We'll be taking some core samples for initial onsite analysis so we can make some preliminary recommendations on next steps back to home base. Dr. Weir will also be investigating some petrobiological anomalies that were picked up in the samples by our predecessor, Dr. Tom Hendsen."

Aimee narrowed her eyes at the tall scientist and Alex guessed she wasn't at all happy with the scientific aspect of the mission having been given priority.

Silex cleared his throat once again before continuing. "The second objective is to find out what happened to Dr. Hendsen, the twenty-eight members of his team, and for that matter, the eleven personnel onboard the initial plane that crashed through the ice. We don't know whether they're dead or just incapacitated due to exposure to one of the dozens of gases that can pool near natural oil deposits. In summary, this expedition has two simple objectives— scientific and possible rescue. However, we know that the ice floes are not policed and can be home to a lot of unsavoury characters like pirates and poachers; hence Captain Hunter and his security detail will be keeping us company."

Following the reference to the security aspect of the mission, Alex noticed Aimee scrutinising his team, and he could read the skepticism in her expression. That's right, Dr. Weir, a lot of muscle and iron just for some poachers. When her eyes made it to him he gave her an almost imperceptible nod. This time she didn't look away as quickly.

Silex continued, "The important thing to be aware of is that we will be doing our work underground. The plane punched through the roof of a large cavern and we will need to enter that opening to complete our work successfully. For those of you like me who have never been rock-climbing or caving before, we are about to get a crash course. Ms. Jennings, can you please talk us through some basics and describe these new clothes we're all wearing?"

Monica walked forward, feeling like a mini superhero in her tight black outfit. In her hands she carried other items they would need in the caves. "Good morning, everyone— this is going to be fun." For a caver or spelunker, the opportunity to explore a new cave system, to find or see something that no one had ever seen before, was a dream come true. For her beloved sport, she would wriggle through the most claustrophobic crevices or scale slippery rock faces in absolute darkness; to her, this was what made life worth living.

"I want to start by explaining what we'll be doing, and then describe some of the materials you'll need, including these state-of-the-art caving suits—thank you once again, Uncle Sam. Caves are like people, really. Some are easy, some secretive and rewarding, and some are real bitches and will kill you if they can. Some caves give you plenty of room, enough to drive a bus through, while others require belly crawls, challenging climbs or dangerous descents. They can be hot or cold, and nearly always dark; they can be dusty-dry, muddy or completely filled with water. We may even encounter ice tunnels where the ice can be soft as a slushy, or dark and blue and as hard as steel." Monica drew in a long breath.

"Professional cavers usually devote plenty of time to training, planning and practising how to use any new gear. We don't have that time, and I've been told that this is just a three-day job, and most of that is travelling. We drop in, locate any survivors, Dr. Weir and Dr. Silex drill a few holes, and then we climb back out—easy." Monica paused for a few minutes to allow what she had said to sink in and check for any questions. There were none— she hoped that was a good sign.

"Your gear is a high-tech military incursion suit being used for the first time outside of a combat environment. They have been modified for cave use and are made up of two thin layers. The first is neoprene with bonded Kevlar threading. It will be waterproof, slippery, for any tight crawls, and tough as hell. It is the closest thing I've seen to flexible body armour. The second layer is for warmth and comfort and has internal battery-powered thermals. It is effectively a survival suit within flexible steel. The gloves and fitted boots also have hardened finger and toe tips and roughened grip pads. Frankly, I'm never giving mine back."

Monica curled her gloved hand into a fist, watching it as a muscle bulged in her upper arm. She smiled at the suit's flexibility and continued with her lesson.

"You will each have a modified helmet that is moulded to your head shape. Remember those security photos we had taken? Well, they captured more than just your smile. This head gear is made of a polypressed ceramic; it's harder than steel but without the weight. Front lamp is a crystal globe behind shatterproof glass. Please don't look someone in the face when you have this on as you will blind them for up to a minute afterwards. There is a box in front of each of you that contains an extra torch, dried food and water, a knife, cord, first-aid kit, space blanket and small whistle. All items are compressed or slim fit and will correspond to a pouch on the belt or elasticised pocket of your suit."

Matt Kerns raised his hand. "Question."

"Let's hear it," said Monica.

"Will we be getting some of those?" He pointed at the extra gear that was slung on or about the bodies of Alex's soldiers. This caused all attention to be focused on the military personnel who had been standing slightly back from the gathered team.

Each of the soldiers had what looked like two hand-guns, one on each hip and more deadly-looking blades than you would have thought necessary for a quick drop in and climb out "fun" expedition.

The look on the soldiers' impassive faces radiated "don't even ask," so Monica turned back to Matt. "You were lucky to even get a penknife, Dr. Kerns," she said, and continued with her briefing. "We have to stick together. No wandering off. No jumping or running. In darkness, depth perception is always skewed. When crawling through tight spaces, keep your arms in front of you, not at your sides. Destroy nothing, take nothing away, and leave nothing behind. I'd normally tell my team not to bother the wildlife, but I doubt that will be a problem on this trip." Monica paused again, but still didn't get any signs of confusion. Good.

"I'll be circulating over the next fifteen minutes, checking your gear and answering any questions. One last important item, if you need to use the washroom, now's the time. These suits are designed to collect your waste—you will definitely not be leaving that behind in the caves."

Aimee couldn't keep her curiosity in check any longer. She had to draw some more information out of the military team.

"There is one thing—if this is a simple science and

rescue mission why do we need six Special Forces jarheads bristling with weapons riding with us on a trip to
an uninhabited continent? No offence, Captain."

"None taken, we've been called worse. Dr. Weir, my
'jarheads' are hand-picked members of the Hotzone All-
forces Warfare Commandos—or HAWCs for short."

Oh good grief, of course. The Major's "hawks," thought
Aimee.

Alex continued. "People, it is our simple task and pleasure to provide the security for this little trip, and perhaps
do some of the heavy lifting for you. The security team
members on this trip are, to begin with, First Lieutenant
John Johnson, my second in command. If I am unavail-
able at any time, all questions and operations should be
directed through him."

Aimee's eyes left Alex to look at the man who he had
just nodded to. At about forty, First Lieutenant Johnson
looked to be the oldest member of the HAWC squad. A
heavily creased forehead and a black crew cut with a touch
of iron at the temples. His heavy-lidded eyes couldn't hide
the formidable intelligence behind them and his bull-like
neck suggested a lot of power to back it up.

Next to be introduced was Second Lieutenant Oscar
Benson, a tall and shaven-headed black man who continued to check his equipment. Aimee saw that two of the
fingers on his left hand were missing; the little finger was
totally gone and the next in line ended at the first knuckle.
Clearly, he hadn't lost those fingers in a pushbike accident.
Mike and Frank "Tank" Lennox were introduced together.
They could have been twins; both had Nordic features and
white flat-top crew cuts, but where Mike was of average
height, Tank was a giant, towering a good head height
above everyone in the group. He looked like he was threatening to burst out of his caving suit and perhaps even turn
green at the same time.

The last man introduced was Second Lieutenant Fuji Takeda. Although his almond-shaped black eyes were impenetrable, he was the only member of the military group to acknowledge the gathered party by giving them a small forward bow by way of greeting. As his head dipped forward slightly, they could see that he was the only HAWC to have an extra piece of equipment. Strapped to his back in a coal black scabbard was the shortened form of a Japanese *katana*, or samurai sword.

Finally, Alex nodded to the last couple of people in his team and gave a small salute. They returned the gesture. "For those who haven't had a chance to meet with them yet, I'd like you to get to know Corporals Margaret Anderson and Bruno Zegarelli. They will be providing medical assistance to any survivors that may be found."

Margaret Anderson had a broad, shiny face that broke into an open smile. She nodded to everyone in Aimee's group. Corporal Zegarelli mouthed *hello* and pulled at the back of his rubberised incursion suit; the man looked compacted in the tight clothing and Aimee guessed a few too many military meals had contributed to his discomfort.

Aimee couldn't help looking from Zegarelli's stuffed figure back to Alex Hunter's physique for comparison, and as she worked her way up to his face she saw a pair of grey-green eyes staring back at her with just a hint of amusement. His face became serious again as he continued.

"Now, in answer to your question, Dr. Weir, seven days ago a light plane crashed into the ice; we do not believe there are any survivors. Following that, just four days ago, twenty-eight men and women comprising a small security detail, two medivac teams and six scientists disappeared at the same site. Our satellites have not picked up any surface activity, however, we cannot see into the hole. We believe they may have either been trapped by a rock fall or succumbed to gases; Dr. Silex has confirmed that toxic vapours can form near surface oil deposits. We will all be equipped with breathing apparatus in the event those gases have not yet dissipated. However, we must also be prepared for the possibility that they were ambushed by a group of non-friendlies. Be advised this continent has no police force and we know it is used as a base for illegal whalers, driftnet fishermen, toxic waste dumpers and a dozen other illegal activities. We're ju—"

"We'll remain safe as long as we stick together, Aimee, and everyone follows instructions. There's no need to be afraid. I'll ensure that the captain and his men perform their security details, and we'll all be home before you know it, right, Captain?" Silex had walked over to take a position in front of the HAWCs, keeping his back to them.

Alex let the silence hang in the air until Silex returned to his position. He ignored the lead scientist and simply picked up where he had left off. "We're not expecting any trouble, just being cautious. We are only here to make sure no one bothers you while you're all doing your jobs. Maximum twenty-four hours on the ice and then we're heading home."

Alex held Aimee's eyes with his own. After a while she exhaled and gave him a single small nod.

"Questions?" Thirty seconds passed before Matt Kerns finally raised his hand. "Go on, Dr. Kerns."

Matt smiled goofily. "I'd like to use the bathroom now." To which Monica leaned across and whispered to him, "Oh boy, look at that face. He so wants to shoot you right now."

Alex raised his voice once again. "We now have twelve minutes to boarding, people. In fifteen we will be in the air." He turned his back on the group and rejoined his men.

Aimee smiled as she watched him walk away. Hmm, looks like Silex isn't going to get everything his own way. Good, she thought.

Alex had said they weren't expecting any trouble, but he wasn't being totally accurate with the facts. The military had sent good men last time; you just didn't make Green Berets disappear without a lot of heat, noise and enemy bodies left behind. Certainly not a task that could have been achieved by fishermen or waste dumpers. If they had succumbed to gases then it was a retrieval mission; if not he and his HAWCs were prepared to meet any opposing force head on. Though his initial brief was to support the scientific mission, Hammerson had told him that he was to assume total command in the event he encountered any form of aggression. He had unilateral authority to engage any enemy.

Now that Alex had a chance to meet and hear from the individual team members he was relieved to find that for the most part they seemed both physically and intellectually capable of the short but arduous mission. The two scientists stood out, but for different reasons. The tall woman, Aimee, intrigued him. He knew from his briefing notes that she was concerned for her lost colleague, and that explained her impatience, but he could also sense a sharp intellect and a degree of impulsiveness and volatility that probably got her into a few arguments. He'd stay close to her; there was strength in her. He couldn't tell yet how she'd react if they found her colleague's body.

Alex was glad it was going to be a short trip as his real concern was for the lead scientist, Dr. Adrian Silex. He felt the man would suffer from some authority confusion if they were there any longer than twenty-four hours, and though Alex would tolerate him and follow his instructions as long as they coincided with his own brief, his men would not. HAWCs would obey the senior HAWC. If anything happened to Alex, then Johnson would lead. His men would ignore any orders from Dr. Silex and he hoped the scientist was wise enough to understand the limits of his jurisdiction and not to push his perceived command. With Alex's men—if they just ignored him, then he reckoned the scientist got off lightly.

# Seven

They sped through the half light of the morning in a swift military SeaHawk-S helicopter. It could take a dozen people and an additional 9,000 pounds of equipment, but as they had little more than slim backpacks for the short trip, they had squeezed the maximum bodies in, and by the look of it, a lot of extra fuel. There were twelve of them: the six HAWCs, Aimee, Silex, Matt, Monica and the two medical personnel.

It was becoming apparent to Aimee that Tom's trip was a larger search and rescue mission with a scientist and a small security detail, whereas this seemed more a strike force with a science and medical appendage. Even the helicopter they rode in looked aggressive. Oscar Benson had delighted in describing the craft's ordnance to her. It was armed to the teeth with a full armament of torpedoes, AGM-114 Hellfire missiles, an M-60 machine gun, an M-240 machine gun, a GAU-16 machine gun and a GAU-17 minigun for good measure. The speed they were experiencing was delivered by two turbo shaft engines, each providing over 1,600 horsepower that gave the sleek beast a speed of nearly 200 miles per hour. Benson had smiled when he finished his description and said, "It can get in quick, deal death and be out before you even hear it approaching." Shit, the lethal team, the armaments; Aimee suspected that the military thought that a little more than built-up gases had knocked the previous team out of action. My ass, they were not expecting any trouble, she thought.

The first leg to Macquarie Island, though the shortest, seemed to take forever. When the door of the helicopter finally slid back, a desolate granite landscape was revealed with a freezing wind that moaned its loneliness to a few wet-eyed seals lying at the grey water's edge. They were meant to stretch their legs, but the cold made the very marrow in Aimee's bones ache and she just pulled her parka hood further down over her face. Mercifully, the HAWCs managed to refuel in only thirty minutes and they shot up once again to complete their trip. No one spoke this time and most chose to simply doze or stare introspectively at their shoes. Even the HAWCs, now wrapped in their white snow coveralls, looked like hibernating polar bears, conserving their energy for the tasks ahead.

In Dante Alighieri's vision of hell, the lowest circle of Hades appeared as a frozen lake that leached all warmth from the human body and spirit. His allegorical imagery of perpetual frozenness was thought by some to be a metaphor for distance from the grace of God's warmth.

Aimee was reminded of those passages from Dante's work as she looked at the flat stretches of white terrain covered by rolling, wind-driven waves of frozen snow and ice. The cold stung her nose and made her eyes water; even her teeth hurt. Before he left, Tom had told her it was the coldest place on earth, with vicious winds called katabatics that could reach 200 miles per hour and freeze-blacken the skin in seconds. Far from God's warmth, Aimee thought again, and took a shuddering breath that seared the back of her throat.

They huddled just inside the doors of the helicopter as the HAWCs quickly unloaded the equipment. Apart from the soldiers, no one was desperately keen to jump out into a hostile environment that stung any exposed areas of the face and made the breath leave your body in white plumes like a flock of small ghosts.

First Lieutenant John Johnson appeared in the doorway and shouted over the top of the howling wind. "OK people, we've been given the all-clear on any gas traces, so no need for the breathing equipment. The drop lines are still in place from the previous mission team, so we'll use those and have a first briefing on the cave floor. You'll actually find it a lot more hospitable down there than up here."

Aimee turned to wave to the helicopter pilot, before it immediately dusted off to the McMurdo American base for refuelling. The additional gusts from the rotor blades barely made any difference to the stinging winds swirling around them.

The team stopped and looked at the enormous hole before them. It dropped away to an inky blackness and no walls could be seen at or under the rim—that meant that where they were standing was probably hollow underneath. Aimee's stomach gave a little flip, and for the first time she felt like refusing to go any further. She steeled herself and tried to bolster her spirits with a little "come on, girl, you're tougher than this" speech. Waiting for her turn at the edge of the giant black hole, it seemed to make little difference today.

By now all the equipment had been lowered into the cavern and two of the HAWCs had dropped over the edge. Another of the soldiers, who had to be Tank given his size, grabbed Monica and Matt Kerns and harnessed them into a drop cradle. The carriage itself was little more than a seat made of straps attached to a winch device bolted to the ice. Tank walked the strapped-in team members towards the edge, briefly held his hand up to his ear to receive some form of communication from the cave floor, nodded to the passengers and then pushed them gently out into the abyss.

When it was Aimee's turn to be lowered into the pit, Tank grabbed her by the harness and gently walked her to the edge. She was thankful for the large man pulling her forward as her legs would have flatly refused her own command to move. The butterflies that had previously tickled her insides had now churned her entire diaphragm into a whirlwind of giddiness that threatened to spill up over her lips. She looked down at her feet, now on the very lip of the black hole, and flashes started to go off in her head. Just as unconsciousness threatened to take her she heard Tank's deep voice close to her ear. "Dr. Weir, don't close your eyes, don't look down; just stay focused on me or the rope." She smiled at him, but was glad he didn't see her expression as she suspected it looked more like a frightened rictus. Tank finally pushed her and she spun down into the darkness. Her mouth filled with saliva and she swallowed hard while concentrating on the rope in front of her; never had rope fibres fascinated her so much.

The relay continued for twenty minutes as the HAWCs rushed to get everyone out of the elements as quickly as possible. When Aimee touched down on the cave floor what immediately struck her was the sheer size of the cavern. Equipment had been unpacked and lights constructed facing primarily outward from their camp, set up just under the southern lip of the ceiling drop area. Truck-sized boulders were heaped towards the centre among some airplane debris; however the rest of the cave was surprisingly bare. It was definitely warmer out of the Antarctic wind; in fact, much warmer than it should have been. The team had removed their bulky snow clothes and now just wore their heated cave suits. As yet, no one needed to turn their helmet lights on as they were still close to the giant column of light that poured into the cave through the ceiling.

Within minutes of hitting the ground Aimee felt the final effects of vertigo leave her muscles, and with her vision cleared she quickly looked about the cavern floor for traces of Tom's party or anything to give a clue to his whereabouts. She could feel a trickle of perspiration under her helmet and as she pulled off her bulky parka, Silex appeared beside her. She turned to him and asked, "It shouldn't be so warm; volcanic activity, you think?"

Silex nodded. "Hmm, it's got to be twenty degrees warmer down here than up there—above freezing easily. It does all make sense, though. The Antarctic is still quite geologically active. We surface dwellers just don't know about it as most of it happens under the ice. In fact, Mt. Erebus is erupting constantly."

"You're probably right. That would account for the ice cap being so thin here, allowing the plane to break through, and also why this cave system isn't totally iced up." Aimee drew in a breath and wrinkled her nose. "Do you smell that? Strange—sharp and acrid, a bit like ammonia."

Silex moved in closer to her. "Sub-surface oils can contain all sorts of natural contaminants—paraffins, cycloparaffins, aromatic hydrocarbons. Hell, I've smelt deep pumped oil that smelled of roses one moment and rotten eggs the next. Every time it's different," Silex tried to look rakish, but ended up just leering. "I love being out in the field."

Aimee didn't like the way he was peering into her face as he spoke. "Aimee, I know you miss Tom and I know you don't want my sympathy, but we'll find out what happened to him. I really hope we can work together and learn from each other. I can help you a lot with your career. In fact, I think you should head up your own company; you know you're good enough. It would be my pleasure to help in any way I can." His head was bobbing up and down slightly, like a heron scanning for tadpoles. He reached out to grasp her upper arm. Aimee smoothly intercepted it with her own hand and turned it into a friendly handshake.

"That's very kind of you, Dr. Silex, thank you." Maybe she had been overly sensitive. Maybe he just has a very different personality to what I'm used to, she thought. He's probably more worried about me than anything else. She released his hand, gave him a small nod and a smile.

"OK, you just let me know if I can help. Well, we've got work to do. And please, call me Adrian!" With that he turned and gave a friendly wave over his shoulder and headed briskly towards the main group.

Monica surveyed the giant hollow carefully. From her experience, caves could be anything from wet and slimy, to dry and dusty, and for the most part unless they were newly formed via earth movement, they were geologically very old. This cave bothered her—it was strange. It had to be millions of years old, but there appeared to be areas that looked recently gouged—although recent in geological terms could mean tens of thousands of years. The ceiling was what she expected, but the ground and walls of the cave looked like something had been dragged along them, abrading every protuberance smooth. Glacier pipes could do that—the heavy, dense ice moving underground and wearing away the rock over a period of thousands of years, but usually they needed more of a slope—strange.

The light from above coupled with their eyes now adjusting to the semi-darkness allowed the farther walls to be seen in more detail. To everyone else it just looked like more broken cave debris, but to Matt Kerns it was a magical impossibility.

"Can't be, can it be? Not Mayan, no, no older, much,

much older." He scurried off from the group with Monica in pursuit, trying to slow him down.

Alex noticed the small commotion and called to Takeda, pointed two fingers at his eyes and then at Matt's disappearing back. Takeda nodded and followed them. Once Matt was in among the fallen debris he stood for a few seconds, waving his torch back and forth so he could take it all in. Though heavily worn, two colossal stone heads, lips full, the noses wide and the faces flat and broad could be made out from the broken rocks. Both were about nine feet in height and looked to weigh close to twenty tons each. There also seemed to be a destroyed dwelling which was actually carved into the wall—not built onto it, but hewn from the very cave wall itself.

"Wow, are these the Mayan ruins you were so excited about back home?" asked Monica.

"Yes. I mean no. Looks a little like Mayan but so much older. Even older than Olmec, thousands of years older, but still with some similarities. Mayan statues are usually carved to represent their rulers as being benign and all-knowing. These look to be in pain or great fear and I don't know what these coils are meant to represent wrapped around them; wait, there's picture writing."

Matt stuffed his torch into his pocket and rushed again to another section, trying to balance among the jumble of debris and take multiple photographs of the artifacts at the same time. The corner of the cave where they worked flared brightly and darkened in time with his camera motor drive.

"You can read that?" asked Monica.

"Pictoglyphs—picture symbols. It's writing, but in a series of images—you don't read it, you interpret it. I doubt anyone today could translate all of it. The problem is the symbols don't represent letters; sometimes they're syllables, words, sometimes sounds or even ideas. Primitive and complex at the same time, but still a whole phonetic language system. Looks like Mayan or Olmec, but the Olmecs had about two hundred characters, the Mayans even more. However, there are some images here I've never seen before. You know, there's probably only two people in the entire world who could even attempt to read this, and one of them is in Central America right now."

"OK, I'll bite, who's the other one?"

Matt had his torch back out. He shone it on his face and smiled. "Stand back, beautiful, this is where the magic happens. Ahhh, if I had more time I could probably draw out more of its meaning. The best I can do is to give you a guesslation, and at this point it'll be heavy on the guessing part. Don't blame me if I tell you it's about a boy with a banana stuck in his ear though."

Matt ran his hands over some of the glyphs, and then changed to another section looking for a place to start. "Interesting. Some of these symbols look Mesoamerican. This single glyph here of two identical kneeling warriors is very similar to one in Mayan that represents a pair of demi-god brothers, from their original creation myth. They were called Hunahpu and Xbalanque and spent their life annoying or outwitting troublesome gods." Matt scanned ahead along the carvings, narrowing his eyes at an image, his lips moving as if working a new word around in his mouth before continuing.

Without turning he started to speak again. "OK, this might well be some sort of variation on one of the most ancient Mayan myths, but as there are so many different character sets I'm going to make a few pretty big leaps here. From what I can translate, it tells a story of a secret or hidden underworld." Matt moved to the next row of symbols and continued. "Anyway, these monstrous underworld dwellers had a mixture of human, reptilian and other animal characteristics. That might mean bits of those animals or they chose to change themselves into all of them at once. It also tells how the king sent an army to journey into a realm of horrors beneath the earth to defeat the enemies of 'All People.' Hmm, don't know what this next one means, or this . . . Strange symbols. You don't have a spare Rosetta Stone, do you?"

Matt had turned around to shine the torch on Monica who mouthed the word *magic* and raised her eyebrows. He chuckled and went back to his translation.

"OK, before they reach their destination they're attacked and nearly all the army is captured or decimated by the ruler of the underworld—the *Qwotoan*. The only people who returned to tell the story were the brothers. Wow, see this? It's a little like the Mayan numbering system. There's a base number, and the dot over it represents it being multiplied by ten." Matt pointed to a symbol with dozens of dots pressed into the stonework above it. "I think this here represents thousands dead. No, that can't be possible, I must be mistranslating."

Matt paused and screwed up his face. "Odd, this last bit looks to have been written later. Even the glyph style is slightly different. I think it just says: 'We are lost, *Qwotoan* comes!' "

Matt knelt down among the debris and sorted through flat pieces of stone that had onioned off the face of the wall. Discarding some and selecting others, his lips moved as he tried to tell himself the story of the ancient civilisation. He was running his hands over a piece of flat stone with faint upraised markings when Monica touched him on the shoulder. He turned and held the small stone tablet out for her to see. It showed a number of small symbols in the ancient icon-imagery of the long dead culture depicting what looked like a warrior tangled in some sort of rope or tentacles. Another smaller image showed an eye looking over a city surrounded by a lot of dots and squiggles.

"What's it say?" said Monica, kneeling down next to him and squinting at the carved rock.

Matt was looking at the stone and *hmmd* to himself before speaking. "It's a little more about the warrior brother's descent to find *Qwotoan* and slay what looks like the 'Devourer' or 'Deceiver.' Why does that name *Qwotoan* ring a bell? Damn, I can't make out all of these pictoglyphs without some more work. This language has some characters that could be Olmec, some Mayan, Aztec, even what looks like some Egyptian hieroglyphs; and this bit here could even be Sumerian. It's all mixed together. This could be some form of root language. But why is it here? Why were they here?"

"And where are they now?" asked Monica. "They all seem to have disappeared."

"This spot is probably just an outpost, but this symbol represents a reference to the 'City'; and this here looks like the Mayan root word for water—'*Atl*,' and the Olmec word for surrounding land. No wait, that could be land surrounded by water." He rocked back on his heels. "You know there are plenty of ancient stories with tales of a lost continent. Antarctica wasn't always frozen under a mile of ice, you know, and many people speculate about what may lie undiscovered beneath this continent's deep ice mantle. Like, just how did fifteenth-century cartographers manage to get hold of maps of the actual coastline of Antarctica which exists under the ice, when our modern cartographers could only achieve this a few decades ago by seismographic means? A lot of these ancient races have legends about their forefathers arriving from the sea after a great catastrophe in their homeland. Their legends talk about their homeland sinking, or 'going below' as it's been interpreted; but what if that didn't mean sinking under water, but going below ice?"

"Dr. Matthew Kerns, you are not going to tell me this is Atlantis, are you?" Monica asked incredulously.

"I didn't say that. Atlantis was Plato's allegorical story; however, in Mayan and Olmec and even Aztec legends, they directly refer to a place called 'Aztlan.' The Mayans originally believed they came to the Americas from an overseas paradise called Aztlan which sank away from sight." Matt gathered his thoughts. "Look, hear me out, there's a section of an ancient Mayan codex called the Troano Manuscript that to this day is still defying a full translation. However, in the 1800s a classical archaeologist by the name of Augustus le Plongeon attempted a partial interpretation. His reconstruction recounted a legend passed down for hundreds of generations about the tragedy of a 'Great Golden City,' which was swallowed in a terrible cataclysm that took place nearly 10,000 years before the writing of that codex."

"Uh, and he said the Mayans knew about this place, did he? What happened to him?" Monica gave Matt a look that radiated a mixture of disbelief and mock gravitas.

"Not exactly. He called the country 'Mu,' but no one would support his work, and of course there was no cross-validating data. For his trouble he was discredited, but look, there is one thing that my studies have taught me and that's extraordinary civilisations have come and gone, but eventually the earth gives them back to us." Matt's eyes burned with excitement.

"I don't believe it. They discredited him just because he called it 'Moo'?" Monica couldn't help laughing and Matt jumped to his feet, pulling Monica up with him.

"Very funny, cavewoman. Come on, we've got to find more evidence, this could be huge."

# Eight

Alex stood on a small boulder and raised his voice so it would carry to all the team members. "Ladies and gentlemen, full team briefing in fifteen minutes. Enjoy your last hot coffee as we will not be taking it into the caves. Please check and pack any equipment you will need; we're going to be very busy shortly." He stepped down without any further interaction. This was not the time for questions and answers.

He turned back to his HAWCs just as Tank handed him a webbing backpack like the ones the others were already wearing. From it he removed a rectangular black box, which in his hands suddenly telescoped forwards and backwards into what looked like a very high-tech Armalite rifle. Alex and his team were ready. They banged their fists together and had just shouted a single "Go HAWC," when Johnson spoke to Alex.

"Heads up, boss." He nodded over Alex's shoulder at Aimee who had her head down and was striding towards them with a look of stern displeasure on her face. But Alex didn't need to be told Aimee was approaching; he had heard her first footsteps before Johnson had even spoken.

"Do you really think it's a good idea to be spraying bullets around in this cave, Captain? Forget about the danger from ricochet, but do you have any idea of how easy it is to ignite a natural gas leak this close to the surface?"

"No, Dr. Weir, I'm afraid I don't." Alex shouldered the rifle and then proceeded to aim at the tail section of the crashed plane and pull the trigger. There was a hiss and a sound like air being blown through a pipe and a small section of the tail fin of the broken plane magically wanged off into the darkness. "No ricochets, no loud noises, no gunpowder. The gas projectile M98 is a variation of the M16 except it's probably closer to a paintball gun. It still uses a gas-powered rotating bolt, and will release up to 900 cyclic rounds per minute at 2,900 feet per second. However, Dr. Weir, the major difference is it doesn't need to have a magazine reload. It simply fires an unlimited supply of super compressed balls of air. It can be calibrated to punch a ball bearing–sized hole through half-inch steel, or set to the size of a softball and knock a man flat from fifty feet. Extremely light and folds away to the size of a dinner plate; only weakness is its effective range is limited to around 250 feet. Shouldn't be a problem in a cave I would think, Dr. Weir."

Alex saw Aimee shake her head as if to clear away some fuzzy thinking. There's that impulsiveness again, he thought. Her eyes softened; even in the darkened cave he could see an almost physical colour change in them as her anger dissipated.

"Sorry, I should have known better. I'm just a little on edge and nervous. Um, I was also probably out of line with that earlier jarheads crack as well."

Alex smiled for the first time. "Dr. Weir, I have a boss who uses language that would make a drunken pirate blush; you don't need to apologise." He went to shake her hand, then drew back and removed his toughened black glove. Seeing him remove his, Aimee did the same before they shook hands.

"Captain, please call me Aimee."

"It'd be a pleasure, Aimee. You can call me Alex."

He kept hold of her hand and looked into her eyes and smiled again. She's beautiful, he thought. He mentally shook his head; forget it, that's not why I'm here, maybe next life. He let go of her hand and she returned to the group and the smell of brewing rehydrated coffee.

Alex turned around and caught his men smiling at him broadly. He gave them a look that made them freeze and drop their heads to continue checking and rechecking their equipment before calling to his Second Lieutenant.

"Takeda."

"Yes, sir."

"Inform HQ we've touched down and will be starting a first sweep at twenty-one hundred hours. Also request any final instructions. Once we enter the cave depths we may lose signal strength."

With that he turned and looked around the cathedral-like vault. Though the all-clear had been given on gases, there was a strange smell he couldn't place. Alex hadn't felt anything like fear for a long time, but something down here was making him feel very unsettled.

"Johnson, take Benson and Tank and recon the crash site. Be back here in twenty minutes. Mike, with me at the science team. Takeda, join us when you're finished with the communications. Everyone stay alert, something's not right."

Aimee handed Alex a small cup of steaming coffee. "A peace offering," she said.

Alex accepted the hot drink and replied, "No need, we were never at war."

"Dr. Silex and I will need to move farther away from the interference of the cave opening to get any meaning-ful readings from the stratigraphic scanners. It's going to be hard enough being so close to the pole as the magnetic waves will create a lot of distortion; we've got to move a little deeper and at least shut out the ionospherics."

Alex could see there was something else on her mind. He gave her time to work up the courage to ask.

"Um, I've been talking to your medivac team. It seems there's one military medic, who is also an engineer, and the other has a biomedicine background—a strange selection for a rescue mission. What gives?"

Alex looked at her for a few seconds, weighing up whether he should lie, and then made a decision.

"Dr. Weir, Aimee, look around." He paused as she briefly looked over both shoulders. "Over thirty people came into this hole over the last seven days. What do you see?"

Aimee looked around again and saw the crashed plane, rock debris and impenetrable darkness leading off to both the left and right of them. She looked back at Alex. "OK, so where are they all?"

"This is not a rescue mission. I don't think there are any survivors to rescue. There are no bodies, no remains, nothing on the motion sensors or heat scanners. It's just us down here. Primary mission objective is unchanged; we are to support your work and then evac in, now, twenty-three hours." Alex paused a moment to let this sink in. "Secondary objective is determine location of initial party and the reason for communications breakdown. But there will be no remains or body retrieval, unless required as forensic samples for further investigation. I'm sorry."

Alex could see the anger building in Aimee's eyes. Here it comes, he thought.

"We are not leaving Tom or anyone else down here in this godforsaken cave. You said yourself, they could simply be trapped by a rockslide. This area is still geologically active, you know. If he or anyone else is alive that would be murder."

As she turned to storm away, she bumped into Alex's elbow and knocked the coffee cup up and out of her own hand. The cup fell to the ground, spilling a long stream of coffee as it descended. Alex's reflexes overtook his commonsense; he just saw the girl about to fall or cover herself in hot liquid and acted. In a single smooth motion he picked the falling cup out of the air and scooped the stream of liquid back into it. With his other hand he caught her by the elbow and kept her on her feet.

Damn, he thought. He remembered the Hammer's directive for being allowed back onto active HAWC duty: "No unnecessary displays of physical capabilities unless to avoid or deflect harm to himself or immediate team members."

He handed the cup back to her. "Phew, that was lucky."

Alex could see Aimee staring at him in amazement and doubted she believed snatching the cup from the air was just good fortune. He needed to be more careful. She opened her mouth to say something just as his men appeared at his side to deliver their field reports.

"Don't worry, Aimee, if he can be found, we'll find him." Alex held her gaze for a few seconds more then released her. He excused himself and led his HAWCs a short distance away.

Johnson was the first to speak. "No bodies, no remains. The plane shows signs of significant collision scarring as you would expect from a crash at velocity. There is some evidence of cranial blood spray in the cockpit from impact trauma, but once again no bodies or even flesh debris."

Tank then added his details from the cave perimeter search. "There are signs of movement down into the southern cavern. Looks like the entire team headed down that way." He nodded in the cave's direction for the benefit of the HAWCs. "Some of the steps are far apart, indicating some of the people were moving at speed. Also, there is evidence of dragging—couldn't make out what, maybe supplies, maybe bodies."

"Captain!" Alex was about to ask Tank a question when the nasal voice of Dr. Silex punctured the ring of soldiers and terminated their debrief. The lead scientist strode into the circle of soldiers and faced Alex.

"Captain Hunter, it's no good, this area is a honeycomb of varying geologies and hollow spaces, and with the significant magnetic disturbance of the pole I won't be able to get any meaningful readings. We need to move; you need to get us deeper."

"Do you smell that, Dr. Silex? Doesn't smell like oil to me."

"Of course I smell it. Are you a petrobiologist? Or even a geologist? Captain, raw petroleum can contain a hundred different chemical contaminants; too many for me to explain to you here and now. If it offends you, put on your gas mask, but we need to get further into the cave. That's an order, Captain."

Alex ignored Silex's officiousness and looked down into the coal black mouth of the southern cave. He did not relish the thought of taking the civilian party in there. There was something else besides a chemical contaminant—something biological about the smell. He could also hear faint liquid noises emanating from the cave depths that had all his special senses on guard. He would have liked to take the HAWCs in first and leave the scientists right here. However, without more information, all he had was a gut feeling and no concrete reason to stall them any longer.

"OK, we can follow the tracks deeper into the cave. This will also give you and Dr. Weir some more depth and shelter from the interference. Benson, you're on communications relay and base camp coverage in the event whatever made those people run down into the cave makes us run back out. Johnson, take point; Tank and Mike, left and right flank; Takeda, rear point, no stragglers. Stay alert, stay in visual with each other." The men nodded once.

"Everyone go to night scope and comms and give me a check." All the HAWCs withdrew from their backpack another item of equipment. It was a small, elasticised piece of head gear with two hardened arms no thicker than wire, ending in a bulb at each end. One end extended down beside the mouth, the other just beside the ear. This allowed normal hearing to be unimpaired. Plug-in ear-pieces tended to reduce stereoaudic hearing and therefore lowered rapid determination of source of sound—fatal in combat situations. On the other side of the head, now folded down, was a miniaturised version of the ATN Patriot night scope—this clipped neatly onto the helmet. With a built-in infrared illuminator, it allowed vision in even total darkness.

The helmet lights were really for the benefit of the scientific team, and the HAWCs would only use them to make the civilians feel more comfortable. However, the soldiers knew that if things started to get "red" they would switch off the lights and become silent, lethal ghosts in the dark.

"Time to get them moving, get everyone packed and ready, let's go." As the men hurried off, Johnson lingered behind and moved in closer to Alex.

"What do you think, boss?" Though the First Lieutenant was older and more experienced than Alex, he greatly respected his captain's capabilities and extraordinary senses.

Alex narrowed his eyes. "That smell, and I can hear something—dragging or sliding . . . fluid movement. We need to stay alert. We're not in Kansas anymore."

John Johnson laughed quietly. "Hey, witches I can

handle, I've been married, remember." He trotted off into
the dark to take point.

On the Antarctic surface, one hundred feet from the hole,
the snow moved. Three white-clad bodies burst from their
concealment and sprinted to the rim of the crater. They
landed flat at the edge of the pit and the largest man thrust
forward a tube covered in white cloth that he held up to his
eye. Borshov used the hand-held surveillance scope to see
over the edge without casting a head-shaped shadow. He
adjusted the magnification and peered down.

Borshov and his men had also been travelling for two
days without stop. First in supersonic jumps across the
Middle East, Libya and Nigeria, crossing the Atlantic and
then on to scream down the coast of Argentina. The Russian Sukhoi S21 was carbonyl ferrite coated and had
achieved speeds of mach-one without showing once on any
watching radar. The Krofskoya agents transferred at Ush-
uaia on the Argentinean horn to a waiting Kamkov helicopter. Its 1,300-horsepower Rybinsk powerplant pushed
it through the freezing air at 220 miles per hour. The
young pilot, just skimming the waves, had turned to Borshov and complained that he was pushing the limits of
the sleek helicopter's range when the giant Russian had
walked to the cockpit and lifted the young man's communication headpiece. He whispered something into his
ear before retaking his seat—the young pilot didn't complain anymore; he didn't even turn to look when he unloaded them onto the snow.

From his scope, Borshov saw that the Americans had
set up camp at the base of the south wall and were just
setting off down into the southern tunnel. He also detected one man was being left behind to anchor the base
camp; by his size and the way he moved it seemed he was
no scientist. If they were with Alex Hunter then they must

be at least SEALs, or worse, HAWCs. This man had to be neutralised before they could proceed.

Borshov knew that the helicopter would wait for them at the abandoned Russian research base at Leningrad-skaya. He didn't care; all that mattered now was Alex Hunter and the mission. Nothing would be recognisable when he left. He'd give the Americans a few minutes to get farther into the tunnels and then commence his oper-ation.

The creature could sense more of the little warm bloods slowly approaching and had tasted them again recently. They were small but once again there were enough of them to nourish it. It was the largest of its kind and had seen many millennia in its warm, deep sea below the ice. The little animals could be mimicked easily but their sounds were still too complex to copy. It reached forward to taste them once more.

# Nine

Benson's orders were uncomplicated—to ensure the team had a fast and clear path of extraction if needed. He quickly checked the SINCGARS radio unit was operational. The small but powerful communication system used LPI, Low Probability of Intercept technology, to obstruct unauthorised transmission intrusion. By using automatic signal hopping, it changed its frequency hundreds of times per second during transmission, making it virtually impossible to intercept a signal. The HAWCs' headpiece units were not powerful enough to communicate directly with command so they were relayed to Benson's unit which pushed them up and out of the cave to another relay point in southern Australia. Satisfied, Benson pulled the flap down over the small box to blanket its winking lights.

He switched off all the camp lighting, unfolded his blackout cloth and covered himself. The cloth absorbed light and broke up the telltale human shape. He did not move, he became part of the cave's natural debris. He had selected a position with his back to the west wall where he had all compass quadrants covered. Just his eyes and gun muzzle peered out from the cloth. In all his years of elite soldiering he had never made a mistake, even when he was captured in Afghanistan and tortured for three days. They had chopped off his fingers, slice by slice, and he never talked, never wavered. In this business, one mis-

take was all that was needed to make the difference between life and death.

The Russian moved around the gaping hole to the eastern
edge. He unfolded his Dragunov SVDS sniper rifle. This
version, with its shortened barrel, flash suppressor and
polymer structure was his weapon of choice for distance
killing. He clipped the silencer into place. The newer,
Russian-designed silencers used baffle chambers to shift
the frequency of the sound beyond the range of human
hearing; it provided an almost soundless kill—less enjoy-
ment for the big assassin, but a necessity when silence was
critical to an operation.

Benson's sixth sense was tingling and he switched to night
vision. He was being watched, but from where? He rapidly
scanned in an arc around his perimeter, then quickly turned
his face towards the ceiling.

The glass-tipped bullet entered his forehead directly
above and between his eyes. On entry the bullet tip was
designed to shear away; it had done its job of maintaining
the projectile's aerodynamics, the remaining slug was effectively a hollow point, broadening inside the skull cavity and turning his brain to soup. Benson fell forward—he
had ceased to exist.

Uli Borshov circled his hand in the air once. The other
two Krofskoya agents broke from their concealed positions in the snow and the three of them raced to the drop
winch.

As the Americans would say, time to join the party.

With his HAWCs spread around the scientists, Alex
should have felt a degree of security for his charges. However, his earlier unsettled feeling hadn't abated and in fact

was growing stronger. He also couldn't shake the sensation that they were being watched, or somehow followed.

Moving away from the column of light the team now
entered complete dark and from over Alex's shoulders the
scientists' torch beams created pipes of light that waved
in all directions. It gave him a chance to scrutinise his
surroundings; for the most part the massive tunnel they
were in was featureless, with few of the formations you
would expect in a large, ancient cave system. The walls,
floor and ceilings were smoothed, perhaps as Monica said
by ice or water, but it still looked unnatural. Even Alex
could feel the weight of the silence; if not for the multiple
footfalls you might have heard your own heartbeat. Alex
could hear that no one was breathing particularly hard as
the clear slope was angling downward. The major surprise for Alex was the temperature—the more they trekked,
the warmer it became.

After hiking steadily for sixty minutes, Alex called a
ten-minute rest break. He ordered Johnson to scout ahead
for five minutes and then report back in. Johnson acknowledged the order with a brief "affirmative," switched to
night scope vision, and disappeared into the still darkness.

From behind Alex, Adrian Silex said in his whining,
nasal tone, "I don't get it, one moment it seems we have air
pockets under us, the next we have water. I can't understand how Dr. Hendsen ever received a positive reading
unless it was somewhere much deeper than here. If we don't
find a testing base site that is on geologically stable ground
I won't be able to receive a clear reading and we will have
wasted our time. Captain, can you please organise for us to
continue onward a bit more quickly?"

Borshov spent time going over Benson's equipment and
caving suit. He needed to know what the American HAWCs
had brought with them and what he would be dealing with.

He held up Benson's M98 and sighted along the barrel. He secreted it among some rocks—a little insurance was a good thing, he thought. The other two Russian assassins wasted little time in destroying communications equipment and anything else that could aid the American team. They looked like three large alien insects in their black head-to-toe infiltration suits. Down in the darkened cave, even their faces were covered with the single lens of the Generation-III cyclops night vision scope extending outwards from their brows. They moved quickly but surely to catch up with the American team.

Borshov looked forward to meeting his old friend again, and seeing if this time his thick American head could hold one of the exploding bullets he was saving.

Alex's comm unit pinged as Johnson out at point reported in. "All clear so far, however the slope is deepening to an incline of about thirty degrees. No sign of the Hendsen party other than the footprints—they just keep heading on into the cave depths."

Alex couldn't help thinking aloud. "Where the hell were they all going? OK, roger that; hold your position, we're coming down. Be with you in about seven minutes."

# Ten

Johnson found an alcove in the cave wall and folded himself in. His training dictated that on field operations you leave as little of your body exposed and undefended as possible.

From the cave depths there was a soft watery sound. Johnson's head whipped around and he strained to hear more. Even with his senses tuned and his electronic equipment at their maximum settings no movement or heat shapes could be detected. He quickly scanned his perimeter and when he turned back to the cave ahead he could now just make out a vaguely human shape about a hundred feet farther in. He remained silent and immobile, even his breathing slowed. The shape moved closer to Johnson's position in a gliding, oily motion.

When the shape was only about twenty feet away Johnson could make out it was a man, but he looked oily or wet; almost like he was covered in mucous or something slick. As the figure came still closer, he could also now see he was dressed in the clothes of the previous rescue party. Johnson adjusted the magnification on his night scope and could make out the name tag: Hendsen.

"Dr. Hendsen, sir, are you all right?"

Hendsen didn't acknowledge him. However, he did seem to move a little closer. Might be in shock or disorientated, he thought. Johnson stood up slowly and walked carefully sideways towards the figure of Hendsen; as he did so he pinged his comm unit and reported in.

"Boss, I got a survivor here—looks to be Dr. Tom Hendsen but he looks kind of strange."

Alex's senses went into overdrive, he turned away and so as not to alert the rest of the scientific team said as quietly, and forcefully as he could manage, "Johnson, you will hold your position. Do not interact with or approach survivor. Is that clear?"

As Johnson was about to confirm his last order, he took a single step back towards cover. His movement triggered an explosion of activity in the Tom Hendsen shape. It leaped forward as if on a spring and smashed into Johnson front-on with a wet smacking sound that echoed back down into the cavern. Johnson felt the juddering impact but was less dazed than he expected to be. Hendsen was an average-sized man and he thought he should have at least been knocked off his feet by the collision. However the mass that struck him was softer than it had a right to be and he found himself held upright and actually glued in place. He reached up with his free hand to push himself away but this too sank into the mass and became stuck.

The acrid chemical smell was making his eyes water and he noticed a thick, fleshy cord extending from the thing's back and away into the cave depths. His comm unit pinged urgently for attention, but he had no chance of responding as even his face was now adhered to the Tom Hendsen shape. The final agony came as several dagger-like tusks extended from the shape and pierced his body. His last coherent thought was of the running footprints, the dragging, the missing bodies; suddenly it all came together.

Johnson managed a single muffled scream as he was

roughly yanked off his feet and dragged struggling into the depths of the cave.

Alex's heightened senses were screaming at him. He was learning to use his extraordinary capabilities to pick up a person's presence when they were in his proximity; and a few seconds ago he could "feel" Johnson out at point. But now . . . gone.

"Johnson, report in." Nothing. "Report in, Lieutenant!" Just static. Nothing.

"Mike, Tank, with me. Takeda, keep the group together and move them slowly up behind us. I don't want any stragglers." The HAWCs sprinted off into the darkness.

In a few minutes, Alex had found the last position of Lieutenant John Johnson. A few seconds later Mike and then Tank caught up and joined him. Though Alex slowed the last dozen paces to approach with caution, no one on the team could hope to keep pace with him when he opened it up. "Tank, eyes forward and cover." Tank nodded and trotted silently further into the cave depths. He had switched to stealth mode so to anyone other than another HAWC he was virtually invisible.

Alex and Mike crouched down and switched on their helmet lamps. The ground showed a single pair of HAWC footprints moving to an area of major ground disturbance. However, this was fairly vague as there was still roughly another dozen sets of footsteps and drag marks from the Hendsen party continuing on into the darkness.

"Contact was made here, a struggle, then nothing." Alex stood up.

Mike looked around and said to Alex, "No blood, no debris; do you think the Hendsen team took him?"

Alex looked at Mike. "Taken a solider like Johnson, in just seconds, with all his skill and firepower? No way; he'd have taken them apart."

Alex looked back down into the darkness. "Do you smell that?" There was the lingering smell of ammonia in the air. Alex went on. "No. He was ambushed and taken by someone or something unexpected and overwhelming." Alex spoke to Mike and Tank who had again joined them, and he also voiced-in Takeda via his comm unit. "Soldiers, we are not alone. Prepare to go hot."

The two teams joined up and Takeda mentioned that the SINCGARS relay module must have been resetting as the line to the surface had dropped out. Alex immediately tried Benson but received no response. A knot formed in his stomach. With tons of rock, and magnetic interference between them and topside he knew losing transmission was to be expected. Still . . .

Alex stood for a moment, looking up at the dark rock above them, as if trying to see through the layers of lime-stone and miles of cave. He was tempted to drag them all out, but he had no information to cause him to think Ben-son was in trouble. He had to assume he was OK and there-fore his priority was to find Johnson. Alex didn't think he had disappeared due to an accidental fall; if he found proof it was a hostile intervention, he'd decide then whether to withdraw or engage. Alex felt a flame light inside him; his senses amplified and the hand on the stock of his gun squeezed until a small popping could be heard from the toughened polymer compound. Not now, he thought to himself; he closed his eyes and smelled green apples until the flame subsided.

He opened his eyes. He'd put it to the scientists, let them think about it and decide if they wanted to proceed or return to base camp. It was still their mission. Alex would try to persuade them to head back so he could run a search for Johnson unencumbered by civilians.

"Listen up, people, here is our situation. We are offline

with HQ, probably due to nothing more than magnetic disturbance. We were expecting this as the polar iono-sphere tends to fragment our signals, resulting in tempo-rary drop-outs in our global comms. There is nothing to worry about, however, what does concern me is that one of my men may have engaged with an unknown adver-sary farther down in the caves not twenty minutes ago—that man is now missing. There are tracks everywhere indicating that the Hendsen party was in motion, or was herded further into the cave system. It is my firm belief that there is significant danger of a hostile encounter if we proceed." Alex looked at the group and gauged their reac-tions. Mostly confusion, but no panic—good.

"Could he have been found by the previous party?" Alex could see the hope in Aimee's eyes as she asked the question. She desperately wanted to find evidence that could lead them to Tom Hendsen. He wouldn't tell her about Johnson reporting that he had seen her colleague; he thought she might grab a torch and charge off into the dark.

"That's a possibility, but we don't believe the previous party is involved in his disappearance." Aimee was about to ask another question but he cut her off—he wasn't ready to share his thoughts on who or what Tom Hendsen had encountered just yet.

"We could proceed, but I believe the best option is for you to return to the base camp temporarily with Takeda. This will allow my men and myself to do a rapid search. If there is no danger and we find our man, we can meet you and return, time permitting." Alex knew a return was unlikely; it would take them several hours just to retrace their steps. Waiting for Alex and then coming back down would not give them enough time to meet the returning helicopter—it certainly wouldn't wait long in below-zero temperatures.

"I'm for returning to base camp." Corporal Margaret Anderson hadn't looked comfortable since they headed into the darkness of the caves, so Alex wasn't surprised that she would vote to leave. He suspected Zegarelli would follow his partner's lead. He was military and would be able to read Alex's signals about the dangers in going forward.

"Dr. Silex, we should probably move immed—" Alex was cut off mid-sentence by the lead scientist who had stepped forward from the group.

"Captain, you said that your man had disappeared. Could he not have simply run off into the dark and fallen into a chasm? This area is honeycombed, you know."

"We don't believe that is the case, Dr. Silex."

"What do you believe, Captain? I didn't hear any yelling or gunshots. Did you see this unknown adversary? What even made you think there was an adversary? More than likely your man got disoriented in the dark and is lost with a broken radio. More plausible than your Special Forces soldier getting jumped by someone hiding in the caves. I know you're champing at the bit to assume command, Captain, but this is still a science-led mission and I say we proceed."

Alex couldn't tell them what he sensed without it sounding like baseless fears, but he would try one last time to turn them. "Aimee, Matt, Monica, everyone gets a vote here. Aimee, can you take your readings at this level?"

"Sorry, Alex, it's like standing on the top of a tall building; too many floors to see through before we actually get to solid bedrock. Dr. Silex is right; too much honeycombing. Besides, I feel we're close. If there is a chance the previous party is alive then we need to find them." Alex nodded and looked to Matt.

"I vote to proceed. There is evidence of an ancient civilisation like nothing I have ever seen. You know, the previous party may have found something and went deeper to investigate." Alex could tell Matt probably didn't think that this was the case, but the hordes of hell weren't going to stop him from investigating his ruins.

Monica just shrugged. "Stable environment, low-angle slope; no problems. I'll go with the flow."

Ah, civilians, thought Alex. "OK, we proceed, but at a more cautious rate. However, if we encounter any form of aggressive interference, this ceases to be a science mission and we evac to the surface immediately." Alex didn't wait to get agreement and as he was about to turn away he caught the narrowed eyes of the lead scientist. He held them for a moment before Silex shook his head and looked away. In that glare Alex could tell the man was silently fuming. Maybe he didn't like the idea of the potential change of mission command or having to return to the surface. It didn't matter; Alex's priority was to keep the team safe, not make friends.

Alex called his men in. They had been silent hulks in the dark, facing away from Alex and the group, sensor units set to maximum as they scanned the depths of the cave. "We go forward. Tank, at point with me. Mike, Takeda, rear-guard, eyes front and back, stay on red." The HAWCs nodded once.

"Let's go, people." The group shouldered their backpacks and marched forward into the yawning, black cave.

# Eleven

Alex and Tank moved through the stygian darkness like phantoms. Tank was about ten feet up and to the left, his huge bulk barely making a sound. Both had their Patriot scopes engaged but Alex was now finding that his own eyes were delivering depth, peripheral and light enhancement that exceeded the military technology. He disengaged the night scope; for light amplification their background illumination was second to none, but the trade-off was in full-field perception. Alex preferred his own eyes.

His mind wandered, either his physical changes were accelerating or they were just flexing like new muscles being tried out for the first time. Only a few minutes earlier a small fury had started to burn within him; he had managed to contain it this time, but he worried about being in a more pressured situation—what then?

Tank suddenly dropped from view. Shit! Alex's mind snapped back into focus. He covered the distance between them in less than a second—an abyss; the cave floor had abruptly ended.

Tank was just over the lip of a drop off into a black chasm, dangling with his back to the wall. The toughened fingertips of his caving glove were buried in the top of a small shelf, the other holding his knife as he tried to reach up and dig it in behind his head for higher purchase. In

one smooth motion Alex leaned out over the rim of the
cliff and took the knife from Tank's hand. Swinging it
around in an arc, he embedded it six inches into the cave
floor with the sound of a sledgehammer striking a rail spike.
His hand now secured by the deeply wedged knife, Alex
grabbed the front of Tank's reinforced caving suit and
lifted. Tank, fully kitted out, must have weighed over 250
pounds; Alex lifted him up and over the lip like he was little
more than a laundry bag full of linen. He sat the big man
down next to him.

"Watch that first step, big fella."

Tank looked at Alex, then at his knife sunk into the
stone of the cave floor. "Been working out, boss?"

"Nah, we were lucky—just got an adrenaline rush
when I saw you go over. You OK?"

"Fine now, but praise the Lord, Ms. Jennings was right
about these suits—you don't need to take them off to use
the bathroom."

They stood on the edge of an abyss that dropped away
into impenetrable darkness. Raising her chin and breathing deeply, Aimee could feel a slight breeze blowing up
from the depths, carrying with it a hint of rich mosses and
humidity. She stood a little back from the edge; there were
two things that made her feel uneasy—swimming in the
ocean at night and darkened heights. Even though it was
much warmer now, she shivered as she remembered the
time five years ago when she attempted to leave a down-
town building late one evening. While waiting for an elevator to take her back to the lobby from the fourteenth floor,
the double doors had slid open to reveal a shaft without
the car. An empty black doorway which led into nothingness. Aimee, daydreaming, had stepped forward and had
only been stopped from plunging hundreds of feet to her

death by a watchful security guard. She had been nauseous for days afterwards.

Twenty feet across the gap the cave continued. Aimee watched Monica crack a glow stick, shake it to get maximum illumination and then drop it over the edge. They all held their breath and waited—and waited. After a while, when the stick had obviously passed out of range of their vision, and no sounds of it hitting bottom could be heard, Monica turned to the group.

"OK, climbing down is not a good idea," she said.

The HAWCs increased the illumination on their torches and the strong lights showed what looked to be piles of clothing or packs on the cave floor over the gap.

"That's them; they're over there." Aimee had stepped forward, her excitement at the chance of finding Tom alive overtaking her fear of the chasm edge. Alex put his hand out to gently hold her upper arm and looked over her head to Monica.

"We need to get over there, Ms. Jennings."

Monica was already looking up at the ceiling to formulate a route. "No problem. I'll cam-crawl across the roof and secure a line to the far wall. We can rig up a rope jerrybridge and relay everyone over. Give me about ten minutes." With that she stripped off her pack and removed a belt containing an impressive array of equipment. "About time I got to try out this new gear."

Aimee thought she knew a little about rock climbers and their equipment. Many Saturday nights had been spent with a pizza, a bottle of red wine and the Discovery Channel for company. She had watched in awe as Edurne Pasaban of Spain, followed by the Italian Nives Meroi and Yuka Komatsu of Japan—three women—had broken the K2 mountain's curse on women and climbed to the top of the feared peak in the Himalayas. She had marvelled at how these small women had ascended the 28,000 feet in freezing conditions while weighed down with all their equipment. She wished now she had paid more attention. However, she did remember the cams—devices with two or more half discs with small teeth that when operated sprang open and expanded into cracks in the rock. They were the tools of trade for rock climbers and mountaineers the world over. Monica's version was slightly different and consisted of four spring-loaded cams with a trigger that looked like it could be easily operated one-handed.

Aimee watched in disbelief as Monica crawled and swung across the cave ceiling, placing cams along the way connected to a soft, twisted fibre rope. In no time she dropped lightly to the cave floor on the other side, still not even breathing hard. It was a simple matter then to set up the jerry-bridge. This was a basic construction that opened in a V shape with hardened plastic plates at the bottom where the V joined. You could simply walk across, placing one foot in front of the other.

Aimee felt her legs go weak at the thought of stepping out onto a rope bridge that was little wider at the base than her own foot. She hugged herself and thought: are we having fun yet? She looked up at Alex; he was absolutely calm and she drew strength from his presence.

After securing the ladder on both sides, Monica crossed back to test the bridge's strength and give the team a quick demonstration of how to cross safely. She stood before them now with her hands on her hips. "OK, this is extremely safe; the bridge ropes are of a kernmantle construction which means they are soft to touch but have enormous tensile strength. Where you will be stepping is a polymerised plastic plate—I guarantee it will not break and actually increases strength under stress."

She looked at Alex. "We're good to go."

Aimee drew in a shuddering breath, took her place in the line and focused on the pile of clothing over the chasm.

Alex nodded to Mike and Tank. They crossed without problem, and while Mike waited on the opposite edge of the crevasse to offer any assistance, Tank trotted ahead to provide some initial recon and some forward cover. The two medics crossed next, followed by Matt, Aimee, Silex and Takeda. Alex took one more look back the way they had come. Strange, he didn't understand enough about his newly amplified senses to know exactly what they were telling him, but he could feel a presence behind them. Was it Benson? He looked forward again and past the group into the caves; there was also something there. Maybe it was the lost group he was sensing. It was confusing; he needed to stay cool, stay focused. He crossed the bridge and ignored the prickling sensation on the back of his neck.

"It's all torn up." Aimee dropped the thermal undershirt back onto the pile of clothing. Belts, backpacks and piles of ripped material, even boots were strewn around. She was shaking her head. "Why would they rip it up? Why would they even take everything off?"

"Disorientation, cerebral oedema, even severe dehydration—a hundred things can cause all sorts of aberrant behaviour, Aimee. Come on, we'll find them." Silex had put his arm around her and rubbed her shoulder. She looked at him and nodded.

"Thanks, Adrian, you're probably right. I'll be OK." She went to rejoin the team but he held her and gave her arm a little squeeze.

"Are you sure, Aimee? I'm here if you need me." His bald head bobbed at her and he was close enough now for her to smell his breath. She compressed her lips in a

tight smile, nodded again and pushed out from under his
thin arm.

"Check this out, you guys," Matt exclaimed from further
down the cave tunnel. There were more of the ancient
glyphs carved into the dark stone of the cave wall. Monica and Aimee stopped as the HAWCs and Silex continued on a few more paces. "These are of a similar style to
the ones back at the cave opening. Monica, look at this,
it's that same symbol I showed you before; the seal of the
two brother warriors—the twins."

Monica came and stood next to him. "What's it all
say?"

"I'm not sure."

"Damn, if only we had that other guy from Central
America." Monica elbowed Matt in the ribs and he laughed.

"Well, I can see the symbols for the brothers and also for
that eye and coiled ropes which is the symbol of the deceiver god—the *Qwotoan* I mentioned before. And there's
more about following the path to the underworld. Other
than that, at this stage it's what we in the archaeology business call a vanished language; the images and symbols are
mostly a mystery . . . and would be to *ev-ery-one*." Matt
turned and shone his torch directly into Monica's eyes as
she mouthed the word *magic* again.

"I wonder where they all vanished to?" asked Aimee.

"I've been wondering the same thing. And I've been
wondering a few other things about those two warriors,"
Matt replied.

The medics, Margaret and Bruno, had joined them now,
and Matt turned to them. "You know, this could be just
coincidental, but there is an ancient Mayan myth about the
creation of the universe that described their version of
heaven and earth and the gods and creatures within it. It
also featured two brave twins, Hunahpu and Xbalanque,

the sons of the blood moon. In the myth, they travelled deep below the earth to their Hades, a place they called Xibalba. Like a lot of ancient races, the Mayan myths were thought to have been handed down from even earlier populations. What if the legend of the brothers wasn't all myth? What if it was one of those stories that was passed down over the millennia and was never a myth at all but the documentation of an actual journey below ground by these two warriors."

Matt was breathing heavily, and he sucked in a deep breath before continuing. "Aimee, you asked where they all vanished to. I've been thinking about that as well. This could be another population disappearance. These Aztlans could have sent out parties to all corners of the globe—that would explain how their writing style was seeded everywhere from the Egyptians to the Mayans. But the rest seem to have just disappeared. The disappearances and the name *Qwotoan*—I've been racking my brain about it; I knew I'd heard something like it before. The first English attempt of settlement at Roanoke in 1587. Over a hundred people disappeared without a trace, and the only clue to their fate was the word *Croatoan* carved into a tree. Do you see the similarity—*Croatoan*, and *Qwotoan*? It could be the same word, but expressed in different languages. If there is one thing that will cross time, geography and races, it's a warning."

The look on Matt's face was as if he had just been handed two stone tablets from the top of the mountain. However, with Tom missing, Aimee was in no mood to hear about inexplicable disappearances. The scientist in her leaped at the vague but fantastical inferences he was drawing from the little data he had to work with.

"Matt, everything you have mentioned has, or will have, a scientific explanation." Aimee saw Matt open his mouth and raise his finger to interject, but whether to apologise or debate she never knew as Takeda interrupted them both.

"Please. They've found something, you must all hurry."

Alex kneeled down beside Tank who was examining something on the cave floor. "It's Johnson's gun. No rounds fired. No blood either, just a lot of skirmish marks and more dragging." Tank looked at Alex with more anger than fear—it was a natural reaction; the team was as close as family. They all knew it was a deadly business they were in, but rated themselves as the best and looked forward to going head-to-head with any opponent. Johnson was one of their finest. So how did he get ambushed, disarmed and carried off? And how the hell did he get across the chasm by himself?

Tank went to hand the gun to Alex, but it stuck for a second. He held the barrel to his nose then offered it to Alex. He didn't need to; Alex could smell it from ten paces back. "Phew, ammonia and it's slimy," Tank said more to himself than to Alex while wiping his hand on his leg.

Alex looked up at Tank's brother. "Mike, go a hundred feet down the cave and hold your position. Report in when you get there and do not engage with anyone or anything." Mike nodded, snapped off a quick "roger that," and was gone.

The entire team had now crowded around Alex and Tank. Alex handed the gun to Aimee. "Dr. Weir, your opinion please."

Aimee touched the substance with her gloved finger, held it up to her nose and sniffed. She also tested its consistency between her thumb and forefinger. "I can't be a hundred percent sure being away from the lab, but I'd say this is ammonium chloride. But there's something else—some sort of biological binder making it sticky that I can't identify without further analysis. Dr. Silex . . ." Aimee held out the gun to Silex but he made no attempt to accept it.

"I'd say it's probably an introduced contaminant. Maybe something the soldier brought with him and spilled."

Alex ignored the scientist and turned to Monica Jennings. "Could this be a naturally occurring substance down here?"

Monica tilted her head. "Maybe, but unlikely. In deep caves, ammonium chloride can occur naturally, but usually in active volcanic regions, and usually near fume-releasing vents. But even then it dissolves quickly. This area doesn't seem active enough to me and that looks fresh. It shouldn't be here."

"Secretion," Alex said softly to himself, remembering the last communication received from Dr. Tom Hendsen and the organic substance he had found but couldn't identify. Alex's comm unit pinged once. "Mike, go ahead."

"I got another drop-off. About a hundred feet straight down to what looks like a plateau with multiple exits leading off from the cave floor down there. At the lip here there's significant ground disturbance and then the tracks seem to end. The Hendsen party seems to have launched themselves off the edge, but I can't see any bodies or debris down below."

"OK, Mike. Look for a way down or signs they could have descended themselves. Stay alert, we're on our way."

Borshov and his agents sped through the dark labyrinth. Like three black wolves closing in on their prey, they travelled lightly and in complete silence. Borshov pushed his men hard; he knew they still had ground to cover before they caught up with the American team, but he was confident there would be no ambush, no hidden detonations or trip-wires just yet. They were not expecting unwelcome company and besides, they still thought they had a man at rear cover.

Borshov stopped his men with a raised hand and, as he had done every thirty minutes since they had set off down into the tunnel depths, withdrew a small box which he pressed down onto the cold ground. A wire trailing from the back of the device ended in an earpiece which he pushed into his ear. The device was a miniaturised seismic resonator. It listened to solid surfaces and amplified vibrations so they could be clearly read. The small LCD screen on the back gave two readings: the distance of the loudest vibration and the direction. The Russian invention was created purely for use by its anti-terrorism units for "listening" though solid walls—a terrorist could be pinpointed simply by taking a single soft footstep.

From the last reading Borshov had taken, the Americans had been just over three miles in the lead, but at their current speed he expected to catch them quickly. He listened again for their footfalls and looked down at the small box for its directional readings. Good, they were still closing, now just over two miles between them. South-south-east with a slightly increasing descent—they must be climbing down at some sections. As Borshov was about to pull his device free from the stone it began to reset before his eyes. It had found another source of resonance. The figures increased rapidly until they stopped at numbers indicating a distance of about two miles, but nearly ninety degrees straight down, and shifting. Borshov closed his eyes to concentrate on the sounds; significant mass, liquid, moving. He pulled the device free. Underground river, he thought.

He gave a short sharp whistle to his agents and sped on again into the dark.

Monica was walking lightly beside Matt, alert to her surroundings, but from time to time dropping deeply into her own thoughts. Be careful, be silent, touch nothing, leave nothing behind; her caving experience made it all automatic now. She used to like nothing more than entering a pitch black cave for the first time, turning out her light and just standing there in the dark, opening her arms wide and just feeling. She would use all her senses other than sight to draw in all the smells, the minute sounds, and feel the weight of the stone around her. She'd done it dozens of times so why now did the thought of switching off her light in this cave give her a knotted, uncomfortable feeling deep in her stomach.

Matt turned towards her and could see the troubled look on her face. "Penny for them."

"It's nothing," Monica said softly.

"Come on, tell Uncle Matt."

"OK, remember how I said that caves were like people?"

"Hmm, yeah, some are easy, some are bitches; sounded like a few girls I knew in high school."

"And some are secretive, that's right. Well, this one is more than secretive; it's hiding something and for the first time in my life I don't feel comfortable in the dark." Matt smiled at her and put his arm around her shoulders.

"Monica, if you're ever looking for an excuse to get me to put my arm around you just ask, OK?"

"You oaf," Monica said through a little smile, but didn't push his arm away.

Alex was the first to catch up to Mike. "What've we got?" he asked while looking down over the lip of the drop-off.

"Only this." Mike stepped to the side and indicated a building-sized stalagmite. About waist high on the column there seemed to be some discolouration about ten feet into the centre of the gigantic mineralised pillar. There were also faint signs that something had led away from the column to the edge of the drop.

"What was that . . . rope?" Alex tried to pick some up but it fell to dust in his hands. "Dr. Kerns, we need you here please."

Matt trotted forward and dropped to his knees. "Wow. This looks like it was once an ancient type of Indian maguey fibre-rope. It's made from a plant like the agave, and look at this." Matt indicated the rope trail from the column to the edge and then over. "It was once wound around that stalagmite, and became embedded, fossilised within the mineral build-up. No idea how old it is though."

Aimee shone her torch on the stalagmite then crouched down beside him, her own scientific interest sparked. "We can get an estimate of its age by judging how deep the rope is embedded within the stalagmite. Looks to be about nine to ten feet in; these things grow at about two millimetres per year, so I reckon that took around ten to twelve thousand years to build up."

"That sounds about right; there haven't been any plants like the agave or any of its ancestors here for over ten thousand years," Matt said, nodding to Aimee. "It could be the brothers again. They could have used the rope to climb down."

"What brothers? Would you like to share your theories with us, Dr. Kerns?" snorted Silex from the rear of the group.

Matt got to his feet and wiped the dust from his hands. Using both his helmet and hand torch he scanned the near walls; soon enough he found what he was looking for—the seal of the warrior brothers. He turned to Silex. "From what I've been able to translate, it seems long ago there was some kind of civilisation here. Before the ice covered everything up it might have been the father and mother of all our civilisations. I think it was being plagued or attacked by something they called the *Qwotoan*, which meant the deceiver or devourer or something like that.

The ruler of this civilisation sent two warriors, a pair of brothers, to take an army and go and battle the *Qwotoan*—I think we've been following in their footsteps. The army was totally destroyed and only the brothers remained. I also think their adventure became a Mayan legend, and by looking at this rope I'd say they hadn't given up on their quest and I reckon they went that way." While keeping his eyes on Silex, Matt pointed with his thumb over the rim to the lower cave floor. Silex gave Matt a look like he had just smelled something bad and turned his back on the young archaeologist.

"Captain. Captain." Silex was clicking his fingers in the air as though calling a waiter to his table. "Captain Hunter, it's like trying to read Swiss cheese from up here. You are going to have to get us down lower so we can obtain better readings. Thank you, Captain, that's all." Tank snorted and Mike looked at his brother and winked.

Alex ignored Silex and walked past him a few paces into the darkness. Alex could sense them now; several of them were coming fast the way they had just come. If not Benson, then who? He closed his eyes and tried to picture the tunnels in his mind.

When Alex had been talking to Hammerson about his strange new abilities the Hammer had given him a copy of a secret naval report titled "Anomalous Cognition in Marine Mammals." The navy had been using dolphins for all manner of experiments since the 1950s due to their uncanny ability to predict or sense danger. The scientific basis was that their unique brains could pick up everything from electromagnetic disturbances to sensitive seismic vibrations long before other animals. Hammerson's inference was clear; he believed Alex was developing this ability. Alex opened his eyes; there they were. Their presence became clearer—four of them, no three, but one of them large. Alex made a decision.

"Ms. Jennings, can you get us down there quickly?"

Monica had been leaning far out over the edge, shining her torch along the wall to the cave floor. "It's a basin. A piece of cave floor that has dropped due to ancient volcanic activity or from water passing over softer material. More likely water by the look of how the cave floor down there has been smoothed and the walls are surrounded by more cave exits. No problem. A straight drop by harness rope; all down in thirty minutes. OK?"

"Make it twenty minutes and drinks are on me." Alex turned away from Monica and called Tank, Takeda and Mike in close. "We've got company, only about an hour out. Not sure if they're hostile, but just in case I don't want to be caught here with our back to this drop, or at the base of the cliff. We drop down, get under cover and take one final look for Johnson and the Hendsen party. Be alert but stay cool; we don't want a stampede down here."

None of the HAWCs asked how Alex knew about the contact; it didn't matter, his judgment and orders were final.

The creature waited. Its great spread-out mass could feel the light footsteps of the little warm bloods through the miles of stone. It sensed more of them moving towards the larger group. It moved upwards once again in anticipation of the attack.

# Twelve

Monica had them all on the lower cave floor within twenty minutes. The area was a cavern junction system where many caves fed into the large lower cathedral where they now stood. Alex moved them briskly out of the open area of the cavern floor and to the south. His equipment told him he was now nearly a mile under the rock and ice and this was as low as he was prepared to go.

Alex ordered Mike to scout further down the main cave to provide forward cover and some initial recon for any further Hendsen party clues. He didn't expect to find anyone alive, especially not Lieutenant Johnson. He knew a HAWC would only release his gun when he was dead, and even then under protest. Against his better judgment, he allowed Matt Kerns to accompany Mike so he could satisfy his curiosity in regards to any archaeological artifacts in the lower caves. However, he told the young archaeologist that the HAWC was authorised to shoot him if he disobeyed his instructions.

"Phew, it's getting hot now," said Margaret Anderson, wiping a sheen of perspiration from her cheeks and forehead.

"Not really," said Monica. "Heating up, sure, but it's still only about forty degrees down here. Unfortunately, our suits are thermally lined and we weren't expecting anything much above freezing."

"Well, it feels like a hundred degrees in this suit. We didn't bring a lot of water and with the low humidity and unexpected heat, fluid loss is going to start to be a problem." The medic was right; Alex knew he needed to watch the liquid consumption.

Over to the side of the group, Alex watched Silex wrench a sheet of clear material from a flat electronic device he had set up on the floor of the cave basin. He balled it up and threw it angrily into the dark. He watched as Monica put her hands on her hips and glared at him with an ill-disguised contempt for his defilement of the pristine cave environment. Silex typed furiously onto a miniaturised keyboard, all the while shaking his head at the results on the small screen.

Alex noticed Aimee standing slightly back from the lead scientist. She was watching him with a look of concern on her face and he walked silently over to join her. "What's his problem?"

"That device is Silex's own design—the supposed next generation of stratigraphic imaging technologies. Where most stratigraphs give you an interpretation of the different densities and morphologies of the stone and can highlight petroleum beds, they still have a high degree of uncertainty. Dr. Silex thinks he has solved the uncertainty equation by generating high-resolution seismic images using a form of spectral decomposition. Theoretically, if there's an oil reservoir, it'll be displayed in 3D with colour-coded rock morphologies, depth and even the reservoir target boundaries—degree of uncertainty: point zero zero one five." Aimee could see some of the jargon was being lost on Alex, so she broke it down further.

"Have you ever seen an ultrasound picture? Well, imagine that grainy, black-and-white image sitting next to a high-resolution colour photograph. According to Dr. Silex, that will be the clarity differential."

"Looks like there are still a few bugs." Alex nodded at Silex who again screwed up another piece of the clear film paper and squeezed it in his fist.

Aimee looked up at Alex and nodded slightly. "Maybe. Mining and oil exploration is a multi-trillion-dollar business; that device could be worth billions. He really needs a successful field test." She shook her head and her eyes softened slightly. "I can't help him. I can determine the purity of any reservoir, its approximate biological decomposition age and even calculate its potential yield. But we've got to find it first. That's Dr. Silex's job."

Alex looked back at Silex in time to see him throw another ball of paper into the gloom. This time Monica set her jaw and headed towards him. Alex groaned and excused himself from Aimee. He moved quickly to head Monica off.

Alex and Monica arrived at the same time Silex was pulling another sheet of paper from his imager. He looked up, and as Alex expected only saw the HAWC's large frame. He came quickly to his feet.

"We need to get deeper, Captain."

"I'm sorry, Dr. Silex, we're around a mile down; that's as deep as I feel we can safely go. Might not feel like it but we've been travelling for eight hours. It's going to take us longer to return as that gentle slope we felt coming down won't feel so easy on the way back up, especially now that we're all tired."

Silex had been screwing up the film paper he had in his hand and Monica was determined to make sure he didn't throw this one into the cave system. She opened her mouth to speak but was dismissed with a curt "piss off." Silex turned back to Alex, hastily unfolding the paper and holding it in front of his face. The coloured swirls and numbers meant nothing to him.

"Look, water. All I'm reading is stupid fucking water.

We are standing on top of some sort of bloody great lake or underground sea. I need to take readings from a different position to validate my calculations or this trip has been a complete waste of time and money. Your instructions were to follow my commands. This is the priority, Captain; we can set aside another few hours for that."

Alex noticed that the two medics had wandered closer, their attention caught by the scientist's rising tone. Margaret Anderson had opened the collar of her suit and was very flushed in the face and Bruno was now wearing her backpack, trying to lighten her load. He was also sweating into the dark rubberised clothing and both had their eyes on Alex. Margaret's expression was pained and he could tell she wanted to start the ascent.

"Dr. Silex, we're performing one final sweep of the south cave for Johnson and the Hendsen party then we'll be immediately returning to the surface." Alex would have rested them all night here and then started the climb out, but he wanted to be away from the open basin before the others arrived. Alex could see the relief on the face of everyone except Silex, whose expression turned from one of officiousness to angry disbelief.

"Oh no, no. If we need to go lower, we'll go lower. We will have hours to spare before the helicopter arrives and my tests have international importance. Captain, if we return to the surface and I tell them that you pulled us out before I could complete my tests, and that you did so against my wishes, what do you think your superiors will say? Let's see, disobeying my orders, no idea on the whereabouts of the Hendsen party and you have lost one of your own men. Is this your first command, Captain Hunter?" Silex pursed his lips and his expression changed again to one of self-importance.

Alex stared hard into the scientist's face, causing him to back up a step. Alex wasn't trying to intimidate the smaller man, but to observe the changing heat patterns on his skin and his pupil dilation. In the gloom, Silex's eyes should have been large dark discs, not the pinpoints he was seeing. This man was becoming hostile and was clearly under a lot of stress—surely there'd be other opportunities to test his device? Strange, thought Alex, he's hiding something.

Alex kept his eyes on the man. He was trying to decide how best to respond without further inflaming him when Silex took another step to the side to look past him at Aimee who was standing with her arms folded and watching from a few paces away.

"Tell him, Dr. Weir, Aimee. Tell him how we are probably only a few miles away from one of the greatest oil discoveries in the last fifty years and we just need to position our equipment in a better geometry to improve the spatial images." Silex looked back at Alex, his eyes wide around their tiny pupils.

Inaudible to everyone else, Alex heard Aimee groan quietly at being dragged in and expected to take sides. "It's possible, Adrian; however, you can feel the heat now as well. We must be very close to some form of geothermic activity, and the likelihood of finding oil or gas occurring near a superheated environment is extremely low. Probably best to head back up and take some broader satellite images."

Silex rounded on her with his mouth hanging open in disbelief. He stepped in close and spoke to her as if to a small child. "Dr. Weir, you know damn well that the heat could be the result of a single volcanic vent and that a large volume petroleum deposit can easily exist shielded by a solid layer of shale. My spectral scanners can detect deposits several miles down and a mile in all directions, provided this idiot soldier is able to get me to a solid, stable position away from this fucking water source."

"Excuse me, sir, we need to start moving into the main south cave. You may find an area that is more promising for your testing. Would you like my men to assist you in repacking?" As far as Alex was concerned the scientific part of this mission was concluding, but he needed to have the scientist maintain an air of civility to his men and the other team members—there could be no conflicts within the party. Cave environments could be extremely dangerous and Alex had a sense that this one was going to test them all before they arrived back at the surface.

Silex shook his head at Alex, and taking Aimee by the arm started to lead her away from the HAWC and the other watching team members. "Aimee, please, what are you doing listening to that army imbecile? He's obviously out of his depth. I recommended to Major Hammerson before we left that we needed more scientific personnel on this expedition, not a bunch of dimwitted Neanderthal soldiers."

Aimee looked at him. "Dr. Silex, I don't know what your problem with the rest of the team is, but I sure as hell don't have the same passion for field testing your new device as you do. The surficial liquid originally identified by Tom must have been that enormous body of water you've been reading. Wrong call, as it happens. This expedition is just about over; the risks are becoming too great."

Silex grabbed Aimee's sleeve, his voice lowering and developing a pleading inflection. "Look Aimee, please, if we prove the existence of petroleum or natural gas deposits in the near area with my new imager we won't need to be making basic wage with the fucking military anymore. I wasn't going to tell you this, but I've been approached by Texegen—they want to buy out my patent. I can make you an advisor, or a minority partner; you'll never have to work again. I need your support here, please, Aimee." He was now holding her forearm with both his hands and was squeezing her skin underneath the cave suit as if to milk approval from her.

Alex was standing ten feet away with his back turned but his sensitive hearing allowed him to catch every nuance of the conversation. He felt like wringing the scientist's neck; the U.S. government funded all of Silex's research and should have first rights to any inventions and downstream discoveries. Alex shook his head and wondered what the man was like before greed and self-interest became his prime motives. He'd let the Hammer deal with him on their return. He turned and watched Aimee gently tug her arm free and respond to him.

"No, thank you, Dr. Silex. I don't think that sounds legal and besides, staying here any longer may just be putting us all in danger."

"Bullshit. You don't have to agree with everything that side of beef says, you know. I really don't understand you; for an intelligent woman you're acting more like a love-sick teenager. You're making wrong decisions, Dr. Weir; maybe you just aren't as smart as Tom and I thought you were." Silex spun away before Aimee could respond.

Aimee stood stunned in the darkness. Disgust and anger flared briefly, and then just as quickly morphed into pity. But it wasn't the kind of pity that made her want to help Silex or offer assistance; more the sort of pity one feels when seeing a scorpion trapped in a spider's web. Sad, but dangerous and repellent, and best to just avoid it altogether. At least she now knew why he had volunteered to come to the Antarctic and why he was pushing Alex and his team so hard to take them all further into the caves. Texegen was a trillion-dollar oil and gas conglomerate and had approached her at GBR several times, mostly just for job offers, but sometimes with much more clandestine propositions to buy raw data and research material. They had a lot of money to spend and she bet they had already spent some on Silex.

He's going to be unbearable on the way back to the surface, she thought, and made a mental note to stay away from him. She'd stay close to Alex. She looked across to where he was standing and caught him looking at her; he smiled and then looked away. That's much better to look at, she thought. She hoped Silex didn't push him anymore as she could tell Alex was trying hard to be patient and firm with the scientist. A few times she had seen the HAWC leader's face darken and his jaws compress as though he was biting back some sharp thought or action and only just managed to keep it locked away. She really hoped Silex was smart enough to see it as well.

Borshov sent his two Krofskoya comrades over the jerry-bridge first. Not that he thought it was likely to be booby-trapped as there was no way that Captain Hunter could know he was being pursued. Nevertheless, he hadn't lived this long by making assumptions.

They couldn't be more than an hour behind them now. Their orders were to retrieve all scientific data, eliminate all mission members and make it look as if a natural disaster had befallen them. Borshov and his team must complete their mission and be gone before the American helicopter returned. Otherwise, they would be left to find their own way back.

"Wow, oh wow," Matt was bouncing from wall to wall deciphering more of the ancient glyphs carved into the stone. "*Qwotoan* flies, or maybe flees, from us while we are protected by the mighty Kinich Ahau; he was the god of the sun. Hmm, this bit's interesting. 'No more does he call to us with our fallen warriors.' Wonder what that means . . . maybe I'm translating it all wrong. Ahh, I need more time."

"Yeah, but does it say what this *Qwotoan* is? Could it still be around, and have taken Johnson?" Mike was talking over his shoulder to Matt as he continued to scan the further recesses of the cave.

"Nope. I think it's just an old legend about one of the gods these Aztlans had. They probably had gods for everything—the sun, wind, rain, disease, harvesting, fire. There is definitely a race overlap here; some of these glyph symbols representing gods are the same in Mayan and these others are almost Olmec. Every time I think I've got it, I look at the next symbol and it skips away on me. But there is obviously a clue here that I just can't draw out yet, it's nearly . . ."

Matt turned to look at Mike and froze. Mike had his gun to his shoulder and was intently watching a figure glide towards him out of the darkness. Matt could feel the hair on his head rise as the soundless figure drifted towards them. "Lieutenant Johnson," he said, "is that you?"

Alex sniffed; he was sure he could detect a faint ocean smell. Yes, definitely salt. He closed his eyes and for a brief moment was back on his favourite Australian beach with warm sun bathing his face, rather than cloistered in the dark beneath millions of tons of rock and ice.

The warm sun vanished with the sound of running feet. Alex heard someone returning from the south cave long before anyone else and he moved quickly into an intercept position. On seeing Alex moving with purpose, the other HAWCs immediately went into a flanking defence to his left and right.

Matt burst out of the black cave and rushed to Alex; his eyes were wide and rolling like a startled horse. It was clear the young man was frightened. Alex grabbed him by the shoulders and gave him a slight shake to focus him. Matt sucked in a few deep breaths and exhaled the words in a rush.

"It's Mike, he's being attacked by Johnson. He won't let go of him."

"Tank, with me." Alex disappeared into the cave darkness like a wraith, moving at a speed no normal human could. He arrived in seconds to the sound of muffled grunts and boots skidding on dry stone. Mike was being dragged into the shadows, disappearing into the gloom, seemingly held tight in his missing comrade's embrace.

Alex's mind worked hard to understand what he was seeing. The figure holding Mike looked to Alex like his missing HAWC, however, there was no warmth emanating from the body and he was glistening like he was drenched in something wet or slimy. The Johnson thing's face was expressionless; Alex thought it should have registered something just from the exertion of dragging a 200-pound man as if he was nothing more than a child.

Tank appeared beside Alex and on seeing his older brother in trouble, charged. He grabbed hold of Mike, and then Johnson, trying to drag them apart. Tank's eyes watered from the stinging putrid stench as his hand became stuck to the figure and he too was pulled off his feet and dragged towards the cave depths. Alex watched as realisation dawned on Tank's face—it wasn't Johnson; it wasn't even human.

Tank was a big man, and Alex didn't think that anyone other than himself could have resisted the force of his attack. At that moment Alex saw the cord—a thick, fleshy umbilical tether protruding from Johnson's back. The two men were being reeled in, like hooked fish on the end of a line.

Alex raised his gun and fired a continuous stream of ball bearing–sized compressed air projectiles that quickly cut through the cord. The air around them exploded with wet thrashing sounds and filled with the acrid smell of ammonia. Mike, Tank and the Johnson thing fell to the ground, and from deep within the bowels of the earth came a deep pounding and sloshing. The cord quickly withdrew, gushing a purple-black liquid as it disappeared into the cold depths of the cave.

"What the fuck was that!" yelled Tank as he lifted his brother away from the cave floor.

Mike was covered in a stinking jelly-like substance and had suffered deep lacerations and puncture wounds. The Johnson thing had released its sticky grip after being severed from the main creature and now lay deflating at their feet. In seconds it was nothing more than a six-foot long fleshy pad, almost colourless, with sucker protuberances. Lining the inside of the pad at the centre of the suckers were extendable tusks that accounted for Mike's wounds. He hadn't just been glued to the creature; he had been hooked to it as well.

Alex could feel his heart hammering in his chest; something horrendous lived in these caves and had been snatching people—the Hendsen party, Johnson, and it had tried to take Mike. He couldn't imagine what the result would have been if it had attacked while everyone was here; he would have lost them all in a mad panic into half a dozen separate pitch-black caves. He sucked in a deep breath and helped the big HAWC pull his brother up off the cave floor.

"Tank, get him back to the medics, double time."

It had not felt agony for countless generations. Its lifespan was measured in thousands of years, but it was not immortal; it could feel pain. Others of its kind had challenged it for dominance of its world and vicious fights were common. The deep cliffs and caves had echoed with the sound of the titans' warring. Now its bleeding would attract the other giants; some creatures much like it, and some vastly different.

Its kind had encountered the warm bloods before and its deep racial memories had always shown them to be food; never had they been able to hurt it. There was no fear; it knew it would regenerate quickly in the warm, dark salty waters below the earth. However, its hunger was not yet sated, and now it felt something else it had not felt for centuries—anger.

# Thirteen

Aimee was prodding the severed mass with one of Alex's knives. "This is impossible; but I can see this is only a small piece of a much larger animal. There's a terminal pad, dactylus and manus, carpal knobs and a partially severed stalk of a tentacle club. I think this is from a very large cephalopod-type creature."

"Cephalopod? A squid? Is that what you're telling us? We're in a cave deep under the earth and we just got attacked by a freaking octopus! Dr. Weir, they don't get that fucking big and they certainly don't live on—or under—the land."

Aimee looked up quickly at Silex, surprised by his fury and the way he had chosen to direct it at her. Before she could respond, Matt knelt down beside her and took the knife from her hand.

"I did my early thesis on aquatic deities and their influence on early cultures and you'd be amazed to know just how many races worshipped giant squid—or feared them. The Norse had their kraken, the Hawaiians their many-armed Kanaloa, the Babylonians had Dagon; there are dozens more. In their legends, they often came to shore and they were big. By the way, Dr. Silex, Babylon was hundreds of miles from any ocean."

Aimee had kept her eyes on Silex who was flushed and breathing hard. She spoke directly to him as calmly as she could. "Adrian, I'm not sure it's a cephalopod creature as we know it; but at least now the ammonium chloride makes sense—giant squid excrete the chemical and are literally filled with it."

While Silex appeared to be on the verge of panic, Matt looked like a schoolboy who'd just been thrown a surprise party. "Hey, that's right. I remember that from some of the cephalopod legends. The giant squid belongs to a group called ammoniacal squids. They have heavy concentrations of ammonia in their systems which gives them a few interesting little tricks. They can be neutrally buoyant and aren't destroyed by the pressure depths. They also have a high resistance to freezing; and they are real smart . . . oh, and very aggressive. Ever seen that sketch of the French ship attacked by a kraken?"

"Oh, bullshit. It still doesn't explain what it's doing so far from the ocean."

Aimee took the knife back from Matt's hand and scraped the blade along the length of the pale mottled lump, collecting a jellied glob of its slime coating. She held the knife up for Silex to see. "I've been thinking about that; there is one little extra advantage of the ammonia chloride being suspended in a gel; it will stop this thing from drying out. I agree it needs water, but it looks to have adapted to be able to leave it when it wants."

Alex took the knife back from Aimee, flicked the slime from the blade and resheathed it. "How was it able to copy us? That thing actually looked like Johnson before we severed it from the main creature."

Aimee looked down again at the six-foot stump of flesh and shuddered. Though her scientific curiosity was aroused by the discovery, she felt uneasy and vulnerable at the thought that they had just rejoined a food chain that mankind hadn't been part of for millions of years.

"This has got to be something that we've never seen

before or at least has left no trace in the fossil record. I don't know exactly how it can copy us, but I have an idea. This thing has been cut off for millions of years and has been free to follow a whole separate line of evolution, one that is limited by a vastly different environment. There are no dinosaurs or even whales to hunt it so its size would be unconstrained by predators. It may have needed to lay eggs or feed above the water, so it evolved an ability to hunt in these caves. And we know squid are intelligent; marine biologists have proved they're at least as smart as dogs." Aimee got slowly to her feet and looked at each member of the group; for different reasons, each one was now staring at her.

"But I think what is more relevant to what we have witnessed here is that some cephalopods actually have an ability to change colour and reproduce patterns and body shape to mimic other species. For instance, the sepioteuthis squid mimics parrot fish. It swims backwards and displays two false eye spots. The arms and tentacles are held together and waved from side to side like a fish's fin. Because the parrot fish is herbivorous, mimicking them allows the squid to get closer to potential prey species that do not consider parrot fish to be their predators. I think this is exactly what is happening here. It's just that we are the prey being mimicked."

Margaret Anderson's eyes were glistening with tears in the reflected light of the torches. Her face was white and she was visibly shaking. "You mean this giant thing is trying to catch us for food?"

Aimee had turned back to the large leaking mass of flesh before them and didn't respond immediately. From this distance, the acrid smell was enough to make her eyes stream and replace her dispassionate scientific observations with an impression of cunning, sheer size and lethality. The thing was covered in serrated suckers the size of dinner plates and from the centre of each, in a retractable sheath, were curved tusks that had obviously been responsible for Mike's deep wounds.

She shook her head; they should have been separated from this thing by millions of years and the thought of being anywhere near the entire creature made her stomach give a little shiver. She half-turned to Margaret and responded without looking at her.

"That would be my assumption, yes."

With the help of the quiet medic Zegarelli, Mike sat up with a groan and gave a weary and very bloody thumbs-up. Alex could see the medic had done his job and the blood loss had been staunched by using a battlefield adhesive that glued the wound back together. The big medic was stabbing him with a hypodermic full of a universal antibiotic and adrenaline as Alex knelt down next to him. Zegarelli shone a small light into Mike's eyes and asked, "What can I give you for the pain, Lieutenant? Morphine, Naloxone, whisky?"

"Give him some salt, he enjoys the pain." Alex put his hand on Mike's back to help him sit up straight.

Mike gave a small laugh which ended in a cough that coloured his lips red with blood. "Just the whisky, Bruno, and make it a double."

By habit, Mike refused all painkillers as they were likely to deaden his reflexes. While he was looking down to fasten his suit Zegarelli caught Alex's eyes. The medic made a small, flat wiping motion with his hand and then pointed straight up. Alex understood; Mike needed to be topside.

Mike coughed again and spoke directly to Alex. "It came at me when I moved. It was so fast and strong; Johnson by himself wouldn't have had a chance."

Alex kept his hand on Mike's shoulder to support him

and nodded. All the evidence pointed to the Hendsen party encountering the same creature. If they had been lured into the deeper caves then surely they were all lost.

"Thank God you made it, Mike; we need to get you back to the surface to properly treat those wounds." Alex stood and didn't need to raise his voice in the cave, now silent as a tomb. "Party's over, ladies and gentlemen. We need to evacuate this area immediately and re-establish contact with HQ. We are not equipped to deal with this type of biological threat."

Matt stepped forward. "Captain Hunter, this is the most amazing find of the century. It makes the rediscovery of the coelacanth look like an old sardine sandwich. It could validate dozens of different cultural mythologies. If I can just get a few shots of the creature, and maybe a small sample we can at least give the next guys something to work with."

Alex could understand Matt's enthusiasm, but had no time for a debate. "Dr. Kerns, every time we have encountered this creature someone has died or been hurt. My priority now is to keep everyone safe and that means getting back to the surface, pronto. I'm sure you can request to return on any subsequent trip."

"But . . . just two minutes."

Alex thought of Johnson for a second and changed his mind. A sample would be needed, at least to develop a weapon for when he returned to kill it. "All right, you have one minute to take photographs of this mess and take a small sample. Everyone else we need to—"

Alex was interrupted by the sound of a sliding, liquid movement from deep within the cave. It gave the impression that something enormous was coming up fast. Alex looked at the group. Without being ordered, Tank and Takeda flattened against the walls and resumed their defensive positions; everyone else had their eyes on Alex.

Most were frightened but still self-contained, only Margaret Anderson looked agitated. She had been standing to the rear looking ashen-faced ever since the tentacle club had been dropped in the middle of the group. She held her hands to her mouth and kept shaking her head as though to make the image of the giant unseen carnivore disappear. Alex could see her repeatedly swallowing and guessed she was going to be sick. She was like a deer on the verge of bolting. Before Alex could get around the group to her, she panicked and ran.

Zegarelli called her name and set off after her. Shit, thought Alex. He motioned to Takeda, pointed at the backs of the fleeing medics and made a chopping motion, indicating he stop them.

"This is a right mess, Captain." Silex didn't want to miss an opportunity to have a dig at Alex.

Alex ignored him and called to the group to shoulder their packs and follow at double time. Tank would bring up the rear. The last to leave was Matt, who was busy slicing off a sample of the tentacle. He tried to remove one of the tusks as well, but all he succeeded in doing was hurting his hand on the scythe-like edge.

Borshov had reached the basin floor with one of the Krofskoya assassins and was already unhooking himself from his ropes. The third assassin was preparing to climb down when the woman burst from the farthest cave, her cheeks covered in tears and her mouth stretched open in a silent "O" of fear. Just a few feet behind her was a man, his hand outstretched as if to catch hold of her. Borshov could tell just by the way they moved they were not HAWCs— good.

In the pitch-black of the caves, Borshov and his assassins were invisible to the newcomers. Borshov pointed with one hand at the man and made a throat-cutting signal to the nearest assassin. He moved quickly to intercept the woman.

There was a faint double *phutt* sound and Zegarelli dropped to the cave floor with two small holes above his left eye. In her panic, Margaret wasn't aware that her colleague now lay dead behind her and she simply thought one of the HAWCs had managed to get in front of her when a darkened shape stepped into her wavering torch light. She didn't have time to realise her mistake and her last conscious sensation was an explosion of pain as Borshov smashed his massive fist into her face.

# Fourteen

Takeda was seconds too late, arriving only in time to see Zegarelli's fallen body and Margaret knocked down by the Russian's punch. He lifted his gun and fired twice before vanishing behind a small stand of stalagmites. Takeda's compressed air blasts took the basin floor Krofskoya agent in the eye and the neck. The second shot was unnecessary, as his first pencil-thin blast of super-compressed air cut a hole from the eye, tore through the skull and exited out the back of his head as a stream of liquefied brain matter and cranial fluid.

Takeda pinged Alex and whispered, "Hostiles have arrived and been engaged. Zegarelli is dead and Anderson now an enemy asset."

Alex ordered everyone to take cover beside the cave wall and for Mike and Tank to take a defensive position against whatever was rushing up from behind to meet them. He hated leaving them here as he was sure, given the choice, all of them would have taken their chances at being shot over being snared and dragged off into the dark by some sort of weird cave creature. He had no alternative, he had a definite threat in front and a potential threat from behind— the definite threat took precedence. He looked quickly at Aimee then vanished into the dark.

\* \* \*

Takeda gave a small start when he felt Alex's hand fall lightly on his shoulder. He was always surprised at how quietly and fast Alex could move for a man of his size. Takeda lifted two fingers, indicating number of known hostiles. He then pointed from his eyes to their positions; one on the cave floor and one up high at the drop-off point to the basin.

Alex assessed the situation instantly; he had strength of numbers, but whoever the hostiles were, they held the high ground and a hostage.

From a concealed position on the basin floor, Alex heard a familiar, heavily accented voice. "*Privet kak Kanitah Hunter, ya soskucheelsya.*" Though Alex could only understand a little Russian, the deep formal greeting and the "I've missed you" was unmistakable. He recognised the voice as belonging to Uli Borshov, Borshov the Beast; the deadly assassin who had put a bullet in Alex's brain and left him for dead. This killer was not here by accident; he was used for extreme red-work, the bloodier the better. Alex felt a door crack open, a rage storm commence to build. A fury was trying to push through that door and explode out to consume the Russian. Alex couldn't allow it; not while Margaret was held hostage and they were pinned down. He needed absolute clarity.

Borshov now switched to his heavily accented English. "I know why you are here, Captain Hunter. I just want your test results; that is my only orders. I hate the dark, Captain Hunter; I just wish to go home. Bring them to me yourself, unarmed, no tricks; you can have your woman back and we all go home, *da?*"

Alex pinged Tank and asked for the group to be brought up. He needed Silex and his data and the additional cover his HAWCs could provide—and he needed to keep his internal demons chained; already they strained and called for war. Alex closed his eyes for a few seconds and inhaled; green apples, but only faintly.

Tank brought the small group within twenty feet of Alex's position, just out of view of the Russian assassination team with Mike remaining behind for rear cover. He joined Alex and Takeda, and handed Alex some of Silex's papers. They were just handwritten notes scribbled on seismic print-outs. It didn't matter; the material was just a smokescreen. Alex knew Borshov was here to kill.

"I'm coming out, unarmed as requested. Be advised, if anyone raises a weapon, my men will take them down." Alex pointed at Takeda and up at the Krofskoya agent on high ground. He signalled Tank to cover him as he walked out to meet the giant Russian.

Alex removed his weapons and stood out from behind the stalagmite. Outwardly he appeared calm, but he knew Borshov's presence meant Benson was dead. His heart rate was beginning to climb—not from fear or nerves, but from his supercharged body gearing up for combat.

Alex knew from experience that Borshov the Beast did not negotiate; he traded in torture, brute force and violent death. Margaret Anderson was simply being used to draw Alex in closer so the Russian had a better chance for a certain kill. If he wasn't careful, they would both be dead in the next few minutes.

Borshov smiled to himself when he saw the American captain step away from his concealment. Uli Borshov knew the odds were against him; his element of surprise had been lost. There was no way he was going to be able to scale the wall without being shot, even if he somehow managed to strap the unconscious woman to his back. He couldn't hope to take down all the HAWCs; they were too good. Kill Captain Alex Hunter, and bury the rest, that would complete the mission.

Borshov spoke quietly into his comm unit—he ordered the concealed assassin to prepare explosive charges for sealing the cave, timed for ten minutes. He was further ordered to stay for nine minutes and fifty seconds to witness him crush Captain Hunter with his bare hands; others must know that Uli Borshov remained unbeaten. Destruction of the American team and crushing Captain Hunter's skull with his fists—perhaps today was going to be a good day after all.

"We meet in interesting places, Comrade Hunter." Borshov was smiling behind the semi-conscious body of the medic. He was holding her by the throat with one hand, his enormous club-like fingers wrapped all the way around her neck. In his other hand he had a wicked-looking black blade held up beside her face.

"Captain Hunter, you have something of mine, you give it back, please."

Borshov was a head taller than most men, easily as big as Tank but with the menacing look of a criminal thug. In his black infiltration suit with just a single cyclops night vision lens pointing at Alex he was enough to make most men tremble at the thought of a direct confrontation, and with good reason.

Alex stared unflinchingly into the Russian's single lens and looked almost bored. "If you give me the woman and surrender your arms, I will let you and your men live today—that will be my only concession."

Borshov laughed slowly. "You are in no position to dictate terms, Captain Hunter. If you don't give me what I want, I will take it."

To press his point he started to drag his knife down the

side of Margaret's face. Blood ran down her cheek as a huge gash unzipped behind the blade. The pain roused the woman from her stupor and the medic moaned and began to struggle.

Alex knew that once Margaret became a liability to the assassin she was as good as dead; he needed to end this quickly. He presumed the Russian's primary demand was for the research material, so he threw the papers at Borshov's feet.

The chains rattled within Alex's soul; the furies screamed and raged to be released. Alex struggled to maintain control; the woman must be free of the beast before he could act or he would trigger a firefight between the Krofskoya and his HAWCs that would kill them all.

"That's everything. Take it, let the woman go."

Borshov didn't bother looking down at the papers. He didn't care about the oil or gas now, the woman's life, or for that matter even his own. His only objective was to remove this insult to his reputation as the world's deadliest assassin.

"My bullet. I want it back . . . now." Borshov tensed. His unblinking eyes behind his night vision scope were like twin chips of obsidian as he waited for the moment when Alex's concentration would lapse, even just for a split second. He knew the timed charges must be ready to detonate any minute now, but that meant little to him. Alex Hunter was either going to die in the resulting cave-in or by his hands.

Borshov started another cut on the woman's cheek. This time Margaret screamed. Alex's eyes slid down to Margaret for less than a second, but in that mere slice of an instant, Borshov's hand shot out like a snake and released the lethal black blade directly at Alex's left eye.

It had been all too easy.

\* \* \*

It was not possible. Where the American captain had been standing there was now nothing but empty air. Borshov heard his blade clatter off into the darkness and in the next instant he felt the woman pulled roughly from his arms. A hand that felt like steel closed on his forearm. A mistake—good, thought Borshov; no man who got within his range could survive against his deadly skills and strength.

From the moment the blade was thrown and the attack commenced the furies were let loose. Alex had been struggling to hold his rage in check when the assassin had mutilated the woman and thrown the killing knife. The voice of an army psychologist telling him to take himself somewhere calm until the rage passed echoed dimly within his head. No, thought Alex, let it come.

Time seemed to move in slow motion around him. His rage built to a cauldron's heat, and with the anger came a flood of biological chemicals into his extraordinary system that fuelled his enormous strength, speed and fury. He was already on the move before the blade had left the tips of the Russian's fingers, circling in to get Margaret out from the danger zone.

Borshov caught movement just at the edge of his scope and almost magically another blade appeared in his hand. He brought the toughened black stiletto around in a short arc, intending to force it deep into Alex's neck. Instead, his forearm was painfully blocked mid-swing. Borshov simply exerted more pressure, intending to force the blade slowly into the American. He knew he had at least eighty pounds on the HAWC and in close combat the odds were in his favour. However, his extra pressure was met with an impossible opposing strength that actually forced his arm away from the HAWC leader. Borshov attempted to use his close quarters, hand-to-hand combat techniques in a flurry of rapid fist and elbow strikes, but each of his blows were blocked and he was in turn struck with what seemed like sledgehammers. When Borshov felt his ribs crack it was time for a change in tactics. He didn't know how the American captain had managed to improve his skills and strength so dramatically, but he was sure he was still human, and all humans could die. If he couldn't retrieve his first bullet from Captain Hunter's skull, he would give it another for company.

At last, Borshov managed to get both his hands on his opponent and quickly lifted the American above his head and then used all his body weight to throw him to the cave floor. Alex hit the ground and bounced from the hard impact, but it was enough time for the Russian to draw and shoot.

Stone chips exploded around Alex as Borshov released a deafening volley of shots in the enclosed cavern. Alex dived and rolled with all his speed and agility to stay ahead of the Russian's deadly aim. He knew he didn't have long; the giant assassin would eventually anticipate one of his moves and he would be hit. By the sound of the bullet impacts they had to be glassine-tipped rounds—there was no such thing as a simple flesh wound from one of those projectiles.

On the next roll Alex pulled a flare from his thigh pocket and in a single spinning motion he struck the base on the ground for ignition and threw it towards the Russian. Light- and heat-enhancement sensory equipment is extremely sensitive and the sudden bloom of the hot red flare rendered the equipment useless—and Borshov blind. The Russian ripped the cyclops scope from his head and brought the gun around to try to re-acquire his target.

\*  \*  \*

When Borshov was able to locate Alex's position he was shocked to find him right there beside him with his gun hand held in a vice-like grip. In the light of the flare Alex's eyes looked red and his face was contorted in a mask of white-hot anger. Borshov brought his other arm around and seized Alex in a deadly embrace, intending to use his larger mass to once again lift the American off his feet. However, before Borshov could brace his legs for leverage, Alex lifted the giant Russian high into the air and then threw him nearly twenty feet down the cave to land with a bone-shuddering thump.

Borshov was momentarily stunned but rolled to his feet quickly; unexpectedly, instead of charging back at Alex, he dived towards Margaret and lifted the semi-conscious woman by the hair. From behind his back he produced yet another hidden blade and was bringing it up to the medic's face when Alex leaped.

On the cave ledge, the Russian agent knew his commander was going to fall to the unnatural speed and strength of the HAWC he battled. He shrugged, time to leave; he owed Borshov nothing.

He pulled back on his belly, out of the American's range of vision and reached up to a small timer, bringing the detonation forward by just a few seconds. He rolled and leaped to his feet, sprinting as fast as he could away from the explosives he had packed on each side of the upper walls. They were an upgraded form of the anti-tank sticky grenade designed to penetrate battlefield steel plating. Though largely obsolete due to the newer toughened armour deployed in conflict zones, the impact force of one of these small portable explosives made them ideal for detonate-and-destroy work by the Russian Special Forces.

He glanced down at his watch and then dived the last few feet to gain cover as the deafening roar of the explosives thumped like a giant mallet against the stone; the shock and compression waves travelling for hundreds of miles in every direction.

Several body lengths separated them, but Alex crossed the distance with ease and landed softly like a black-clad ghost. He struck out with a *kizami tsuki* flat-hand blow at a speed far beyond any normal soldier's capabilities. In one fluid movement he forced the giant Russian's forearm up past Margaret's face and on towards his own. The wicked-looking blade skimmed Margaret's forehead and buried itself in the orbital cavity of his eye. As Borshov was falling to the cave floor like an empty sack, their subterranean world erupted in a cyclone of heat and thunderous noise. Everything was chaos, everything went black.

# Fifteen

On the other side of the world Hammerson sat in his office and watched the steam rise off his coffee. The fresh cup sat next to an identical one that was also full, but cold. This one would probably end up the same.

Arcadian and the team had fallen into a grey-out several hours ago. For headquarters it was the worst sound you could receive from a field unit—the hissing crackle of dead contact, no reception, not even confirmation of a working communication device. After the first hour Hammerson had ordered men and machinery down to the McMurdo base at the Antarctic. Something had gone wrong and support needed to be there where they surfaced . . . if they surfaced.

Hammerson re-read the intercepted transmission from the Russians down on the ice. The Leningradskaya base was awaiting orders for a covert evacuation—they had men down there, too, and Hammerson bet they weren't there to lend a hand. Too late and too soon to do anything about it, he narrowed his eyes and continued to stare at the rising steam.

Immediately after the fiery plume from the explosives, hundreds of tons of rock and debris caved in to close the exit for fifty feet from the edge of the drop-off. Large and small boulders fell to the cavern floor making ground-shaking thuds as they either shattered or bounced off into the darkness. Aimee dived for cover, waiting for the sounds of the rockfalls to die down as the echoes continued to travel away into the numerous feeder caverns for minutes afterward. If it was dark before, now it was doubly so as even the torch lights had their range limited by the thick palls of dust filling the air.

Aimee was the first to rush forward to check on Alex as the dust began to settle. She had seen the last minute of his battle with the large Russian and couldn't believe how fast he had managed to move. In the dark she had had trouble keeping up with his reflexes and bursts of speed and wondered briefly if it could be some form of military steroid the soldiers were taking. In the red light of the flare his face had been terrifying and if she hadn't known for sure it was Alex in combat, she would never have recognised him.

The luminous glow from the flares coupled with the smoky dust in the air gave the cavern a hellish appearance. She centred in on Alex's voice and the sounds of rocks being moved out of the way. As she approached, she saw Alex lifting rocks from the prone body of Margaret Anderson. He bent at the knees and grasped a stone the size of a man and lifted it aside as if it were no more than an empty box.

Aimee halted and stared; it couldn't be real. She had read of instances where people in extreme stress situations had lifted cars but Alex's face was calm; there were no signs of any stress. When Aimee reached his side he wasn't even breathing heavily, just looking down with weary resignation. Margaret's body lay like a broken doll beneath the tons of debris.

"Bruno?" she asked.

Alex looked into her face for a few seconds and shook his head slowly.

* * *

The remaining HAWCs were quick to assemble around Alex, and even Mike was back on his feet. Though his bleeding had stopped, he was gritting his teeth to keep the pain under control. "Is everyone OK?" Alex raised his voice and surveyed the dust-covered group. They had all switched on their helmet lights and the beams were like train lamps swinging back and forth around the large, choking cavern.

"OK? OK? No, we're not fucking OK! We're trapped miles under the ground. We have several people dead, a bomb's just gone off and there is some sort of creature trying to eat us. Oh yeah, and who the hell were those guys who were trying to kill us?" Silex looked down at the crushed body of Margaret. "I mean, did kill us. They knew you, Captain; what did you bring down on us? I'd say your mission management is about as bad as it can get. Anyone else want to take a bet on how long the captain can keep the rest of us alive?"

From the corner of his eye Alex saw Aimee closing in on Silex, her head shaking as if in warning to the fulminating scientist.

"You asshole, Silex! We'd all be dead a dozen times over if it wasn't for Captain Hunter. We only came down here to the lower levels on your instructions, so shut up or God help me I'll knock you down myself." Aimee was shaking her fist right in Silex's face and with the dust covering her from head to toe, and her once soft blue eyes red rimmed and glaring, she hardly looked like a woman you'd want to mess with. Silex's head jerked back in surprise at the sudden onslaught from his rather mad-looking fellow scientist.

Alex recognised the anger in Aimee. He still felt its traces himself. He had just brutally killed another human being; it shouldn't have mattered to him. As an elite soldier he was trained to disconnect from sympathy, empathy or any regret for a fallen foe. But he felt something; something else. It had felt good to obliterate the giant Russian. And now, something inside him wanted even more conflict, more war.

Alex needed to head this off. Though he felt like throttling Silex himself, an intergroup conflict in these circumstances could be fatal. He called out to Monica, who was scurrying around peering into the cave mouths, presumably to see if any led back to the surface.

"Ms. Jennings, we need another route back to the surface. Any suggestions?"

Monica rejoined the group. "Well, there is no breeze coming from any of the large caves. There's also no cooler air in any of them that would indicate a path to the ice surface either, and there's no discernable upward slope. All that leaves us is a choice based on direction. My view is we head north which takes us towards the coast and away from the interior which we know is covered in several miles of ice, as well as rock. So . . ." Monica pointed to a medium-sized opening. "That one."

"All right, sounds like as good a plan as any to me. Any alternatives or objections? OK. Mike, get fifty feet down into our exit cave and see if we still have something large and slimy to worry about. Takeda, Tank, check our Russian friends for anything we can use. Everyone else, gather everything we may need into your backpacks, non-essential items remain here and we travel light. We leave in two minutes."

Alex watched Silex turn away and check his bulky backpack. He knew what he was doing. "Sorry, Dr. Silex, essential equipment only. The electronics are non-essential and must remain here."

"No! I am not leaving this device here. It's a prototype

and represents millions of dollars and years of research. I demand to be allowed to take it with us; if the device stays, then we all stay."

"That's your choice, Dr. Silex, but everyone else will be sticking together and finding a route back to the surface. I won't try to drag you along." Alex looked back at the cave where the creature had attacked them and then looked back at Silex. The inference was clear: you'll be here by yourself and that thing is just down in there. Silex looked at Alex with a mixture of fear and hatred and turned to find Aimee; she shook her head and turned her back on him. Silex ground his teeth and then began to swear under his breath as he tore off his backpack and roughly ripped the image resonator and several other small boxes from the webbing and flung them over his shoulder. Alex watched them loop slowly in the dusty air before bouncing and cartwheeling across the fallen boulders, giving off a spray of sensitive electronic debris as they went.

Alex turned away from Silex to face the tunnel where Mike had just disappeared. He knew the injured HAWC was hurting and now he had just been sent by himself back into a cave where he had been attacked by a creature from a nightmare. Mike hadn't flinched as he rushed to follow his instructions. Good man, thought Alex.

Aimee came up beside Alex. "Are you OK?" She laid her hand on his arm and looked into his face.

Alex nodded in Silex's direction. "I get the feeling he doesn't like me anymore. But I feel safer with you here—you can be pretty terrifying, you know." He smiled and she smiled back.

"Who were those guys that attacked us? Dr. Silex was right; they did seem to know you."

"They were Russian Special Forces. I've come across the big one before. He shot me and left me to die on the other side of the world. I can only guess they were sent to retrieve or destroy the work we're doing. The world is hungry for oil, Aimee, and how the world gets it is of secondary concern these days. Anyway, forget that, how are you?"

"Don't worry about me. My dad always said I was steel wrapped in velvet. I'm tough."

"Good, I think we're all going to need to be tough before we see daylight again." He put his hand on her shoulder and squeezed. She looked like she wanted to say something but didn't know how to start. Alex's comm pinged. "Mike, report in."

"All clear and quiet."

"OK, come back in, we're moving out." Alex turned towards the chosen tunnel and hopefully their path back to the surface.

It heard the boom of the falling rock and hesitated. A cave-in was one of the only things it feared. Also, the noise and vibrations made it impossible to hunt in the caves. It held its place and waited until it was sure there were no major rock falls that could crush it. It could smell the floating debris and dust from the cave and also detected the scent of fresh blood but could not risk entering a weakened cavern. It would take another route, as it sensed one of the little warm animals moving fast through the upper passages.

Pieter Dragan had been a Krofskoya agent for three years and had never failed a mission. He was not sad that his comrades had been killed. Borshov was a psychopath and made killing a prolonged game to savour, when it should have been quick and surgically efficient. His time wasting had been his downfall; too bad.

Pieter was racing back to the American's jerry-bridge

when his night vision lens picked up a flicker of blurred movement, and then a human shape appeared standing beside the bridge at the edge of the ravine. It was a girl, and she was holding what looked like a baby. Pieter flattened himself against the wall; there didn't seem to be anyone else and the girl looked harmless and a little lost; she also looked dripping wet.

The girl didn't move or speak and when Pieter called to her, she seemed to glide a little closer. Maybe she came from the airplane crash and had been wandering around lost all this time. But how did she get down so deep by herself—and in the dark? Pieter stood up and called to her again, in the few words of English he knew. "Hello, who are you please, you identify, yes?"

The girl shape leaped forward and crashed into Pieter with a wet smacking sound. The pain was excruciating as several dagger-like tusks pierced his flesh. He could not push himself away from the girl as she seemed covered in foul-smelling glue and now even his face was stuck to hers.

Panic set in as he was pulled by an unbelievable strength towards the edge of the rift. His last vision through his night scope was of being hoisted over the cliff edge and drawn down into the blackness where something large and liquid-sounding waited hungrily in the depths below.

# Sixteen

Alex distributed the useful items and food among the remaining non-military team members. The long rifles he
left behind; though he would have liked the extra firepower,
he decided instead to travel light and fast. He also managed
to recover one of the handguns which he gave to Aimee.
Silex protested, but there was no way Alex would put a
loaded firearm into that man's hands. He figured that even
though the guns fired hard impact rounds as opposed to the
HAWCs' safer compressed air armaments, the danger from
the creature far outweighed the danger from ricochets.

Alex checked his watch; it was only twelve hours until
the chopper arrived to evacuate them. He knew the pilot
wouldn't be expecting to hear from them until they were
at or near the surface, and when they weren't there he would
wait several hours and then call it in. That meant they
probably had around fifteen hours to make it back to the
surface—a walk in the park, if there were no more cave-
ins, and if they didn't stop from fatigue or hit a dead-end
or were attacked.

The team marched in silence through the dark for several
hours until their cave abruptly ended in a jumble of fallen
rocks.

Monica put her hands on her hips and looked over the
pile of broken stone, nodding to herself as though she'd

been expecting it. "It's a boulder choke. In simple terms it means the passage has been filled by rocks in some ancient collapse."

"And she's the expert? Great choice—four hours walking for nothing. Now I guess we walk all the way back and take door number two." Monica ignored Silex and clambered over the fallen boulders until she found what she was looking for at the very base of the pile.

She went straight to Alex. "As I expected, it looks like there might be a way through, a small choke hole, but I'll need to check its length and depth."

"Do it," Alex said.

"Give me twenty minutes." Monica looked at Alex and caught his expression. "OK, give me ten." She removed her backpack and placed it on the ground in front of a small opening between the boulders. From the pack she took a small stick of red chalk which she held between her teeth. She tied a rope around her waist, and prepared to dive head first into the hole when Matt grabbed her ankle.

"Just one thing." He got down close to Monica and whispered in her ear. "Be careful, come back." She smiled and with her chalk drew a little red heart on the back of his caving glove and then, pushing her backpack in front of her, slithered forward and disappeared.

Everyone seemed to hold their breath as they focused on the small opening in the wall of stone before them. The only sound was a slight whistling coming from Silex's nostrils as they all willed Monica to return safely. Aimee used her arm to wipe a trickle of perspiration from her eyes and tried to swallow; it hurt. Her throat was dry and sticky—Margaret had been right, water was going to be a problem. Her eyes were like glass as she thought of the two cheerful medics. Bruno always wanting to lend a hand; looking like an overstuffed sausage in his cave suit—executed for trying to rescue his colleague. And poor Margaret—Aimee shuddered at the thought of her final moments at the hands of the brutal assassin. It's over for them now; they're probably better off, she thought. The rest of them were all trapped deep beneath the most isolated continent on earth and were being stalked by some carnivorous creature that lived down in the labyrinths and was snatching people away to devour them. It made her feel sick, and she shuddered again.

Aimee thought of Tom and almost cried out for him. Poor Tom—had he and his team been stalked and snared in the dark while they ran and screamed like blind rabbits in the caves? Had they become nothing more than morsels of food for the leviathan hiding somewhere beneath them? She felt the trickle of a tear run down her cheek and let it fall.

In just under twelve minutes Aimee saw a light begin to appear in the choke hole, indicating Monica was returning. Matt was there first to pull her out.

"OK, it goes all the way through, but it's a tight squeeze. Alex and especially you, Tank, are going to have to hold your breath in some places. Everyone try not to touch anything on the way through. This fall probably occurred hundreds of thousands of years ago and is not likely to move. However, there is still a chance that the rocks that have already fallen are poised dangerously one on top of each other. An inch or two can make all the difference. Our slide through the choke hole could undermine the supports of the whole pile, and cause it to suddenly collapse into a new shape, which may be far too small for us to squeeze through. Or worse, it could collapse into a solid compressed mass—and we really don't want to be under there if that happens."

Monica checked everyone's cave suit for unnecessary items or bulges. "OK, we need to stay close together so we can actually see each other's feet. Take off your packs and push them ahead of you. Take it slow and don't panic. If you get a little caught up just breathe slowly and unhook yourself. There will be people in front of you and behind you to help. One more thing: avoid my red markings. I'll go first."

Aimee slithered out of her backpack, and holding it in front of herself folded her arms around it. The size was comforting and also meant no one saw that her hands were shaking. She closed her eyes and silently mouthed to herself, *if Monica can do it, I can; if Monica can do it, I can*. She really wanted to be home now.

She jumped when Matt bumped her elbow as he stepped forward, intending to go into the hole next. Alex overruled him. "Sorry, Matt, Takeda goes next to give us all some cover on the other side. Tank, you go last. Can't have you corking us all up now, can we?"

Tank laughed. "Don't mind none; I reckon you'll have wiped it all clean by the time it's my turn."

Aimee looked at Tank's bulk and hoped his good humour was matched by luck. She hugged her pack and waited for her turn.

The first thing Aimee noticed as she wriggled through the tiny tunnel was how easy it would be to get claustrophobic and lose it in such a confined space. You were continually banging your head, elbows and back on the jumble of fallen boulders. Some of the rocks were the size of houses, some were just rubble all pieced together like a giant's jigsaw puzzle. Monica had placed a red chalk "X" on some of the rocks, indicating a weak spot or pivot point and these were to be avoided at all costs. Every time Aimee came across one glaring out of the dark her heart gave a leap at the thought of being buried alive, or worse, ending up crushed like Margaret.

Monica had said it was only about fifty feet, but she already felt she had been crawling for twice that—distance was hard to judge in such tight quarters. Perspiration ran down her face, creating more little streaks in the dust around her eyes and the air was already thickening from her hard breathing. It would be so easy to lose it in here.

She was fifth to go through, behind Silex, and mercifully he had slithered through rather quickly. The thought of him getting stuck and her spending the last few hours of her life trapped in a choke staring at Dr. Silex's skinny legs was almost too much to bear. When she finally emerged into Monica's waiting hands she felt such an unbelievable mixture of elation and relief that she almost burst into tears.

In no time Mike and Alex popped out of the hole and everyone gathered around waiting for Tank. Alex kept his eyes on the hole and said, "He's struggling. He's as strong as an ox, but about as flexible as a piano." Alex got down on his knees and shone his torch down into the hollow. Tank must have dropped behind as he was still quite a way in.

Alex's comm unit pinged. "I'm hooked up on something." Alex turned to Monica. "He's caught." Monica immediately drew two soft elasticised ropes from her backpack and shot back into the hole. She reappeared moments later, leaving the two ropes trailing into the small opening.

"Yep, he's wedged in about fifteen feet back. I've tied the ropes around his wrists. We're going to have to give him a gentle persuasive tug. He's ready for it."

Alex pinged Tank. "On the count of three, big fella, give a push. One, two . . . three."

The entire party pulled on the ropes but there was hardly any give. Then from deep within the boulder choke there was a very slight screeching sound like a truck putting on its air brakes, followed by a hollow grinding. Although there was no visible movement from the outside, they knew this would not be the case where Tank was stuck.

Mike yelled his brother's name and went to dive into the hole. Alex grabbed him in a bear hug that was impossible to break. They all waited. After just a few seconds there was silence again. There was no dust and no tumbling rocks. The boulder choke had simply shrugged and settled back down again for another few eons.

No one even exhaled as they stared at the small choke opening; and then to their surprise a very large body shot out of the hole like a cork. Tank was coughing and laughing. He got to his feet and dusted himself off. He looked at the team, all standing there with their mouths open.

"What? It's only a small mountain, it's gonna take more than that to flatten me."

Mike stepped forward and punched his "little" brother in the chest. "Okay, you're the baddest—for now."

Alex ordered a rest and food stop. The dark was disorientating and time was measured not by clocks but by fatigue. They ate dried fruit and some chocolate and Alex was pleased to see that his HAWCs were joining in some good-natured banter. He and his team had been trained to keep a respectable distance from civilians and regard them as invisible, or a means to an end—to be retrieved, delivered or expended. However, Tank's escape had been the first piece of good fortune they'd had for a long time and he guessed they would all need luck and each other's help to get back to the surface.

Alex sent Takeda ahead with Monica to scout out the area and he sat by himself and checked his equipment. He removed his glove and placed his bare hand down onto the stone and closed his eyes. There was no sliding, no vibrations; other than Takeda and Monica, nothing was moving. He had reached out with his extraordinary senses and couldn't feel any cold presence nearby. For the moment they were secure. He looked into the dark where Monica had just disappeared and thought to himself, *Come on girl, find me an exit.*

Aimee came over and sat beside Alex while Silex watched like a snake from the dark, his wet lips moving as if mouthing secret obscenities at the pair.

"What're our chances?" Aimee asked.

"We'll be OK." He couldn't tell her of his fears. They had food and water for only another few days and battery life for even less. The HAWC night vision goggles would last a little longer, but that was it. He didn't want to think about what would happen if the lights went out for good.

"Things always work out. You'll see."

Aimee looked up at him. "How can you be so confident and calm all the time?"

Alex gave a half smile and turned to her. She rested her chin on her hand and even in the dark her eyes were luminous in her dust-streaked face. What could he tell her? Though it was his job to keep a unit in the field motivated, the real reason was difficult to explain. Alex knew he should already be dead, but had survived and literally risen a different being. Risks and danger held no fears for him anymore as he felt destiny, kismet, karma, whatever you wanted to call it, was keeping him safe for some specific purpose. He didn't believe for a second it was to die in these caves. He would see the sun again.

"Do you believe in fate, Aimee? I do, and I know we'll make it. Besides, it's been over twelve hours since we communicated with HQ and by now Major Hammerson will be bursting the eardrums of the entire armed forces to get more military bodies down here. Stay close to me and don't worry."

Monica appeared looking very pleased with herself. "Everyone this way, I've found something," She led them quickly down the cave and to a gigantic hole in the rock floor.

Monica immediately set to pegging in around a large belay rock. Silex was immediately at her side and hissing into her ear. "What are you doing, we're not going down there. Are you crazy? That'll just take us deeper. We need to be going up, you know, where the sun shines. Not down."

"Dr. Silex, you hear that?" Monica had held up her hand to quieten the scientist and the entire team stopped what they were doing and listened. Nothing could be heard except for their own breathing.

Alex was the first to speak. "Water, running water."

"It's a cave stream, quite a large one by the sound of it. I'm not making any promises because it could just disappear through another boulder choke that we can't get through. However, it could also flow out at the coast."

Alex stood at the edge looking down thoughtfully. Silex stared at him and smirked, probably thinking Alex was racked with indecision, while he was in fact using his senses to get an impression of what waited for them down in the dark depths. He didn't want to let Monica rappel down first, and his men could just as easily have achieved it, but she was the specialist and better equipped to give them an idea of the descent's safety and risk factors.

"OK, Ms. Jennings, but I want you to borrow Mike's comm unit so we can stay in touch. Mike will be coming down right behind you. Hand the unit back to Mike and then do a near-perimeter survey and report in. Got it?"

Monica nodded and started to rig up her rappelling harness using low-stretch kernmantel rope with a friction brake to control her speed. She didn't have the time or the rope to set more safety cords, or cow tails as they were called, but did use a sit-stand rig to ensure the rope wouldn't rub against any jagged rocks.

She looked briefly at Matt. "Once again into the wide black yonder." Matt gave her a thumbs up and looked as cheery as possible in the situation as Monica stepped back into the abyss.

The shaft was complex with many ledges, lumps and spikes. She descended slowly, watching both the wall and the rope and keeping a lookout below for the yet unseen floor. There was no echo, just the faint musical sound of the water as it tumbled over a hidden stream bed below. At about fifty feet down she hit the floor of a second large chamber. It was flat-based, worn very smooth like a giant tabletop. She still couldn't see the stream, but it was louder now. It was also much warmer and the humidity had encouraged traces of moss to grow on the walls.

She unzipped her suit a few inches and spoke into her comm unit. "Captain Hunter, you're good to go. Careful on the way down as there are some protrusions, but I'll be at the base guiding Mike down."

Alex held up his hand to Mike who was already rigged up and waiting for the word to drop. Before he descended Alex walked over, checked his rigging and spoke to him. "How're the wounds?"

"I'm OK. They're starting to bleed a little again, but when I get down to the bottom I'll give 'em a little more coagulant gel."

"Good enough. Can't have you bleeding away any more energy, can we?" Alex nodded and slapped him on the shoulder. Mike stepped back into the shaft. He descended quickly, Monica's light giving him more depth perspective than she had.

One after the other they descended, leaving only Alex at the top. He hadn't bothered to rig up and instead unfastened the rope from the belay boulder and let it drop down into the hole. He heard Aimee's panicked voice from below.

"What just happened? Did it break?" As the rope coiled on the ground at their feet Aimee shone her torch back up the shaft. Monica gently grabbed her by the arm and pulled her out of the way.

"Aimee, he knows what he's doing. He just saved me from having to climb back up there. We need that rope and can't afford to leave anything behind we might need later."

Alex climbed down the wall like a spider; there were enough protrusions to afford him plenty of hand and toe holds and his caving suit was specially toughened on the fingers and toes for just such a climb. He was confident that Monica could have ascended without trouble, but it would have cost them at least another ten minutes and at this point Alex was keen to save every second they had and use it for escape.

Monica shone her torch in a slow arc around them. Caves were amazing places. There were magnificent formations all around and above them; straw-like calcite stalactites and huge piles of what looked like frozen pink froth lumped around like melted candy. As a general rule, the larger the cave, the older it was. By that standard, these caves were truly prehistoric. It was like being in some giant child's garden made from coloured stone. Rocks that looked like icicles, trees, statues, or the delicate designs of lacy flowers in shades of white or cream, or blues and reds from the dissolved minerals trickling from miles of stone overhead. At any other time Monica would have been lost in delight at this caving wonderland—for now, survival was the priority.

The cave ended abruptly at the bank of a wide and slow-moving river. It looked shallow, but cave pools and streams could be deceptive due to the clarity of the water—a stream where you could easily pick out every tiny pebble on its bottom could actually be over six feet deep. The upside was that there were rarely hidden jagged objects under the surface—the smoothing effect of thousands of years of polishing by the moving liquid.

"What now, build a boat from rocks?" sneered Silex. It was an obnoxiously posed question, but they were presented with a problem—they had no raft and there was no river bank or beach to walk along. They couldn't cross to the far side of the river as it ended in a sheer rock wall—in fact, the cave they were in ended at the river.

Monica was standing on the bank looking downstream. She turned to Silex, not caring that she was staring into his face and blinding him with the bright beam of her helmet light. "Well, we need to follow that river and we don't have diving equipment or a raft with us, so you're right, we do build a boat—but not from rocks, Dr. Silex, from people. There is a caving style for travelling down streams to ensure everyone stays together in the dark. It's called the Disney method—everyone sits one behind the other holding on to the person in front by their feet. We rope everyone's waists together and create a set of human train carriages. We'll also need an anchor—someone who is tied to the group but set about twenty feet back to act as an emergency brake. Usually they're the biggest member of the team." Monica turned to wink at Tank.

Tank smiled and said, "Shucks, I didn't even have to volunteer."

"We also need a driver; that'll be me."

Alex quickly overruled the caver. "Good idea, Ms. Jennings, but I'll sit out in front this time. The team is going to be too heavy for you to steer and I'm better able to sustain impacts. However, I'd like you to be right behind me, guiding me and telling me what to expect."

They all turned to look at the river. None of the team particularly looked forward to getting into the black water and floating into the impenetrable darkness that loomed ahead. However, everyone realised that going back would be even worse.

Takeda took a reading downriver with a portable echo distance display unit and spoke back to the group. "Straight run for about two miles then it either bends, dips or stops. No narrowing I can detect."

"OK, people. We travel the straight distance and stop for rest when we get to the bend. Let's keep moving."

Monica wound the soft rope around Alex's waist and then left a vacant loop for herself to climb into. She looped in Matt, Mike and then Aimee. Takeda went next, then Silex and twenty feet back, Tank as the anchor man. Tank had already removed a small collapsible grappling hook from his pack and tucked it and its rope tether into his front suit pouch. They were ready.

If it wasn't for Alex leading the way, they may have all hesitated a few minutes while working up their courage. As it was, before they had time to think he was wading into the water, and all being tied together, they had to follow.

Rocks moved; then more. A low groan emanated from under the rubble. A large flat piece of stone flipped over like a door opening and a black-clad figure sat up.

Borshov slowly pulled the knife from the orbital socket of his eye and felt something warm and jellied fall to his cheek.

In the darkness he felt the ragged hole and cursed in old Russian. He resheathed the sticky blade and pulled a small light from a pocket as he rose to his feet.

# Seventeen

It was slower going than many of them expected. Though the stream travelled at about three knots their weight and bulk meant they travelled closer to two knots. At this rate Monica estimated they would be in the cold water for an hour; not great, but there was no choice. The thermal lining in their suits would provide some protection, but eventually the cold would seep through and start to slow down muscle reaction time. Any longer than that and hypothermia would set in.

The only sounds were the slight tinkling of the stream and a few whispers from among the team members. Matt kept both hands around Monica's waist and Monica in turn dropped her hands to cover his. For the most part, except for the odd bump it was a fairly smooth ride.

Several times the team passed little black sandy beaches and heard scuttling sounds off in the darkness. But when they turned their torches in the direction of the noise, there was nothing there. From time to time they also witnessed small flashes of light on the walls of the cave. Monica leaned forward to Alex. "Bioluminescence, or cold light; probably small cave organisms or fungi. If we get enough, maybe we can do without the torches."

Alex had requested they keep moving their arms and legs as much as possible in their restricted positions to ensure they kept their blood flowing right down to their extremities. It was easy to become numbed, and it was this numbness that allowed Mike not to notice that the water had diluted the gel over his wounds and they were once again beginning to bleed.

In the stream his faint blood trail moved ahead of them, at three knots to their two. In the dark and with such a small amount of blood it could not possibly be noticed; not by human senses anyway. After about fifty minutes in the water, Mike noticed his wounds were becoming almost unbearably itchy. It was not for a HAWC to complain about hunger, pain or discomfort. He had slept in snow, hidden in a steel drum in hundred degree heat and been camouflaged under mud for eighteen hours; he would wait until they reached a rest point as instructed by their team leader.

At last they reached a suitable rest point just a few hundred feet before the stream veered around a huge fallen boulder. A small beach of black sand curved in a crescent at the base of the rock wall. They all stood up in the waist-deep water, stepped out of the rope loops and struggled up the bank on cold stiff legs. Though they were shivering the team was in good spirits and looking forward to some rest, and perhaps some more chocolate. Takeda immediately took to lighting a miniature propane heating unit. Each of the HAWCs carried them; they could be used for emergency lighting, as an incendiary device, or in Takeda's case, a way to heat his precious green tea. Alex allowed the small break in the rules as Takeda was the most serene and efficient warrior he had ever come across; if the tea helped, then he could have it.

Aimee was the first to notice the changes in Mike. He was bent over and his robust frame was smaller and seemed somehow shrunken. Where the rope had previously been looped tight around his lean muscular body, his waist had not yet snapped back into place. He looked deformed, soft.

"Mike? Mike, are you OK?" Aimee grabbed his arm and turned him around.

On hearing Aimee raise her voice, Alex rushed over to where Mike stood unsteadily on his feet. In the harsh light of Aimee's torch his face was slack and looked like wax. Alex stared into Mike's eyes and asked, "Second Lieutenant Mike Lennox, what is your immediate operational status?"—a command any of the HAWCs would have instantly responded to.

Mike coughed and fell forward. Alex caught him and lowered him to the ground, turning him over onto his back. Mike's body was different—he felt lighter and less substantial. Mike coughed again, then again harder. This time some redness appeared on his lips. The team gathered around and bathed Mike's prone body in the combined light of multiple helmet beams.

"He's bleeding internally." Alex rolled him onto his side to assist his breathing and this time Mike began coughing continuously. Blood spots appeared on the black sand, and then with the next racking cough a rush of a red gelatinous fluid gushed from his mouth to pile on the sand next to him.

"Oh shit, there's something living in him." Silex jumped back; there was no scientific curiosity, just a base human reaction to a severe parasitic infection. The disgust was clear on his face as he unconsciously began wiping his hands on his sides. Silex was right, among the piles of jelly beside Mike's face there was a mass of worms, each about six inches long, writhing on the sand. The black and red mess had undoubtedly come from the flesh and blood the worms had been consuming from inside Mike.

Tank pushed Silex out of the way and cradled Mike's head while Alex reached down and undid the straps on his caving suit. The sight that met their eyes made even the battle-hardened HAWCs wince, and Tank moaned at the vision. Where there were once wounds, there were now ragged holes that were alive with worms. Mike's stomach and chest cavity must have been full of them as the skin moved across his bones in an unnatural rippling manner. His jaw worked as though he was trying to say something, but it wasn't clear whether it was actually Mike or the worms sliding beneath the muscles in his neck and face.

"Dr. Weir, what are those things, leeches?" Alex himself wasn't keen to touch Mike until he knew what they were dealing with.

Aimee had the back of her hand across her mouth; disgust and fear distorting the features of her face.

"Dr. Weir? Aimee?" Alex reached out and touched her arm.

"I, I don't think so, more likely down here they're some form of nematode."

Aimee crouched down and tried to concentrate on Mike's condition, hoping scientific curiosity would override her revulsion.

"Can we get them out of him?" Monica asked the question, although it was plain to everyone that even with the best medical care he probably stood little chance, and down here he was as good as dead. In the few extra minutes they stood around him he seemed to further deflate and shrivel as his flesh was being consumed from the inside out.

"I thought nematodes were microscopic things that lived in the soil," Matt said.

"There are tens of thousands of types of nematodes and more than half are parasitic. Most are microscopic, but some are bigger, much bigger. There's one species that can get to about thirty feet—it parasitises the sperm whale. These things have been around since the Cambrian and like our giant cephalopod, have probably been trapped down here for millions of years."

"Yuck, those things were in the water with us." Monica was stripping off her suit and checking her body. Everyone quickly did the same.

"I think we'll be OK. Mike was the only one who was hurt and bleeding. These things are little more than mouths on the end of a fleshy pipe. They must have sensed Mike's blood in the water and homed in on him," Aimee said.

Mike's eyes were like glass. They bulged up from his face and then began to sink into his sockets just as there was an almost inaudible *phutt* sound, and a small dark hole appeared in his forehead, not made by the parasites, but from Tank who fired a pulse projectile into Mike's brain in an act of mercy for his brother. No one recoiled or even winced; it was the right thing to do.

"Permission to dispose of the body?"

Alex didn't have to think before responding. "Permission granted, soldier."

Tank lifted what was left of Mike. From once being a man who looked like he weighed in at 200 pounds, Mike now looked a quarter of that. The worms dropped freely from his sleeves and ankles where the suit wasn't fully closed. Tank walked with the body to the corner of the beach and knelt beside him. He looked to be talking to his brother one last time. He stood, crossed himself and removed his own propane cylinder from his backpack and proceeded to spray Mike all over. Tank depressed the ignition stud and Mike's body flared yellow as the highly flammable propellant burst into life. As the suit burnt and peeled away there was an insane thrashing all over his body as the parasitic worms reacted to the destruction of their home and last meal.

\* \* \*

Tank rejoined the group but his head, like his spirits, was down. Alex walked over to him and grabbed his shoulders. "Tank, he made us all proud. He was one of the best we ever had, I'm going to miss him; we all will."

Tank gripped Alex's forearms in both his hands. His lips were clamped together and his eyes shut tightly. Tank and Mike had been inseparable their whole lives. They had looked out for each other and shared everything, from pushbikes to being in the same football team and on to military training. They had regularly topped their classes in strategy and combat and they were both delighted to be selected for second-level training to become Green Berets. Then, after distinguishing themselves on complex missions they were further assigned to fifth-level training to become US Navy SEALs. In just another two years they had been invited to join the HAWCs and had attended tenth-level training under Major Jack Hammerson. Tank wrenched his arms away from Alex and brought his hands up to the side of his head as through he was about to scream only to bring them down hard on Alex.

Alex caught and held the bigger man's wrists easily. Though Tank outweighed Alex by fifty pounds, Alex was far stronger. Alex knew the big man was not wrestling with him, but with the pain of his loss. Tank's face was contorted in a suffering that only a person who has just lost someone very close to them could understand. When Alex felt the pressure let up he released Tank's arms and allowed him to walk off down the beach to gather his thoughts. Alex would let him mourn for a little while, but would not let him withdraw into himself. Everyone was needed now, especially his remaining HAWCs.

Alex saw Aimee approaching him along the beach. When she reached him she stood silently for minutes, just watching Tank's massive form moving off into the dark. At last she spoke. "It's all going bad, isn't it?"

He thought for a while and then turned to her. "I can't say this is exactly how I saw things unfolding, Aimee, but we've got to keep moving forward. If we do that we have a chance."

"Even though I said that the nematodes were only attracted to Mike because of his bleeding, I can't know that for sure. They're a species that has been isolated down here for millions of years and I don't know exactly how they are going to behave. Though none of us are as severely wounded as Mike was, there are other entrances to the human body." She paused for a moment, looking over her shoulder at the group. "Alex, no one wants to go back in that water. We already know those worms are not top of the food chain and I certainly am not keen to meet any more links in that chain."

Alex expelled a breath of air between his lips. "Aimee, we're still a long way from home and things might get even rougher before they get better. I don't want to go in the water again, but we can't go back and we're not dying on this beach, either. I'll need your help to keep everyone's spirits up. Despair—that's our main danger now."

Aimee gave a weak smile, nodded and went to rejoin the small group. Alex called Takeda in close and also Tank, who still looked morose and withdrawn.

"Lieutenant! Tank, there'll be plenty of time for giving Mike a proper send-off when we're on the surface. Right now we need to get these people back into the daylight." Tank nodded, still not yet trusting himself to speak. "Takeda, give me a forward recon down that beach and report in on what you see. Take Ms. Jennings with you. Tank, you go back to the upstream end of the beach and give me a secure rear perimeter. I don't want anything else sneaking up on us—report back in T-minus twenty minutes."

The two remaining HAWCs synchronised their watches with Alex's then turned and trotted off to their allotted tasks. Alex looked back at the group. Matt, Monica and Aimee were talking and finishing off their chocolate. He knew Aimee would do her bit and keep everyone rallied. A little farther down the beach he noticed Silex staring at him and mumbling to himself. The man was shaking, but Alex didn't think it was from the cold; more likely stress—that was worse. Alex had seen men in battlefield situations have a full autonomic nervous system collapse and go into seizures; he had also seen them blow their own heads off, as well as those of the people around them. He hoped the man could hold it together. Though he had retrieved many of the medical supplies, he didn't relish sedating the scientist and having to carry him to the surface. Alex shook his head. Oh boy, could this get any better?

Takeda and Tank came back to report in to Alex at exactly the same time. Takeda had Monica in tow—he nodded to her to proceed with the update.

"OK, about a mile down the beach the tunnel ends at another boulder choke. However, the current is still fairly strong so my guess is the choke is either not solid or long, and then the river continues on straight thereafter."

"What are you suggesting—a cave dive? We aren't rigged for that." Alex knew it would be hard enough getting the team back in the water at all, let alone diving beneath it.

Monica shook her head emphatically. "Not a chance. In normal caving, if you get lost, you sit down, have a chocolate bar and wait to be found. However, in cave diving if you get lost, you run out of air, lose your orientation and drown—I hate cave diving. Normally in a cave when I have clients with me, I demand that no one damages the cave or its surroundings. However, this time I think I'm more than happy to suggest we might be able to get over the top of the choke if we dig and dislodge some of the medium-sized rocks."

"Sounds like a plan to me." Alex called them all together. "Everyone, Ms. Jennings may have found a way forward. We may have to do some digging and I'd like to think we'll all lend a hand. Gather your things, we're moving on."

"Captain Hunter?" It was Silex, licking his lips and looking more nervous than usual. "Will we have to go back in the water?"

"Maybe, and if not now, then probably later—it's the fastest way for us to travel and conserves a lot of our energy. Dr. Silex, time is our greatest enemy now and we need to get through these caves as quickly as possible." Alex was about to turn away, then had a thought and turned back to the group.

"Is anyone bleeding?" Everyone shook their head. "Good, but I'd also suggest that if someone needs to go to the toilet, please do so on dry ground. Though our suits are designed to absorb waste, I notice a few abrasions appearing in the material; so . . ." Alex didn't need to say anymore. Just the thought of the worms invading where and when a person was most vulnerable made everyone decide to try and squeeze out any last drops of urine before they potentially had to re-enter the stream. They only separated as far as was needed for modesty and Aimee, being the last one in the line, thought she heard something break the water's surface away in the dark, something that had to be much larger than any invertebrate worm they had encountered.

Within five minutes they were ready to go. The small group walked in silence to the choke, with the only sounds the scrunching squeak of the black sand beneath their feet. Alex and Monica took the lead. As Alex walked along the narrow beach beside her he looked down at his legs which were covered in a black shiny mineral. "What is this stuff?" he asked her. "It's sticking like glue."

Monica wiped her finger down her leg and brought it up to roll some between her thumb and forefinger. "Probably magnetite; it's a mineral that's crystallised from basaltic magma. Usually where you see it like this it has weathered out of the basalt and has accumulated as sand on beaches. It also indicates prehistoric volcanic activity; never expected it down here though—that and a lot of things. By the way, it's not sticky, but slightly magnetic— keep it away from your electronics and weapons otherwise it will cause them to lock up."

"Good point. Gentlemen, pack your weapons and keep them away from the sand—it's magnetic particles." Tank and Takeda nodded and pushed their rifles over their shoulders into their packs.

The team moved slowly in the darkness and after twenty minutes they came to the choke. It blocked the cave and the stream ended in a slight belly as the water had to slow down in front of the huge pile of tumbled stones. On the surface slight whirlpools could be seen where the water was being sucked through the choke via small crevices. Monica waded in along the edge of the cliff wall and leaped up onto the choke, scrambling to the top. She scurried back and forth for a while then rejoined the team. "Good news; it's an apex choke—smaller at the top. At the centre, the debris is smaller."

"Can we blast our way through? We can set our rifles to produce a broader air projectile that could provide a non-explosive hammer effect." Monica thought about it for a while, and then turned back to Alex.

"My view is we hold back on that as we don't know

how stable the ceiling is. First let's try to tease the rock out and pass it down via a human chain. It's slower, but there's less chance of bringing it all down on our heads."

Alex nodded. "OK, how do you want us organised?"

"I'll go up first as I've got a better idea which stones to pull free. Tank should be with me in case I need his strength to pull some of the larger ones out."

Matt quickly interrupted. "I'd like to offer to be up there with you as Tank might just be too heavy on the top of the pile. Also, I'm very strong—did you know I was the only guy at college who could bench-press two hundred pounds?"

Monica blew a strand of hair out of her eyes and smiled. "All right, Hercules, come on up."

# Eighteen

Matt climbed nimbly to the top with Monica; for all their hardships he still looked to be enjoying himself. "I also came third in a hot dog eating contest in my final year, but I'm holding that one back for now."

Monica whistled. "You're a very talented man, Mr. Gym Jock, now let's dig."

It took them longer than expected. Even though most rock piles formed a basic pyramidal shape, the top of the boulder choke still needed about ten feet of digging and hauling down and along the human chain. First Monica crawled through, and came back quickly to report they could wriggle through to the next open cave—it also looked like they might avoid getting wet.

One by one they crawled through, this time with Tank managing to avoid getting hooked up. On the other side, they found themselves in a large domed cavern with what looked like stars twinkling on the ceiling. Matt looked up and said to Monica, "Bioluminescence again, huh—bugs or moss?"

"Let's find out." Monica clapped her hands loudly. In the cavern it sounded like a rifle shot and all the lights in the ceiling winked out at once.

"Aw, the nasty cave woman turned off the stars," said Matt.

"Wait for it." Monica pointed up and sure enough the

lights came back on. "Glow-worms probably. Or maybe a hundred other things we've never even seen before."

The small team continued on for another thirty minutes in the darkness and most managed to forget their predicament by marvelling at the wonders of the cave. Enormous limestone formations towered above them, looking like the organ pipes in the Vatican cathedral. There were dripping shoulders of stone like giant angel wings and vast columns reaching from floor to ceiling where a stalagmite and stalactite had joined, some easily a hundred feet high and as wide as a house.

Their beach was narrowing, and they were being forced to walk closer to the water. It was Monica who first noticed the changes.

"It's getting warmer again, and the stream has stopped flowing, and hey, look." She pointed into the water. "This is very rare. I've only ever heard about it in caving chat rooms."

It was a strange effect, the stream seemed to float. It looked like a stream on top of another stream.

Matt knelt down to look. "It's like magic."

"It's not magic, you boy scout." Silex managed to make the normally innocent term sound like a curse. "It's a natural phenomenon called a thermocline. It's either where warm water overlies colder water, or where there's a geologically active floor site. Means it could be toxic as well if hydrogen sulfide is dissolved in the water. This could be more bad news."

"I don't think so." Aimee had also knelt down now. "It's not warm enough to be a thermocline and there's no build-up of minerals to suggest there's sulfide in the water." Aimee removed a small vial from her backpack and took a sample of the lower water level. She sniffed it and then dipped her finger in. She looked at Alex and winked and put the tip of her finger to the end of her tongue. "Yep, that's salt." She got to her feet. "It's a halocline, which is a stable boundary between seawater and fresh water. They usually occur where an underground river flows towards the sea. Seawater backs up into the cave, and the less dense fresh water flows smoothly above it for a distance. It's safe." Aimee picked up a small pebble and tossed it in. Two sets of ripples formed—one set on the surface magically seeming to float above a second set a couple of feet under them.

Monica stood with her hands on her hips. "If it's salt water meeting the stream's fresh then that's good news. We must be going the right way."

Alex looked at the group. Aimee's helmet torch was yellowing. He hoped Monica was right; the dark was fast catching up with them.

In another hour the scent of salt could be detected in the air and the stream's double layer combined into one. Monica had been walking for a while with her head tilted up and she called to the group to stop. "Guys, we need to check something. Could everyone turn their torches off for a few seconds?"

One by one their helmet torches went out. Aimee noticed that Alex hadn't used his light for ages and couldn't remember when he ever had it on. She saw him give some quick signals to Tank and Takeda who both pulled lenses down over their eyes; infra-red, she guessed. Seconds passed with nothing occurring and Silex started to complain in the blackness. Aimee noticed that his voice had moved as he had taken the opportunity to get a lot closer to her. Creep, she thought, as she *sshhhhed* him in the dark.

After a few more seconds the bioluminescent stars appeared again on the ceiling, then on the walls, and after a minute, they could actually make each other out in the cavern. They were no longer in the sightless black of the cave, but in a soft blue twilight.

"Cool," Matt said, looking up, and to perform his own test clapped his hands just once very loudly. It came as such a surprise that even the HAWCs swung around towards him with their rifles raised. Immediately, and as he expected, all the cold lights went out, leaving them once again in the impenetrable darkness. But what no one was expecting was to hear the loud splash from the other side of the stream. Everyone switched their helmet torches back on and some lit up their handhelds for good measure.

Alex spoke to his HAWCs while never taking his eyes off the stream. "Something large entered the water about a hundred feet farther down—eyes on. Everyone else get behind us." The stream, which had been as flat and calm as ice, suddenly lapped up on the sand.

"Surge wave, something's coming towards us in the river. Get ready." The group backed up and positioned themselves behind the HAWCs who had their rifles pointed at the river surface.

It happened quickly. The smooth stream surface exploded as the thing charged out of the water like a shiny, black torpedo. An enormous mouth opened to display a zigzag of deadly teeth at the front of a twenty-foot-long muscular body. It powered itself at Alex on squat legs, aiming to take him round the waist. None of the HAWCs flinched; three rifles fired at once, sending highly compressed bullet-sized projectiles of air into the long body. Holes ruptured along its head and flank and the creature thrashed and thumped heavily on the sand for a while before trying to retreat back into the stream. Tank fired one more round between its eyes and it dropped still on the shore, its flattened tail still in the water and its great shovel-shaped head falling to the sand leaking greenish fluid.

Everyone stood in silence for a few seconds until Matt spoke. "I love this place! This is like fucking Pellucidar. Do you know what this is?" he asked wide-eyed to the still panting group.

"Looks like a cross between a shark and some sort of alligator," said Tank.

"I used to keep Mexican walking fish when I was a kid; looks like the daddy of one of those," said Monica.

"I think it's a dinosaur. Man, oh man, it was a real live dinosaur!" Matt was beside himself.

"Close, very close, but not reptilian or saurian. Long scaleless amphibious morphology, shovel-shaped head, short but muscular legs; I think it's a labyrinthodont." Aimee moved to the head and lifted the mouth to display an upper and lower jaw that when brought together made the teeth slide past each other like scissor blades. The surface of the palate was covered by tiny raised denticles, similar to shark skin. By looking at the mouth and teeth, once the creature got something into that maw, there was little hope of it escaping. In fact, Tank was right; it did look exactly like a shark's mouth.

"Wow, welcome back, big guy." Matt ran his hands down the slimy body. "Once we started finding life, we should have expected something like this."

Aimee nodded. "Monica was close about walking fish. These are the grand-daddies of today's salamanders and newts and last lived right here in the Antarctic. Everywhere else they were out-competed by the crocodiles, but it was way too cold for crocs down here and the labryinthodonts once thrived. Of course, this was over a hundred million years ago. But one thing no one would have expected—it's black," said Aimee.

"I know, deadly but beautiful, isn't it." Matt responded, still looking lovingly at the dead creature.

"No, I don't mean that as a fashion statement. I mean it shouldn't be; it shouldn't be any colour. We're miles under the surface in total darkness. All the creatures we've seen so far have displayed all the expected troglomorphies associated with their adaptation to a subterranean life. Things like loss of pigment, loss of eyes, longer legs and other enlarged sensory organs. This thing is an ambush specialist; it hunts using sight."

They all looked at the fist-sized black eye on the side of the large head—it jerked. Matt and the others leaped back and the HAWCs raised their guns. The creature started to move slowly back into the water, tentatively at first then with a rapid jerking. It wasn't moving under its own strength. It was being dragged back into the depths by something else unseen.

"It's the blood, seems to be a very attractive commodity down here. I think we better go now." Alex instructed them to double-time it for a few minutes to clear the feeding frenzy zone. The cold light from the cavern was extinguished as the loud sounds of thrashing and ripping could be heard from where the small group had just been—nothing would be wasted down here.

In a little while their heartbeats slowed and Alex allowed them to return to a walking pace. But regardless of the team's comfort level he had to order all lights be switched off. Batteries were becoming a prized possession and Silex had already been caught trying to buy Matt's spares. They could never navigate their way back to the surface in the dark.

Once their eyes grew accustomed to the strange blue glow it was quite comforting to have a 360-degree light source instead of relying on narrow beams. After a while it was Matt who voiced what they could all sense. "It's getting even lighter." He was right; the dim blue gloom was turning to an evening-like twilight.

What they now entered could not be called a cavern, or a cave, cathedral or any of the other descriptions applied by cavers and geologists to underground openings or pockets. It could only be described as a world.

"Pellucidar is but a realm of your imagination—nothing more." Matt had been the first to speak and break the sense of awe at what they were seeing.

"Maybe Edgar Rice Burroughs knew more than he was given credit for," said Aimee in a slightly hushed voice.

Matt went to rush forward but Alex held up his hand, flat and open-fingered to indicate to Matt that he hold his position. Alex tried to reach out and sense danger but his consciousness was overwhelmed by the massive life forces emanating from the realm before them.

They stood at the mouth of the cave on the curve of a black beach, where the stream emptied into a vast dark ocean. The colossal hollow's roof and walls were lit with an abundance of the eerie bioluminescent light, making it a permanent twilight. Huge chandeliers of lichens and primitive mosses hung from the ceiling hundreds of feet over their heads and draped the walls like ragged sackcloth. The walls they could see in the near distance were cliffs that had dozens of openings just like the one they had exited from, and the horizon, even though they were in semi-gloom, could not be seen. There was evidence of old rock falls but mainly the slick walls were smooth and draped in mosses, lichens and primitive-looking plants that resembled slime moulds more than any earthly flora. For the most part they were white or translucent, but now and then one would be blood red or cobalt blue, indicating it had tapped into some mineral vein and was converting the rich minerals for its own use.

The underground sea itself was not a dead sheet of glass, but alive with small ripples that appeared on the surface, indicating life was very busy beneath its surface.

Matt turned to Monica. "How can this world exist down here? It's unbelievable. Looks like it's been here forever."

"Well, there are enormous cave systems all around the world that are fantastically old even by geological standards. There's the Ursa Minor in the Sequoia National Park, St. Michaels in Gibraltar, or the Jenolan Caves in Australia that are supposed to be nearly four-hundred million years old. But this could easily top all of those."

"It's warm, and feels like jungle humidity. There must be geothermic activity keeping this underground water body in solution even though it's buried under the coldest continent on earth. Or perhaps the heat from the earth's interior is keeping the sea from freezing—a form of geothermal heat radiating up from below and warming rocks on the underground seabed." Silex was wringing his hands and seemed to be talking to himself. He licked his lips constantly now, and they had become chapped and cracked. He rambled on.

"Hmm, yes, I'd say the ice sheet above would also be acting as a blanket, protecting the lake from cold temperatures on the surface. The heat source probably gives it the basis for its food chain in the near dark. Similar biospheres occur close to deep vents miles under the ocean, you know."

Alex was looking at Dr. Silex with concern. "Let's get further up onto that beach and rest—I'm not happy being this close to the water. Tank, get me some readings." Alex needed to keep them all moving and focused on getting to the surface. As soon as someone started to give up hope, a malaise—or worse—would set in.

Tank reached into his backpack for his small radar unit and fiddled with the buttons before pointing it at the ceiling and then turning it in a wide semi-circle. "OK, we're just under three miles down; we have moved that much again from our initial insertion point." Some more fiddling. "The body of water is . . . well, it must be over a hundred miles in length as it exceeds this device's readings, and about fifty-five miles wide, depth unknown. There are . . . there are multiple movement signatures in the air above and below the water—varying sizes. Christ, some of them are huge—maybe whales, at least that big anyway."

Alex looked at Aimee. She shrugged and narrowed her eyes—he knew what she was thinking; they still hadn't come across the creature that attacked them and owned the rest of the tentacle they hacked off. God help them if that thing wasn't top of the food chain. Meeting something that size in a cave was one thing; you had a wall at your back and it was defendable, to a degree. Out in the open they were just more food for the taking.

"Let's move. Single file. Takeda, lead us out, please."

Alex looked into the distance through his scope and used its maximum magnification to try to find a safe place to rest. He spotted a ledge about a mile down the black beach that looked like the perfect site—up from the water line, dry and with a slight overhang making it defendable. Alex's senses tingled—they were not in their world anymore and danger was everywhere.

# Nineteen

Viktor Petrov sat up in his king-sized bed and sipped from the gold-rimmed china cup. The black, smoky-flavoured Russian tea singed his lips and he blew across the rim to cool it. He thought deeply about the information contained in the intelligence reports that were now fanned out over his red silk sheets. The Russkaya Station in western Antarctica had indicated a seismic ripple from near the site where Borshov and his men had entered the ice. Petrov knew that ripple could only be man-made.

Petrov took another sip of tea and stared straight ahead, his eyes fixed on a spot thousands of miles from his bedroom as he thought of the possible outcomes of the underground explosion. It could mean one of three things. One, Borshov had succeeded and the Americans were dead; good. Two, they were all dead—the big oaf had blown himself and everyone else up; still good. Or three, Borshov was dead and the Americans had survived. Lower probability, but the worst possible outcome for Petrov if true.

He'd put more feelers out and monitor every single blip of electronic traffic coming off the ice. But as a little insurance he'd transfer some of his accounts offshore—it might be a warm winter after all.

Monica moved up to walk beside Aimee; her eyes were wide as she tried to take in all the sights, sounds and textures of their fantastic environment. "In all my life I've never seen a cave like this. No, in a thousand lives, I don't think *anyone* has ever seen a cave like this. It smells primitive, alive."

They rounded a small outcrop of boulders and saw a new black sand beach alive with movement—dozens of long-bodied spider-like creatures were scuttling away from the group. Each of the crustaceans was easily over three feet in length with a flat, heavily armoured insectoid-type body.

"Lobster, anyone?" asked Matt.

"Yuck, centipedes more like it," responded Monica with some disgust. The clicking of their shells and the quick nervous way the creatures moved did remind the group of a hive of giant insects rather than some type of edible sea creature.

"Dangerous?" Alex asked Aimee as he and the remaining HAWCs kept their guns pointed at the scuttling mass on the beach.

"No, I think they're some type of marine arthropod. I'm guessing more frightening to look at than harmful, but down here who knows?"

"They still look like lunch to me." Though Matt had a slight joking edge to his voice, after nearly twenty hours of bitter dark chocolate the thought of real food made a few stomachs complain. None of the small group were on the verge of starvation just yet, however, Alex knew it wouldn't be long before they would all be seeing lunch in every fish and beast. Not yet, thought Alex, but it might be a good idea soon to start working out what was edible in the event they had to spend a little more time down here than they wanted.

"Takeda, clear me a path; exercise extreme caution."

Takeda gave a small bow and headed down the beach towards the swarming mass of scuttling chiton. Alex could have asked Tank who would have simply opened up with his pulse rifle and blown the creatures to bloody atoms in a few seconds. However, Alex didn't think covering the dark sand in blood and gore was a great idea given the feeding frenzy they had witnessed in the river cave. Besides being too messy, he knew Takeda loved the thrill of the hunt. He was a born hunter; many times they had been on jungle missions and he had slipped out into the darkness to return with fish or game caught with little more than his shortened hunting blade or bare hands.

Takeda slowly approached the swarming mass. Long eye stalks ending in shining bulbs swivelled to watch the small biped approach. The creatures started to part in a horseshoe shape around the man, not retreating, looking more like they were encircling the HAWC. One of the largest of the creatures, closest to Takeda, coiled its body, opened a pair of plate-sized front claws and raised a deadly looking tail spike to point it at his chest.

In one fluid motion, Takeda drew his sword and removed the tip of the creature's tail. Whether or not it was poisonous didn't matter, he was taking no chances. On the backward swing he plunged the blade into the centre of the creature's head. There was a muffled crunch as its claws and tail dropped immediately; the blade must have pierced its central nervous system. Takeda withdrew his blade and re-sheathed it. The other creatures hadn't moved and instead started to close in on Takeda once again. This time, however, it seemed the body of their fallen fellow creature was their goal.

Takeda backed up a step and looked closely at the dead creature as the rest of the swarm moved in on it. Its shape bristled with spines and armour plating; black eyes on segmented stalks grew a foot long from its spade-shaped head. Its feet were sharp pointed spikes covered in bristling hairs and what was left of the tail tapered to a point.

With its black and green mottled shell it was a fearsome-looking creature. The swarm quickly reached the body and claws like giant toothed shears chopped and tore at the gristly frame. In seconds the four-foot-long creature had gone from a boiling mass of frenzied armour-plated bodies to a blackish pool of blood staining even blacker sand.

From up the beach Matt turned to Aimee. "You said harmless, right?"

"Well, I wouldn't want to step on one in the shallows, but then normally you wouldn't unless you were around about two-hundred million years ago. Looks to me like one of the extinct varieties of sea scorpion. They were normally sea-floor dwellers but they could also live on land. Still think they look like lunch?"

Takeda saw that the slaying had started a feeding frenzy among the creatures and actually drew them more tightly together. He drew his sword again and swatted one hard on the head with the flat of his blade. The clang of his toughened steel sword against the thick exoskeleton echoed off the cliff walls and was carried away into the low mist rising off the warm water. However, it worked; the creature scuttled out of the way. Takeda struck again and more of the creatures parted and slowly headed towards the water.

Whether it was the noise or the vibrations from the sword blows was hard to say, but they were moving. Not quickly enough however, and when Takeda halted for a second or two the creatures tried to move back up the beach, either changing their mind or preferring the sand over the water. Takeda waved his free hand and brought his sword down again on the tail of one large retreating sea scorpion. This time he uttered a loud "Yaa Yaa," to try to squeeze more speed from them.

Alex and the team moved forward as Takeda finally

managed to clear the beach. Alex watched Takeda travel farther down the sand, closer to the lapping inky sea. At last the creatures were now in flight and their rapid jerking movements hinted at panic as they crawled over each other to escape. As they picked up speed and were scuttling back into the water, disappearing beneath the surface, the clacking of their spindly sharp legs was replaced by hissing as they hit the water at speed and continued on into the depths.

Alex noticed that there were large wet areas of the beach, each about fifty feet in a rough circle, that the scorpions seemed to avoid. In fact, they were taking great pains to detour around them. Some were taking longer to bypass the slightly raised circular shapes and looked to try to head back up the sand, so Takeda moved quickly to head them off. One of the larger creatures swivelled its eye stalk backwards and on seeing the two-legged predator almost on top of it, decided to cross the empty, wet-looking circle. It got no more than five feet onto the circle when it stopped dead, but not because it had decided to freeze. Rather, it looked glued to the spot.

Alex felt his heightened senses jump and they allowed him to react immediately—this was danger. He shouted for Takeda to halt; unfortunately, Takeda only heard the command after he too had taken several large steps onto the circular pad; he stopped and looked down.

His feet had sunk in and were stuck fast; it was like fly paper. Takeda tried to remove his feet and then used his sword to try and cut himself free. The pad started to draw itself towards the centre of the circle, which had dropped into the wet sand to display a ragged black-red maw. It was some type of enormous living creature that was buried beneath the sand and was using the pad as a trap for unwary animals—a trap that was now being reeled in and sucked down into the dark orifice of its mouth. As the carpet of flesh was tugged violently from under Takeda he was tipped over to land flat on his side. Now, rising back to his feet was impossible as he found most of one side of his body trapped fast.

Alex raced down the beach. He stopped at the edge of the pad and fired his rifle into the round "tongue." It had no effect; Takeda was now only ten feet from the centre and he could just lift his head to observe the sea scorpion disappear inside. The pad stopped for a second or two and a crunching could be heard as the scorpion was pulverised by a still hidden, powerful set of jaws beneath the sand.

Alex fired again, this time into the centre of the hole, but it still had no effect. He was about to leap forward onto the moving pad, planning to use his enormous strength to pull himself free when Aimee cried out. "Don't, we need you with us."

Takeda had not uttered a word or a cry. He looked at Alex and shook his head. Alex nodded, understanding the unspoken communication and said quietly into his helmet comm unit, "Farewell, my friend," followed by a single word, "Grenade."

Takeda reached into his belt pouch, pulling free a baseball-sized metal ball. He held it close to his chest and closed his eyes. He was roughly pulled into the maw and just as a sickening crunching began, there was an explosive *whump* from beneath the sand. A small ripple of shockwaves ran across the sand that made Aimee and Matt fall to the ground.

The dim bluish biological light in the cave immediately went out and left them in absolute darkness.

"Be patient and quiet. Wait for it. Wait." Sure enough the lights started to wink back on. A small patch to the right, then larger, then to the left, then all back on. "I don't think these ancient glow-worms or whatever they are down here are used to loud noises."

"Them and me both," replied Matt with an ashen face. "What the fuck was that? What was that thing?"

Tank was clearly distressed at losing another of his buddies and began pacing at the edge of the smoking hole. Alex looked around; the team was gathered down near the water's edge, except for Silex who had remained far up the beach with his hands over his face.

Silex heard Tank's questions and came stalking down the sand. "What is it? It's our punishment, that's what it is. We're all dead and in hell, don't you know? We must have died and now we're stuck in hell and are nothing more than bugs in a giant spider's web waiting to be devoured. We're going to be pulled to pieces and eaten bit by bit. Ask that imbecile soldier." Silex's cracked lips had begun bleeding. With his chalky white face and the gloom of the cave, his appearance had taken on that of a mad clown.

Alex had taken a step towards Silex without even realising. He too was shaken by the loss of Takeda and one of his hands had formed into a fist which vibrated from the enormous pressure. Aimee stepped in front of Alex and gave the scientist a sharp slap across the face. He staggered for a second and gave her and Alex a look of such murderous intent that the furies in Alex screamed out to accept the challenge. Silex noticed Alex's large bulk drawing silently near and burst into sobs. "We need to go, we need to go, we need to go." With his hands up beside his face he lurched up the beach, repeating his plea to himself.

Alex knew that Dr. Silex was becoming a liability to the group. Normally, he would simply sedate the scientist and carry him out, but circumstances made that option impossible. His behaviour was creating an added burden—he would have to be watched and kept under control. Usually,

Alex would send one of his men after Silex to return him—against his will if necessary. But given the scientist's fragile state, he was liable to go screaming down the black beach if Tank went near him. And if it was Alex who went after him . . . well, best if he stayed away from the man for a while. Alex looked at the small group; Matt Kerns looked the most harmless, he could go. He'd have to be quick, though; they needed to be under cover and Alex figured things would probably get a lot worse for all of them before they got better.

Alex's senses prickled. Since the small explosion he knew they were being watched by a thousand eyes. If they thought they might have been able to sneak along the shoreline undetected before, they had announced their presence with a loud ringing bang now. He hoped it wasn't a dinner bell. He looked down at the smoking hole one last time. Blood and gore had begun to ooze to the surface and wash down towards the water. He knew what that meant.

"Everyone move, double time."

Aimee felt like she was floating, disconnected. Tom and his party seemed to have run down into these low caves and they still hadn't found any trace of them. If this place could kill the HAWCs, how could Tom have survived down here? He was no outdoorsman and she doubted he had ever slept rough in his life. Her eyes were beginning to blur from tears when Alex came up beside her and spoke softly.

"So, what do you think that thing was?"

Aimee pushed thoughts of Tom out of her mind and tried to focus again on where she was. Wondering where he was and what happened to him wouldn't get any of them out of this alive. "Impossible to know exactly. Nothing like that exists up on the surface, and as far as I'm aware nothing in the fossil records indicate anything like it ever has. It could be some form of tubeworm below the surface of the sand with a modified fan that acts like a trap across the surface. In effect it was like a giant tongue spread over the sand that was triggered by the sea scorpion and Takeda stepping on it. One thing I do know, it was a very large ambush predator designed to catch very large prey."

Alex expelled a breath through his lips. "Hard to tell people to keep a look out when we don't know what to look out for. I could sit on a rock that turns out to be some creature's nose."

"You're absolutely right—and in a way Silex was also right about the spider's web. Down here we're not top of the food chain; we're just something else to eat. I don't think it's going to be very long before all of us are screaming like Silex that it's time to go home."

"I know; nearly to the ledge. Let's have a rest and something to eat and make plans for getting us the hell up and out of here."

Borshov had been walking for hours. The cave he had chosen had at first narrowed and descended to what he could only assume from the readings from his resonator was a rushing river given its size and movement. However, the cave had quickly started to increase its upward slope and now he found himself climbing up into darkness.

The blood was congealing on his cheek, but it continued to dribble thickly into the back of his throat. He swallowed; he needed the liquid, and the protein.

Borshov cursed once again every one of the American HAWC's descendants all the way back to Adam and Eve as he tried to focus his mind away from the miserable throbbing in his head and face. He didn't know how the hated Captain Alex Hunter had been able to defeat him so easily, but he knew there were other ways for an assassin to execute a foe.

Borshov rested for a minute on the steep rock face and spat a gob of gore into the void. He would not underestimate him next time.

# Twenty

Tank climbed to the ledge and surveyed its interior. After several minutes he appeared at the edge and called them all up, adding, "Might be something you'll find interesting up here, Dr. Kerns."

The ledge was shaped like a platform roughly fifty feet long and about the same in depth. The back half of the ledge was sheltered by an overhang making a shallow indentation in the rock face. It gave the team better shelter and a feeling of more security, and for the HAWCs it meant they didn't have a 360-degree defensive field to maintain. Monica and Aimee set to portioning the last dried food packets for each of the team members.

Tank took Matt to the rear of the small cave and showed him the far wall, just over a mound of stones. It had some small glyphs similar to those they had seen on their descent.

"It's another message from the brothers. No, wait; I think it's a farewell to one of the brothers from the other." Matt ran his hands over the slightly raised markings on the wall and spoke softly. "Little brother. The gods rejoice at your bravery in battle. Your name will sound in the halls of Aztlan forever. I cannot hope to defeat *Qwotoan* and must climb back to the light to give my warning to the sun king. The Deceiver will not stay in Xibalba. It finishes with the sign for Hunahpu." Matt looked down at the pile of stones. "Holy shit, this must be the grave of his brother, Xbalanque. It wasn't a legend after all, it was all real!"

Matt dropped to his knees and began carefully lifting away the larger rocks and then the smaller stones until he was left to brush away pebbles. After a while he uncovered a small fossilised skeleton, no more than five feet long. Lying across the ribs was a small dagger made of a golden metal and what was once a short thrusting spear, it was now little more than a stain line of powdered wood and brown rust across the mineralised bones. Under the skull at the base of the neck were coloured stones and small pieces of gold that must have hung around his neck at one time. His arms and hands would have been folded across his chest, but it was obvious that his was no peaceful death. His left arm was sheared off above the elbow, leaving a splintered mess of his humerus. His left foot was missing and his skull showed multiple depressions—the tiny warrior's death must have been a brutal one.

"Amazing, he made it all this way with just a sword and spear," said Monica.

"Made it! He looks like he was hit by a fucking train. I hardly call that making it." Silex was again working himself up to a state of high agitation.

Matt responded as calmly as he could to Silex's fury. "Well, his brother had the strength to cover him up and write his death story. I figure Hunahpu headed back to the surface and we need to follow."

"I think your stupid little Indian has probably been long digested over 10,000 years ago, and the trail will probably lead to nothing more than another pile of chewed-up, fossilised bones somewhere."

Alex stepped quietly forward. "That's enough, sir, this isn't helping. You've got to pull yourself together or you're not going to make it."

"I'm not going to make it? What does that mean—you'd leave me here? Shoot me in the leg, is that it? You're going to try to cast me off so you have more food and water for yourselves. I'll tell you something, it won't be me that dies next." Dr. Silex's stare was that of a man unhinged and dangerous. Alex put his hand on Silex's shoulder, turning him round so he could bring his face very close to the scientist's so that only he could hear. "Dr. Silex, my job is to keep you all safe. But if you look to endanger the rest of us, then I will no longer regard you as part of the group and my protection duties for you will cease. Do you understand me, sir?"

Silex spun out of Alex's grasp and briefly turned to hiss something inaudible, then retreated to the back of the cave. As Alex watched him go, a small flame burned within him. He closed his eyes for a few seconds and pictured a golden beach with sparkling water and crashing blue waves—it all seemed a lifetime ago.

Several miles out on the black sea the water lumped as something large broke the surface. It stayed there for a few minutes, hanging in the water, its enormous body supported by fluid-filled sacs providing neutral buoyancy at any depth it chose. It had sensed the blood trail and felt the compression waves from the explosion. It could not yet detect the source of the scent but could sense movement on the water's edge. The opportunity to feed close to its home and not have to hunt in the upper caves was too attractive; it slid silently below the surface and propelled itself swiftly towards the beach.

After scanning the surrounding walls for several minutes, Alex called the group together. Silex refused to join them and sat at the back of the small cave, watching the team from under his lowered brows.

"OK, there are multiple caves all around us—one or more must lead back to the surface. I figure we don't have too many opportunities to make a wrong choice and double back. So, how do we narrow our search and make a higher value choice the first time?"

Monica was the first to respond. "Should be simple really; there are two indicators we can use. The first is change in temperature. The further we descended the warmer it became. Therefore, we should choose a cave that seems cooler than the rest, signalling that it leads to more topside Antarctic surface temperatures. The second, unfortunately, runs counter to the first. Warm air rises. We need to find a vent that is channelling warm air to colder temperatures. It will be like a wind tunnel. If the wind is strong, this will mask any colder air we could detect at this level."

"Any others? Dr. Kerns?" Alex could see that Matt had something he wanted to share with the group.

"There's a third indicator as well. Though we crossed paths several times, I don't think that Hunahpu came down the river the way we did. We know from the near-surface caves that at least one of the brothers returned. If we find any carvings or glyphs indicating the place he made his ascent then it's definitely the right cave. Or at least it was ten thousand years ago."

"OK, good. If we find one of the tunnels with two of the indicators you mentioned then the chances are high it's the one we need. Tank, give me some density readings starting from our present position in a two-mile grid search. Everyone else, we've got about ten more minutes of rest time before we need to push on."

Mumbling to himself, Silex focused on Alex's back with a look of such venomous intent it almost sent tangible waves of loathing across the cave floor. "You've forgotten who's in charge, you grunt. This is mutiny. Just want the applause and the girl. Nice day's work, glory-boy. Well, you aren't going to hobble me and leave me for the spider crabs." While the main group was huddled at the mouth of their small cave ledge, Silex reached into the uncovered grave mound of the fallen warrior. He tested the blade against his hand and finding it still intact he slipped it into his belt pouch. He mumbled once again to himself. "You just wait, you just wait."

After a few minutes Tank was able to report that one of the larger caves, about a mile and a half to their west, was showing air movement in a single direction. Warmer air was being sucked in at a rate of about five knots—not significant, but enough to indicate a pretty good updraught.

"Temperature change?" enquired Alex.

"None I can detect, but as we expected this could simply be because of the constant warm air being drawn through the tunnel," replied Tank.

Alex looked towards the large cave opening that Tank had indicated—it was not the easiest cave to get to. There was a section, about 200 feet in length, where there was no beach; the water came right to the cliff wall. They would have to either scale the rock face, or wade through the shallows—if they were shallows. He didn't think the team would relish the idea of swimming in that water or even wading through shallows, given Mike and Takeda's fate.

Alex turned to the group. "OK everyone, we have a route selected based on Ms. Jenning's insights on air movement. Unless we have any better ideas I suggest we break camp and move off immediately." Alex waited for a few seconds, scanning the strained and dirt-encrusted faces before him. With the exception of Silex, they looked tired but still fairly strong and Matt was now openly holding hands with Monica. He hoped he could get them both safely to the surface so they could share a happy ending—something good had to come out of this.

They repacked and prepared to make their way along the shore on the first part of the trek. Alex could see the fatigue etched into their faces as they all groaned to their feet and started to walk—all but one. "Please keep up with us, Dr. Silex." Alex waited for him to catch up; he wanted to keep the group together, but more than that, something in Silex's eyes convinced Alex that this was not a man to have at your back.

In the near dark the small group walked silently along the black beach, the squeak of the sand particles beneath their cave boots making a noise like they were a small group of rusting robots in need of oiling. Everyone was tired and looking only at the sand at their feet; the group was retreating into their own thoughts—all except Tank and Alex, who were on high alert, never taking their eyes from the sand, water, cliffs and ceiling. This was an extremely hostile environment.

Aimee thought of Tom again. Did he make it here? Was he still alive by then, and did he climb down or was he dragged? Maybe he had hidden; could he still be . . . No, that was silly. He wasn't alive anymore, none of them were.

Matt and Monica also walked in silence, but sneaked a peek at each other from time to time to smile and give reassurance. Matt was worried about Monica and thought he would need to provide protection for her, while Monica knew she would have to be looking out for Matt. They were determined they would get to the surface and be sipping drinks on a warm beach before the week was out.

Dr. Adrian Silex was also silent, though his cracked lips continued to move in a feverish monologue of hate. His mind formed wilder and wilder conspiracies—they were planning to steal his imaging technology designs and then leave him here to die like an animal. Why was it that only the soldiers had guns? They were supposed to be taking orders from him, now they seemed to be the ones giving orders. If he had a gun he'd be the one giving the orders again. If anyone was going to be getting out it was him— everyone else could go to hell, and he might just make damn well sure of that.

Alex tried to keep the group as close to the cliffs as he could and away from the unfathomable black water. On the glistening walls in among the hanging fronds of mosses and lichens, lice-like creatures the size of his fist wriggled into crevices to hide as the small group passed. At the water line, something brightly coloured caught Alex's eye. He called a halt, leaving Tank to stay with the team. He carefully approached the water. Lying still on the glass smooth surface was what at first glance looked like wood, but it had tendrils of orange material through it. There was more than one; roughly about ten feet long, they must have been organic as they were giving off a disgusting ammonia smell that made him hold his breath. Looking across the surface of the mess, Alex could see hundreds of the worms they had encountered in the upper caves that had so effectively ended Mike Lennox's life. Some of them were as thick as his wrist and looked like small blind snakes.

Alex kneeled to get a better look and could make out metal objects that might have been rock climbing cams, coloured canvas and perhaps the broken handle of a gun. Alex knew Aimee was approaching before she kneeled down to examine what Alex was looking at.

"It stinks." After Alex spoke he turned to look at Aimee; a single tear was streaking her dirt-stained face.

"That's Tom's jacket in there. I've only ever seen this

type and size of excretion as coprolite—fossilised shit. Oh god, this is all that's left of him and probably the entire party he came here with."

"I'm sorry, Aimee. I know he meant a great deal to you."

Aimee sniffed and wiped her cheek, then looked up at Alex. She started to laugh softly as tears welled in her eyes.

"You know, if anyone knew how to get himself into shit, it'd be Tom."

Alex smiled at her as she looked back down at the large excreted packages. "At least now I know and can stop worrying. His suffering is long over." A strong ammonia smell engulfed them. "Phew, that smell is a mixture of the cephalopod feces and ammonia. They compress and package all the indigestible items from their meals and expel them."

"Great. Don't tell me we're right in the creature's lair."

"Maybe, maybe not—they're very rare. Cephalopods usually hide them or deposit them away from their homes to throw off predators. However, they're usually tiny, so I doubt predators exist for these things." Aimee rubbed her eyes as if to clear away the image of Tom's last seconds on earth. "This thing has got to be hundreds of feet long and though it might not be close, this must be near to where it lives. We need to get out of here or we could end up in the next pile that it excretes."

"I hear you. Let's go."

# Twenty-one

They came to the end of the beach and stared fearfully into the small bay that blocked their path. As expected, no one wanted to wade into the water to test its depth. Monica cracked her last glow stick and threw it out towards the centre. The water was crystal clear but the stick sank until it was just a dim, glowing dot some fifty feet down. There could be no wading; they would have to swim.

Aimee had also been looking into the water, but at something that looked like rice washed up onto the black sand. She walked quickly down to the water's edge and scooped up a handful, sorting through it and squeezing some between her fingers as she brought it back to show Alex. "This is strange. These look like abyssal shrimp. They're still quite fresh, but all dead. These things only exist in deep water, and I mean deep; down to the hadal zone, twenty thousand feet plus. You see them all the time when they're drilling in the ocean trenches. Strange, the water's far too warm for them down here. These guys are from our world, not this one." Aimee looked down into her hand. "Hmm, how did you guys get here?"

"Could they have been washed in somehow?" Alex looked quickly into her palm at the small crustaceans and then turned to focus again on the dark water in front of them.

"Washed in?" Aimee seemed to ponder the question as she walked back up to where Matt was standing.

Alex noticed the team was standing well back from the small inlet. After what he suspected lurked in those depths even he was against taking to the water. Looking up, all Alex could see was an almost vertical rock face covered in some odd-looking plants and mosses. He knew his great strength could carry him across the cliff with minimal handholds but wasn't sure about the rest of his group.

Monica, who had also been looking up at the rock face, moved down the beach to Alex. "There are plenty of choices. How high do you want us to go before dropping back down?"

"I don't know how far up we need to be to feel safe, so I'll take the route that's quickest and anything above the water line," he said.

"OK, the safest wall traversal I can see starts at the sharp rock just there and goes vertical for twenty feet, then travels across to that reddish-looking bush, and then continues up again for another ten feet." Monica continued to map out the cliff trail for Alex; he admired her expertise as handholds and ledges he missed in his quick scan were now visible once they'd been pointed out by a rock climbing expert.

"It's only about a hundred fifty feet or thereabouts, but we'll need to climb vertically in some areas and given our level of fatigue that's going to be extremely taxing. I'll hammer in a guide rope, but whoever is bringing up the rear will need to unhook the line so I can draw it forward and re-use the tether."

"I'll do that." Alex volunteered as he knew he was the only one other than Monica who could get across the wall without any guidelines.

"I'm going next to Monica." Matt was quick to offer to keep close to her so he could do his best to keep her safe, and Monica was happy for him to be there so she in turn could keep watch over him.

"OK, Dr. Silex, you go next, followed by Tank, and then Dr. Weir." Alex wanted either himself or Tank to be close to Silex at all times. He was becoming more remote from the group by the hour and Alex now considered him another potential danger that must be contended with.

The climb was not quick and, as Monica said, it was very tiring on already exhausted muscles. Though the fingertips of their caving gloves afforded an excellent grip, it was slippery, and every inch of the way was covered in moss or greasy, moist lichens. Startled cave lice like armoured many-legged rats scuttled out from handholds or leaped past their faces to the water below. Monica guided them along the easiest path she could have found and, true to her word, every ten feet she inserted a cam and threaded a guide rope for handholds. She hitched the rope at chest level so the team could stay flattened to the wall—a height that proved very useful as some of the ledges they inched their way along were less than a foot wide.

After climbing, crawling and inching their way forward for over an hour, they stopped to catch their breath. They were over halfway across the stretch of dark water and they found themselves on a slightly wider shelf. The small resting ledge afforded them space to crouch or sit down carefully as its two-foot width was perhaps the widest place they were likely to encounter on the climb. If not for their fatigue and concern for their predicament, they would have said the view was almost magical. In some places they still could not quite make out the ceiling of the giant underground cavern as it was indistinct in the heights and obscured by a light mist. The enormous black sea stretched away into the distance and they could see hundreds of beaches like their own—some barren, others moving with the sea scorpions they had previously encountered, and some with other strange animals that would have been a paleobiologist's dream. While they watched, high up in the mist something with the wingspan of a small plane looped down and back up to disappear again into the primeval fog.

"This place makes the Galapagos Islands seem boring. Imagine a biological expedition here to map and study the environment. How many new species would they find, or old species we haven't seen for millions of years? And what secrets are beneath that water." Aimee seemed to be musing to herself. "There may even be ancient species that have followed some completely different evolutionary path and turned into something totally new by now."

"After what we've seen, I'm thinking they should bring a harpoon cannon," offered Matt.

Under Tank's enormous weight the ledge silently cracked and was held to the rock face only by tendrils of the strange ferns that grew all along the cliff walls. It just held as he passed, but when Aimee set her foot firmly with all her weight on the weakened rock it gave way. At that precise moment she also took both her hands off the rope so she was tipped outward as the ledge disappeared from under her. She flailed her hands back at the rope but she had already moved too far out from the rock face and was beginning to fall.

Alex flew towards her and caught her by the wrist, managing to swing her down and back up to the ledge. Alex watched as her pistol flipped up and out of her belt and pinwheeled towards the water. "Grab on," he hissed through clenched teeth. It wasn't that Aimee was heavy, but the angle he held her at while precariously holding the rock ledge with one hand made it a very difficult manoeuvre. To make matters worse, loose rock was falling around them and a fist-sized chunk struck Alex on the side of his head. Luckily the damage to his skull was minimal due to his cave helmet but his infra-red scope was knocked off and fell slowly to the water nearly fifty feet below.

Aimee couldn't stop shivering. She felt her reserves were almost gone now. She hated heights, she hated small places and she hated the dark. She kept her face pressed against the cold stone wall for a second until her heart rate slowed and then looked up at Alex. He immediately made her feel calm. Who was he? How could he be so quick and never seem to fatigue or falter?

Monica clambered back across the rock face, passing over Matt and Silex as she scaled nimbly down to hold Aimee close to the wall. "OK, I've got you." Monica had Aimee round the waist and both of them were able to rest and slow their breathing against the cliff; however, they now found themselves about ten feet below the main group.

After Alex had released his grip and let Aimee drop into Monica's hands, he was about to lower himself down to their ledge when he noticed the wave—it wasn't large, no more than a foot high, but it shouldn't have been there. There were no winds or moon to pull any tides down here. Something large was coming at them under the water.

Matt had clambered down as well and brought the end of the rope with him. Aimee had settled enough to begin climbing again, and Monica was planning her new climb path now that she, Matt and Aimee had to take a different route across the rock face.

It was at that moment that Silex decided to act—Tank

was preoccupied with watching the group beneath him and Alex was looking down at the water below. Silex edged himself closer to Tank and in one swift movement he unclipped and withdrew his sidearm. The polymer-framed 9 mm was a light, lethal-looking pistol and was a no–gas compression model. Tank reacted instinctively and reached for his holster; it was a mistake. Silex had been hoping he would do this and responded by swinging his other hand at Tank's now exposed neck. In the scientist's hand was the golden dagger from the fallen Aztlan warrior and he struck with the speed of a snake. Tank managed to bring his shoulder up slightly and avoid a death strike into his carotid artery but the knife still plunged several inches into the trapezium muscle bunch between his shoulder and throat—painful and potentially debilitating but not lethal, especially for someone with Tank's enormous muscle mass. However, it threw Tank off balance and he started to slip. He fell to his knee but managed to keep his other hand clamped around the rope. Silex took off across the rock face, throwing all caution to the wind, or perhaps with the carelessness of the insane.

Seeing Silex's attempted murder of his HAWC, Alex almost screamed with rage. He felt as though his chest was about to burst as the furies demanded he go after the scientist; he wanted to tear the man limb from limb, to utterly obliterate him. They should have gone another way, he should have been watching the man; but then he would have lost Aimee, he would have lost them all. He couldn't be everywhere. He held on to the cave sill and brought his fingers together; some of the rock broke off and exploded to dust in his fist. Not now, he thought. He breathed deeply and the rage began to settle again.

Monica went to go after him but Alex yelled to her.

"No, leave him. We've got enough problems. Tank, can you make it?" Alex held his position as the giant HAWC got back to his feet.

"I'm OK, just feel stupid for letting that little weasel ambush me." He went to pull the knife out and Alex called for him to stop. Though the knife embedded in his shoulder would be painful as hell and would be even more so with movement, if he withdrew it now and couldn't pack the wound he would lose a lot of blood before it could be closed. Losing blood meant two things down here: with the loss of blood so went your strength; and more important, it rang the dinner bell for every strange monstrosity that inhabited this world.

Alex doubted Silex was going to be able to get very far, and he preferred to have him in front of them rather than at his back. He looked down to see if Aimee, Matt and Monica were ready to proceed when his eyes were drawn to movement below them. The water only seemed like ink because there was no sun to give it colour or depth and the sand beneath it was also black; in reality it was almost totally clear. Now Alex could see the outline of an enormous moving mass just below the surface, and what was more disturbing was that the mass had focused an intelligent eye the size of a car on the small group.

"Everyone freeze, we've got company." Alex quickly weighed up his options; they still had about ten minutes of climbing before they would be down on the opposite beach. He knew he could clamber higher and out of reach easily, but he doubted anyone other than Monica could keep up with him. Tank was wounded and wasn't going anywhere quickly, and without ropes Aimee and Matt would certainly fall. They could either stand and fight or get across the cliff face, and given the size of the thing coiling itself for an attack below them, standing and fighting would mean a very short battle indeed.

Alex spoke to Tank. "Soldier, hold fast but prepare to engage on my order." Alex knew Tank might not have seen what he had and he needed the big HAWC to be mentally preparing for battle. Even with the knife in his shoulder and the dozens of bruises and scrapes all over his body, Alex saw Tank's jaw set and his eyes darken; Tank had entered combat mode.

As Tank was checking his armaments and Alex was looking down again towards the water, Aimee screamed. Seemingly floating up toward them was Tom Hendsen.

Despite the danger, Alex marvelled at the creature's ability to mimic a human form. In the sub-light environment it really did look like a person, right down to the colours in the clothing. He could now understand how it so easily lured people to its embrace in the dark.

The Tom Hendsen figure seemed to hang there in space, waiting for something, for some sign. He remembered the encounter that Mike had with the creature in the upper caves, and how it had only leaped at him when he moved. As an ambush creature and one of the few down here with sight, it was probably keyed to attack on movement.

"Nobody move a muscle." Only Alex's eyes moved as he watched the human form glide close to him, then down to pass over Aimee and Monica.

Silex reached the beach and looked back up to where his former team members were still stranded high on the rock face. He blinked a couple of times to remove the sweat from his eyes and also to clear his vision of what had to be a hellish hallucination. Reaching up out of the water was a tentacle whip as thick at the base as a redwood tree, but tapering at the tip to what looked to be a human body. The owner of the massive appendage was still hidden beneath the water but by its size the creature had to be enormous.

Silex looked back at his colleagues and giggled. "Can't let that tricky Captain Hunter evade his fate this time, can we?"

He raised the handgun and fired at Alex twice, then turned to run along the sand.

The twin boom of the handgun was like thunder in the cave. This was no silent gas projectile being fired but a hard round with explosive chemical propulsion. Two things happened almost simultaneously—the creature snapped its lure away from the team on the cliff face, and the lights went out.

At first Silex could not see what was coming. The creature propelled itself so silently and smoothly along under the water that it would have been invisible even in the twilight of the glow-worms. He continued to run across the black sand in the dark, oblivious to the danger. The first he became aware of a change in his circumstances was when he suddenly became engulfed in a marine-ammonia smell that made his eyes water and his nasal passages sting. Slowly the lights winked on and with them a clearer image of what now stood before him—Tom Hendsen.

"No, no, no, you don't want me; there are more people back there. I already wounded one for you, Tom. You know I hoped that one day we could work together. I always admired your work; your research was always impeccable."

Silex slowly raised the gun until he had it pointed at the face of the figure.

"You know, you really should watch that Captain Hunter and that co-worker of yours. There's something going on there." Silex grinned and blood spotted his chin from his cracked lips. He double-gripped the gun and pulled the trigger.

The boom of the gun's report made Silex's hand jerk upwards and the bullet slammed into the facial area of the human form in front of him. A small hole had been punched into the flesh, but no blood flowed and no pain showed on the placid, wet-looking face. The Tom form rushed forward and slammed into him. He wasn't knocked from his feet as the tentacle club was exuding its sticky paste. In addition, large hooks embedded themselves into his flesh. He was snared as effectively as a rabbit in a steel-toothed trap. Silex was pulled from his feet as the horror from the deep dragged itself free from the dark water.

For the first time the group saw the creature clearly—it looked like a squid but was different. Two long, whip-like tentacles and eight thick muscular arms extended from its head. From just behind its enormous eyes it was encased in cone-shaped armour plating that was dragged behind it. Nearly the size of a 747 jet plane, it looked to be easily 160 feet in length and a sick, mottled green colour. It lifted the screaming scientist towards it, briefly holding his wriggling form up to the emotionless disc of an eye and then used the longer tentacle to hand him to the shortened feeding appendages. These commenced to strip him of as many of the inedible pieces as could come away easily; his back-pack and belt and his caving suit were roughly torn free and with them probably a good deal of his skin. He looked raw by the time his still struggling form was passed towards the centre of the tentacle mass. The thick arms opened to reveal hundreds of inward-pointing teeth like some sort of gigantic rasp. Silex screamed as he was gently lowered into this jagged maw. Mercifully, the tentacles closed over the disappearing form of the scientist so the others would be spared watching him be ground up and devoured.

Matt and Monica both moaned and Aimee kept her forehead pressed against the cliff wall. Alex heard Monica praying softly, hushed words calling for deliverance from damnation. Both HAWCs remained impassive, only their eyes moving quickly over the large beast, probing, searching for tactical weaknesses. The diversion also gave Alex the opportunity to get the team off the cliff face while the creature was occupied with the scientist. Up here they were as good as dead as they couldn't stay motionless forever; at least on the sand they had a slim chance. His destination was a small cave right at the base of the cliff on the dry beach. It was only half a mile away, and it looked defendable and much too small to accommodate the large hell-snail. Monica was the first to land on the sand and it took all her willpower to stay focused on getting Aimee and Matt down and not look over her shoulder at what was happening to Silex. Tank and Alex arrived next, and Alex had to yell to stop them all either freezing or collapsing to the sand in terror. He pointed to the small opening in the rock face and yelled again for them to put their heads down and head for the cave. Aimee was too slow; Matt, Monica and Tank were already shooting along the dark metallic sand while Aimee was only just climbing to her feet on wobbling legs. In a fluid motion Alex closed the distance between them and scooped her up under his arm; his legs were pumping hard, throwing glittering black sand out behind him in a plume.

The creature detected the movement and shot its long whip-like ambush tentacle forward again. This time, just as Alex dived into the cave, he turned to see the figure of Dr. Adrian Silex presented to try to entice them from the cave. Considering they had just witnessed the scientist being peeled like a grape and devoured, looking at him now was like seeing a returned soul that had been condemned to hell. Silex was now trapped forever, united with some terrifying creature miles below the earth. Perhaps this was his punishment after all.

# Twenty-two

The group huddled at the back of the cave. It was only about twenty feet deep but narrowed considerably so the creature could not hope to wedge itself inside. Unfortunately for the group, it didn't need to get its entire body into the cave and Alex knew too well what sort of power it could use to drag them out when it determined its lure wasn't working.

The cave was dark, and when the faint glow from the cold bioluminal light was blanketed by the creature's huge bulk the darkness was almost total. Even in the near complete darkness Alex could still see the leviathan and was glad only Tank could see what he could—just outside the cave, an enormous eye began to peer into the gloom where the group had taken refuge. This was a monster of legend, perhaps the grounding of all the tales of sea monsters. Maybe every hundred generations a movement of the earth's crust opened a rift that allowed one or more of these things to be released into the surface ocean to steal sailors from the decks of their great ships—the mythical kraken incarnate.

The Silex lure stood silently at the cave mouth just off to one side, seemingly imploring them to come closer. Because of their enhanced vision the HAWCs could see the other club snaking along the opposite wall of the cave as it hoped to catch them off guard while they had their attention focused on the human form.

"Aim for the area of the club attaching itself to the tentacle, see if you can cut it off. I'll take a body shot and try to blind it." Alex sighted at the giant eye.

"Roger that." Tank aimed at the tentacle snaking its way towards them like a giant, wet-looking slug. The air in the cave was becoming an eye-watering ammonia soup and the only sound was the terrified breathing from the team behind them. The creature started to move faster and Alex barked, "Fire!"

The sound inside the cave from the gas projectile rifles was like soft clapping, but outside there was a sudden pounding commotion as hundreds of tons of flesh moved to cover itself. Tank didn't manage to sever the club from its base but ensured it was a ragged mess when it was quickly withdrawn. Alex aimed for the eye but a moment before he fired the creature moved, turning part of its armour-shell casing towards them. Though his projectiles could punch a hole through solid steel, the biological armour plating could easily be several feet thick.

"Cease fire." Alex waited to see the result of the push back, hoping it would discourage the creature from any further attempts to get at them if it thought it was going to be too much trouble or more pain than it was worth. However, several of the shorter, stronger tentacles reached into the mouth of the cave and began to pull the rocks away from the walls as it attempted to enlarge the cavity. They were far from safe. It was going to dig them out; it would peel open the cave like a tin of food to reach the tasty humans inside.

Again the HAWCs fired but the creature moved faster than anything that size should have been able to. Once again it withdrew its thick tentacles and turned its shell to block the cave. The HAWCs needed to keep firing into the same place on the giant beast to cause any real damage. The creature would soon re-emerge and resume tearing rock away from the mouth of the cave. At this rate within the hour they would be torn out like oysters from their shells.

Matt inched his way along the cave wall to Aimee. "Hunahpu must have had some weapon other than his spear and knife to drive these things off. Could it have been some form of natural toxin?"

Aimee shook her head. "Maybe, but probably not enough to worry something that big. I'm not sure what this thing would fear."

"Damn, he must have used something we haven't thought of. How could he have made it all this way and perhaps even escaped with just a gold knife and short spear? Think, think. His army is gone, his brother is dead, he'd be running, holding the torch . . . Hang on—of course. Fire. He had fire! Kinich Ahau wasn't just the god of the sun, he was the god of fire as well—why didn't I think of that before? He must have used the flaming torch to keep it away."

Matt darted forward, keeping a hand up over his face to shield himself from the flying debris. He crouched down behind Alex. "Fire. I think they must have used fire to drive the creature off."

Alex stopped shooting and thought for a few seconds. While Tank kept up rapid firing to try to slow the creature's demolition of their hiding place, Alex moved to the rear of the cave. From his backpack he removed his portable propane canister and broke open the back of his rifle.

"What's the plan?" Aimee had scurried over to Alex in the dark and put her hand on his forearm. He looked down at her. She looked tired and frightened and he wanted to give her a reassuring hug, but now was not the time.

"Whoever designed the gas projectile M98 never expected the adversary to be a giant squid, especially one that has its own armour plating. We might as well be throwing rocks at that thing."

"That thing looks like an orthocone." Aimee hugged herself as if from the cold even though it was over seventy-five degrees in the cave. "I knew this deep biosphere had been cut off for millions of years, but it must have been in isolation for more like hundreds of millions. That creature attacking us is an orthocone squid, the giant ancestor of all squid and octopus. It was the top of the food chain for millions of years, until it got knocked off by things like the megalodon shark. Down here it has been shielded from competition, from potential predators, from meteor impacts and any other mass extinction events in history and has been allowed to grow to an immense size."

Aimee looked at Alex and anger flashed in her eyes as she went on. "I know it wasn't Tom, but for a minute back there I thought it was. Tom, Dr. Silex and who knows how many others are now nothing more than some form of lower-order memory in the brain of a creature that shouldn't even exist."

Alex reached out and put his hand on her arm but remained silent. He let Aimee speak, knowing she had more to say.

"This is not just a little by-road on the evolutionary path; this is like a whole new world, as alien to us as another planet. We don't belong here, Alex."

"I'll get us home, don't worry." Alex was glad it was dark as he didn't want her to see his eyes in case he betrayed some self-doubt at the chances of their escaping. He filled the projectile compression chamber with the propane gas and quickly shut the casing.

"I'll need your help." He removed his lighter from his pocket and handed it to her. "All you need to do is hold that under the muzzle of the rifle so the flame is just floating in front of the barrel. I'll do the rest."

He was impressed; she didn't flinch when he asked her to move closer to the giant creature. They moved into position as close to the cave mouth as they dared. Though Tank had succeeded in shooting through and amputating several of the tips of some of the tentacles, the cave was now much wider than it was only minutes before. Alex nodded to Aimee who ignited the small lighter flame.

"Show time." Alex depressed the trigger.

The result exceeded his expectations and made him smile grimly. The compressed balls of air now had a high proportion of propane gas in their makeup and ignited when they passed through the naked flame. The range would have been severely restricted as the gas was causing the compressed ball of air to expand and the flame slowed the projectile, but still it was a spectacular result. A stream of flaming balls shot rapidly from the gun muzzle. Even slowed down, they moved faster than the eye could see to give the same effect as a thin-beam flamethrower. It looked like a burning laser that spread its gas innards on contact with the beast.

There was an explosion of activity at the cave mouth. The orthocone extracted its tentacles in a boiling mass of confused and seared flesh. As the final hooked club was being withdrawn, the image of Silex appeared, followed immediately by Tom Hendsen, then another man in a jacket with the word "Buck" across the chest, and finally the visage of a young woman holding a baby before it retreated back to the water leaving a stink of charred meat and ammonia.

There was silence in the cave before Tank yelled. "Wow, I gotta get me one of those."

Alex walked cautiously to the mouth of the cave. The sand was deeply furrowed and large chunks of pale, mottled-green flesh littered the area. He was soon joined by the rest of the group. Monica clamped her hand over her nose and mouth.

"I get thc feeling you don't think we've seen the last of our multi-armed friend." Matt was looking up and down the beach for signs of the giant predator.

"Aimee, could that thing grow its arms back?" Alex asked, without turning around.

"Yes, cephalopods have enormous regenerative powers. In a few months that thing will be as good as new. It'll be back, Alex. Squid and octopus are smart; it won't keep making the same mistakes."

Alcx turned to her. "Neither will we. In the military there's something we call conflict education. In battle you want one of two things: to win outright, or to survive with greater knowledge. Every encounter with a new foe is an opportunity to be better educated for next time. We actually learned a lot today: its body is soft and vulnerable, it feels pain and shies from heat, it has an armoured body that reduces its manoeuvrability. We don't have to kill it, Aimee; we only have to stay out in front of it."

"Adapt or die—sounds like survival of the fittest."

Alex nodded slowly, "That it is, Aimee, and speaking of adapting, you said that thing could regenerate in a few months—what about days? Do you remember in the upper caves we severed one of those long tentacles it's using to try to lure us closer to it? This thing had two fully functioning clubs. I've got to assume it's not the only one of its kind down here. One was a big enough problem; more than one and we might not be leaving."

Alex also didn't think that they had seen everything that made up the food chain, but kept that to himself as he needed everyone to stay positive about their chances of escape to the surface. Alex looked across at Tank and realised that the big soldier was still going strong with a 10,000-year-old knife sticking out of his neck.

"All right, big fella, time for some minor surgery on that neck. And no tears, OK?"

After Alex closed the last stitch in Tank's neck, he called them all together to repack and continue on to their destination cave. No one believed that they had seen the last of the giant beast and they remembered what Aimee said about it learning from its mistakes—next time they might not be so lucky.

The rest of the trek across the wide dark beach was slow and made in either rapid sprints between potential defendable positions, hunkering down to check for sudden movement from any direction, before sprinting off once again. It took them well over an hour to reach the mouth of the large cave that was set back from the shore line in what looked to be the widest part of the beach. The mouth was paved with a floor of crushed debris, giving it the look of a gravel driveway with pieces of quartz reflecting the blue glow from the ceiling far above them. Even though the cave was dark and its size meant that they could be followed by any number of large creatures, the slight breeze rushing past their faces filled them with hope.

Monica stood in the huge opening and inhaled deeply. The cave was enormous and made the giant Deer Cave in Borneo look like a mousehole. Most importantly, it tilted upwards at a fifteen-degree angle—not much, but at least it was heading in the right direction. The faint breeze blowing past meant no smells could be detected and small sounds hidden in the darkness were muffled or disguised in the updraught—however, the very movement of air meant that the warmth was being dragged towards a cooler air pocket. It was as good as they hoped to find.

The final piece of comforting evidence to indicate they

were heading in the right direction were more flaking glyphs carved into some broken stone at the edge of the cave. Thousands of years ago they had been carved into the wall, but had since crumbled to the cave floor. They paused for a break while Matt set to putting all the pieces together so they could hear the stone talk once again of the small warrior whose footsteps they were following.

"He's still being chased. It says *Qwotoan* still taunts him by showing him the spirits of his lost kin. OK, this looks like . . . the moving, or could be . . . shaking ground has opened a door to the sun land, that could mean Aztlan or the surface, and now *Qwotoan* will find them and devour them all. There's some more but I can't make it out. This was meant to be a warning." Matt sat back on his haunches and ran his hand over the ancient glyphs.

"Do you think he made it?" Monica had hunched down beside him and was looking at the broken stone as well.

"Not sure. Someone made it back to carve the story in the first cave. But it could have been anyone. We may never know whether he made it home or the creatures caught up with him; or even if they followed him all the way to the city. This area must've been undergoing shallow earth tremors around that time and one or more quakes opened the cave system that allowed the creatures to start to attack Aztlan and its people. Then, just as suddenly, another earth movement sealed them in or destroyed their city." Matt rocked his head from side to side. "Of course, Aztlan could still be on the surface, but buried beneath a mile of ice. I still think the 'sinking' could be a reference to the ancient city disappearing below the ice as opposed to beneath the sea. At this point it doesn't matter; at least we know we're headed in the right direction."

Aimee peeled back the dressing to check on Tank's wound—though she could tell he was trying to mask the

pain, he must have been in agony from the deep lacera-
tion. There was also an odd yellowish colour starting to
spread around the gash that worried her. After replacing
the dressing and dispensing some all-purpose antibiotics
she walked over to Alex.

"I've been doing some thinking. Did you see the last
lure the creature showed us in the cave—the girl with the
baby? Her clothes were old-fashioned . . . I mean really
old England or something."

Alex looked at her, knitted his brows and *hmmd* at her
to go on.

"These things copy what they've digested. Well, she
obviously wasn't one of the recent teams that came here. I
think they have been able to get out in the past, and I think
I know how." Aimee looked over her shoulder at Matt and
Monica and lowered her voice. "Those abyssal shrimp I
found can only live in the deepest ocean areas in the
world. The Antarctic Sandwich Trench is over 25 000 feet
deep and is just off the coast. Remember you asked if they
could have been washed in? I think you might be right. I
think there is, or was, an open vent, a deep ocean well-
spring that flushes water in from the trench." Aimee folded
her arms across her chest as though cold.

"You think there's another way out, under the water?"
Alex looked intently into her face.

"Maybe not anymore, maybe only sometimes, and not
for us. These giant cephalopods can take crushing depths
and freezing temperatures. Matt mentioned earth tremors.
I think when the Antarctic plates shift, a vent may be
opened allowing these things out, or back in. That girl was
probably taken a long way away, and a long time ago."

"Aimee, you said yourself they're cave dwellers now.
We've never encountered anything like these things."

"I think they always return here, but we might never
see them anyway if they stay in the deep sea trenches or

seek out other underwater cave systems." Aimee looked over her shoulder at Tank.

"Oh great. Well, let's hope the vent is closed or only wide enough for shrimp now." Alex wondered what the Hammer would make of all this.

"There's something else that's worrying me. That wound of Tank's."

"Deep?" asked Alex.

"Yes, but that's not what worries me. I think it's a type of infection, but nothing I've seen before. The chances are extremely high that there are microscopic life forms down here that we've never encountered. There's also the chance that the knife had some sort of toxin on it. The poisons shouldn't still be viable now, but whatever was on that knife stayed in there after we extracted the blade and it certainly isn't getting any better with the antibiotics we've got. At the rapid rate the wound seems to be degrading, I think he'll need professional medical care within twelve hours."

"Great. Keep a look out for ladders or black cats, will you? I don't think we need any more bad luck."

Tank knew Aimee and the boss were talking about his wound. It took all his great strength and a warrior's force of will to keep his focus away from the thumping ache that was spreading from his neck and down his side. It wouldn't be long until his arm was useless and then he would be a liability to the group when they needed to be moving quickly. He would not let that happen.

# Twenty-three

"Let's keep moving, everyone." Alex ordered.

No one needed to be told twice; everyone wanted to feel the sun on their face again and avoid becoming part of the local food chain. They shouldered backpacks and prepared to climb up into the large cave. Inside the cave the walls and floor seemed to have been ground smooth by something continually coming out or going in to this part of the cave system—not a good sign.

Aimee helped Tank get to his feet. His entire shoulder and arm were now numb and there were bluish, thread-like tendrils blooming up around his neck. Under his ar-moured cave suit his body was a mass of darkened lumps and veins as the ancient bacteria converted his body for its own use. Aimee had done all she could; she had loaded his giant frame with penicillin and changed the dressing on the wound. However, it was clear that whatever was in-vading his body was winning the battle.

Tank ground his teeth from the pain and cursed to him-self. The hair from his head and eyebrow on the wound side was falling out. This was not the way a HAWC should meet his end, brought down by something too small to even be seen by the naked eye. He masked the excruciat-ing pain from Alex—if the boss saw he was badly wounded, he would feel obligated to help at a time he needed all his energy focused on getting them out. He unwound Aimee's arm, thanked her and when she wasn't looking he brought his clenched fist down hard onto his thigh. The new pain brought a flood of adrenaline and some clarity. Just a little more time, just a little more.

Alex could smell it now; the creature had been in here. This cave was not going to be a sanctuary and he only hoped that the beast was behind them. He didn't relish the idea of having a giant carnivorous creature between him and their potential escape route. He looked back towards Aimee and Tank.

Alex's unique senses detected a pressure change. There was danger approaching in the near dark, and this was not the place to be caught out. He quickly scanned left and right. Out of the mouth of the cave in the distance he could make out an enormous V-shaped wave pointed directly at them and closing fast across the sea. Something very big was coming at them at about eight knots under the water.

"Time to move, people. Now!"

There was a booming crash as something hit the shallow water like an aircraft carrier running aground. Everyone jumped and, as if on cue, the lights went out again. This time the noise continued as something gigantic was heaving itself up and out of the water with a sound like a hundred waterfalls. There were no guesses as to what its goal was or who it was after, and the continuing noise meant the lights were not going to come on any time soon.

Alex no longer had his night vision scope equipment and he no longer needed it. He turned to the source of the noise as images started to appear. He remembered the discussions and endless reports from the medical teams when his eyesight started to change. He knew normal human beings had a poor ability for night vision in near total darkness. In some animals, like dogs and cats, biological night vision is ten times more sensitive than in humans, and other animals can perceive heat and cold changes in thermal density. They could build up an image that is not quite seeing at all. The scientists had called it "sensing."

The changes to Alex's brain were again delivering to the limit of human physical capacity for light and heat vision sensitivity, and the images that were displayed to his brain were alarming indeed. A cold mountain was heaving itself from the warmer water and dragging itself up the beach with a scrunching squeal of crushed sand. It had just under a mile of open ground to reach them, but it confirmed to Alex why there was little large debris around and inside the mouth of the cave—this creature had been up and in here before, and this time the cave was large enough for it to follow them.

Torches flicked on in the cave and though Alex would have preferred the darkness, the team needed the light for comfort. With Alex leading the way, they all moved quickly back and along the side of the cave—all except Tank.

Alex turned to Aimee and yelled over the crushing of stone, "Keep 'em going."

He took a few steps down towards Tank. "Move it soldier." When there was no reply, Alex started to bound across the rocks just as Tank pinged him on his mike.

"I'm staying, sir. I can't keep up and I'm too big even for you to carry for long. I can at least give you some more lead time—but you've gotta go now. Please don't make me disobey an order." There was a pause as Alex thought about how to respond before Tank pinged him again. "It's been an honour serving with you." The comm unit pinged one last time signalling the conversation had been terminated. In the distance, Alex saw Tank pull the device off his head and fling it away into the dark.

Alex could see the creature drawing closer. Trying to drag the giant soldier out against his will would be difficult, especially when he knew that what Tank had chosen to do was exactly what he would have decided to do in his position. Alex gave a half smile and spoke softly to the HAWC's back.

"Good luck, soldier. It's been my honour to have a man like you on my team." He drew in a deep breath and shouted with all his strength, "Go HAWC!" It was his unit's battle cry; and with that Alex turned and sprinted to catch up with the remaining team members.

Tank didn't feel fear; Alex's shout still reverberated around the cave and once again he felt strong. He had injected several CCs of pure adrenaline into his leg from his backpack med-kit and his body was drawing on its final energy reserves in anticipation of the coming combat. He alone had a night vision scope and, like Alex, could see the approaching leviathan and knew what that meant to the group. His whole upper body under his suit was strangely lumpy and his skin crawled to the touch. The side of his face near the wound was slack as the muscles had atrophied under the foreign bacterial attack. His strength had been leaving him and he knew it was only a matter of time before he needed to either lie down or be carried—neither was an option as far as he was concerned. He didn't have a chance of winning this fight, but if he could give Alex a few more minutes' head start, then he would have done his job.

He took his position against the side of the cave and filled his rifle with some of the liquefied propane. In one hand he held his lighter close to the end of the barrel and the other rested lightly on the trigger. Without taking his eyes from the advancing creature he whispered to himself,

"See you soon, little brother." He took careful aim at the large sticky eye now filling the cave mouth and simultaneously lit his flame and pulled the trigger.

The small team had stopped and were waiting for both HAWCs when Alex appeared out of the dark. "Let's go."

"Where's Tank?" Monica was looking over Alex's shoulder as she asked the question.

"He's giving us a chance, Ms. Jennings. Let's make it worthwhile." Alex went to turn away but she stopped him.

"Will he be able to catch up to us? He was hurt."

Alex just stared at her. It was Matt who spoke first. "Ah, shit. Tank, too? Shit, shit, shit." Matt rubbed the back of his neck and walked away into the darkness shaking his head.

Monica was about to speak again when Alex cut her off.

"He knows what he's doing, he's—"

There was an explosive *whump* that made Monica cringe, followed by darkness and silence. Aimee looked at Alex, then dropped her eyes.

Alex turned back down the cave, his face a mask of stone. He knew that the small war Tank had been waging had been decided; he could already sense the outcome. "Let's go."

Matt walked close to Monica, whispering to her continuously. After many minutes he was rewarded with a smile, then a small laugh. It was many more minutes before they noticed the difference in the cave. It was almost sterile compared to the scuttling and crawling abundance of life they had seen in the outer subterranean world. The dripping mosses and glistening lichen ferns had disappeared. Not only was the cave devoid of life but it was unexpectedly dry and smooth.

"No moisture; that could be a good sign—means we're

headed for a drier atmosphere and hopefully the surface."
Monica was determined to remain optimistic.

"Excellent, now if we can just keep up this sprint pace
for the next eight hours or so, in the dark, and stay ahead
of the monster chasing us, we'll be just fine." Matt kept a
good-humoured lilt to his voice in between his ragged
breaths. But he, like the others, knew that at any moment
they could reach another choke or find that the end of the
tunnel had long since been iced over.

Alex was also formulating alternatives in the event they
got to an impassable blockage. His major concern at present was the lack of cover afforded by the worn, smooth
cave. If they were run down by the giant creature now, he
didn't like their chances of surviving in a stand-up fight
when their only firepower was what he carried and a couple of grenades.

The grinding, pulverising noise was continuing from
the way they had come, which meant they were still being
pursued. Up ahead there was a slight narrowing of the cave
and Aimee turned to Alex. "It's bottlenecking, it can't pursue us if the cave gets any narrower."

Alex didn't get it. How could the creature have first attacked them in much smaller caves, or for that matter, have
made it all the way to the surface to attack Aztlan when it
was of such an enormous size. There was no way it could
get that hard shell into smaller caves. "Ms. Jennings, please
scout ahead and everyone continue with the pace as is.
I'm just going back to check on our friend and perhaps see
if I can slow him down a bit."

"I'll come with you." Alex could see a look of alarm
on Aimee's face.

"Not this time. I can move at twice the speed of all of
you, and I can rejoin you very quickly, but only by myself."
He moved nearer to Aimee, removed his cracked and
dented helmet and wiped sweat from his forehead before

whispering to her, "I'll be OK; they'll need you to lead them." Alex pulled his comm unit and headset from the helmet and stuffed it into a pocket. He dropped the helmet to the ground and disappeared into the dark like a wraith.

In the darkness Alex moved swiftly and lightly; he could hear and see almost everything around him, and what he couldn't see, he could sense. The grinding was continuing and he needed to see how the creature was going to force its way through the first narrowing it was about to encounter. He also wanted to place one of his last grenades in its path and perhaps encourage it to change its mind and stop following them.

Alex blended back into a tiny alcove in the wall of the cave and watched the leviathan approach. He was astounded at how it laboriously pulled itself forward, dragging its giant shell behind it. It was colder than its surroundings and gave off a slight green glow. Its two tentacle clubs waved out in front of it like insect feelers probing the way ahead and maybe even tasting the air for chemical traces of the small humans it hoped to devour.

At the first junction, Alex could see that it was going to have trouble forcing its gigantic form into the slightly smaller cave. Though the cave itself was still large enough to drive a couple of eighteen-wheel rigs through, it was going to be an impossible squeeze for the giant cephalopod.

The two waving tentacle clubs were feeling the junction and assessing its size. The creature halted and seemed to be ruminating over its next step. Good, thought Alex, it's too small, isn't it? If it tried to drag its way into the smaller cave it may at the least slow down its progress so much that they could leave the creature long behind them.

Then there came a liquid sucking sound from the creature and Alex watched in dismay as the giant slowly pulled itself free from its shell. Mucous flooded down around it and Alex could smell sea salt, decayed meat and dozens of other unidentifiable odours that emanated from the beast's soft body. Just like a hermit crab it could obviously move in and out of the shell at will—that explained how it was able to pursue them into smaller caves.

Now free from its shell, the creature gathered its smaller tentacles underneath it and lifted its mottled, bulbous frame upwards. It now looked more like a giant pulsating spider than a sea creature; freed from its shell it was much more agile and moved rapidly forward. Its speed had more than doubled and with its boneless body it could no doubt squeeze into very small crevices and would be able to send its attacking clubs forward to scoop his team out of the forward caves.

OK, at least it will be without its armour plating and should be more vulnerable. Alex planted his timed grenade pack on the cave floor and set it for just three minutes, then turned and sped into the dark after his small team. He doubted the grenade would do much more than cause the creature to hesitate for a minute—he needed more explosives to do any real damage to something that size, but decided to preserve his other charges for more strategic attacks or any demolition work that may be required.

A thousand feet farther into the cave Alex stopped and turned. The muffled explosion told him that his charge had gone off at the right time, perhaps even right underneath the creature and he hoped it would give them a few more minutes' lead. Their pace was going to have to double now if they wanted to escape their pursuer, and Alex needed to devise some further ways of slowing or stopping the creature. He had the feeling that they would tire long before it did.

\* \* \*

The creature could sense the movement of the tiny warm bloods far ahead, and also the presence of one of them close by. It could not yet see or hear the small creature, but knew it was near. As the giant pushed quickly forward, now free of its shell, the anticipation of the kill and of the feeding made it reckless; the detonation caught it right over the top of the grenade. The small but powerful explosion blew a ten-foot, thousand-pound chunk of flesh from the end of one of its muscular tentacles. It curled the tentacle stump and folded it close to its body. It registered pain but also knew that the wound was not lethal and it would regenerate quickly. It continued its advance but was more watchful for the small creature that waited by itself. This one was dangerous and needed to be taken first and quickly.

# Twenty-four

Aimee's legs were burning and fatigue was turning to nausea inside her. Matt and Monica were probably fitter than her but she could see their shoulders slumping and they hadn't spoken for a while. Aimee knew physical fatigue wasn't the only danger; it was the emotional exhaustion that set in after the adrenaline washed out of the muscles and brain.

"Let's go, guys. I want to be lying on a beach somewhere by the weekend." She sucked in a breath and smiled broadly at Matt as she overtook them on the slope.

"Go, Wonder Woman. Can you carry me?" Matt chuckled as he said it, but both he and Monica increased their pace to keep up with her.

Alex quickly caught up to the team; they had made good progress. The slope was increasing steadily and though this gave them all reason to feel they were heading in the right direction, it was proving much more exhausting than before.

Alex knew their bodies were tiring but with the creature in pursuit they couldn't afford to rest for a moment. The cave was narrowing even more but was still easily big enough to accommodate fifty men walking shoulder to shoulder and the roof was nearly out of sight in the darkness. The cold blackness of the cave meant they had relied solely on their torches and helmet globes, and now these too were wearying and yellowing into the gloom.

For several more hours they climbed, before exhaustion demanded a break. Alex turned and listened intently. Far behind them he could just make out the sound of pursuit. His electronic movement sensors were useless in a twisting cave as the density and compression waves became distorted and muffled by the airflow and cave bends. He had to rely on his extraordinary senses alone and this was still proving difficult as the creature without its shell was almost silent and now much more cautious. Alex was also beginning to think that the thing chasing them was not just some oversized prehistoric brute but had an intelligence that enabled it to learn, plan and perhaps even try and trap them.

Monica pointed out the jumble of debris on the cave floor. It was the first sign that there had been geological movement in and around the cavern for many millennia.

"Please Lord, deliver us from dead ends." Matt was trying to inject a little levity into their situation, but he could not have crafted better words to reflect how they all felt. The thought of having to backtrack gave them all a feeling of dread. Though they had not seen or heard from the creature for some time, they could pick up the vibes from Alex, and the way he kept stopping to stare into the darkness behind them let them know that they were far from safe.

The shards of fallen rock were growing in size, with some now the size of houses. It made the trip slower as they constantly had to zigzag in and around the debris. The slope had reached an angle of about twenty-five degrees and their thigh muscles were screaming for a break. Alex quietly but firmly urged them on; he could not let them stop until they found a spot that was concealed or at least defendable.

They were slowing and Alex decided he had to set another ambush for the creature. He needed to give them some more time. Just as he was about to disappear into the dark he heard Monica call. She had found a rift in the cave—a huge, jagged tear in the black wall with a hint of an earthen smell coming from within on the slight breeze.

Aimee used the deep earth sonar as Alex had taught her and came up with a reading of half a mile before it encountered a bend or obstruction. There was still a good deal of airflow originating from the narrow cleft so the odds were it wasn't a dead end.

"Looks fairly new, maybe even under twenty thousand years—that's just a few seconds on the geo-clock. This place must still be active to a degree and I can't be sure it will be safe for us." Monica was giving her professional speleological view of the dangers involved but they were not in any normal caving scenario.

Without a second thought, Alex just shouted one word. "In!"

Monica then Matt followed by Aimee entered the ten-foot-wide rift. Alex hung back for a few extra seconds and surveyed the entrance—it looked far too narrow for the creature to fold itself into, but without its shell or any discernible skeletal mass he couldn't be sure exactly what it was capable of. Nevertheless, he guessed it would send one or more of its tentacle clubs into the crack to try to hook them out using the vicious talons embedded in their tips.

They were no more than a hundred paces into the rift when Alex became aware of a cessation of air movement. Without alerting the team and without slowing them, he stopped and stared intently into the dark, using all his senses to try to determine the cause of the change in air density. Though he could not see outside the rift, he could sense that a large presence had blocked the entrance they had just come through. The orthocone was trying to squeeze its enormous bulk into the small crack in the cave wall. There was a groaning and some debris rained down on the group. Monica paused and held up her hand to stop, fearing that it was their footsteps that were setting off some sort of small earth tremor, but Alex overrode the instruction and urged them on. He alone knew that the creature was trying to widen the fissure in the wall.

The liquid stealth with which the creature had pursued them so far was abandoned and replaced with a ground-shaking crashing like the charge of a hundred elephants. Matt and Monica looked at each other, then back to Alex, momentarily blinding him as they directed their torches into his face. Alex turned and closed his eyes for a second to get some night vision back, but when he opened them it became clear to him exactly what strategy the creature was going to use. A gigantic tentacle was moving quickly down the tunnel; as it came forward it knocked car-sized boulders out of the way like a child would do with its toy building blocks.

This was not the place for engaging the creature. Their armoured caving suits would either be snagged by the razor-sharp hooks on the tentacles or they would be crushed as the creature knocked a boulder on top of them. Alex fired a stream of compressed gas projectiles into the club tip, but he knew that this would only slow the advance.

"Ms. Jennings, find us some cover, double time. Everyone else follow her—now!" Alex was running and turning to fire every few seconds. He was aware they only had a few minutes before they were run down or crushed when he heard Monica call from just ahead.

"Careful under here . . . it's a floating choke."

Alex could see what she was referring to. The rift they were moving through was only about twenty feet wide, but suspended over a narrowing area was a table-shaped slab of stone of immense proportions that held tons of debris above it. Aimee had dropped back to Alex and looked at him with her determined, grime-streaked face.

"Are you thinking what I am?"

"Oh yeah, time to shut the door."

They all passed under the choke and Alex yelled for them to keep moving as fast as they could and to stay close to the walls to avoid any falling debris. He turned and calibrated his rifle to deliver fist-sized compressed air punches to the weakest point in the choke and depressed the trigger. A constant stream of air projectiles was focused on where the choke met the wall. The high-velocity compressed air hit the rock face with the power of a pneumatic sledgehammer. In just under three seconds, Alex managed to do what the rocks had tried to do in their original rush to the cave floor tens of thousands of years before; they came boiling down with a thunderous crash. He threw his rifle over his shoulder into the backpack strapping and leaped forwards, bouncing nimbly over and through the falling stones. Tons of rock and debris collapsed around him. The impact, when it came, was like being hit by a car. The centre of his back was punched by a rock the size of a bowling ball travelling at about forty miles per hour. The breaking sound from his back was lost in the crash of the rock slide, but Alex was knocked to the ground.

He lay on the cave floor waiting for the dust to clear. His senses told him there was no more airflow and that most of the debris had fallen, totally blocking the narrow cave. He doubted whether the creature could bring enough power to bear with just a single tentacle to force a path through. They were safe for the moment.

Alex sucked in a deep breath and spat out some dust. He slowly got to his feet and flexed his upper body; he hurt and something crunched at his back. He pulled off his pack and pulled his rifle free. The once sleek M98 was a crumpled mess. It had been made from thermopressed polycarbonate—stronger than steel but as light as plastic. The impact had shattered the casing. Better you than me, he thought, and dropped the crushed gun at his feet.

Aimee was waiting just behind a large boulder with her canteen for him to take a much needed swallow.

"Well, looks like we can rule out doubling back from now on. Let's take ten minutes." They all fell to the floor. Now that the adrenaline was subsiding in their systems, exhaustion was taking over. Muscles screamed, feet throbbed and backs ached. Alex lay down flat and closed his eyes. He gave them ten minutes, so he would sleep for exactly eight before rousing them to continue the next stage of their journey back to the light.

"It's a door." Matt was dwarfed by the structure.

No one else spoke for several seconds as they looked in awe at the seamless transition from natural rock creation to man-made structure. The rift walls suddenly smoothed, and then were blocked by a twenty-foot-high stone door. The panels were intricately carved with images of kneeling human figures and glyphs similar to those they had seen earlier. The massive structure stood out from its surroundings, not only due to its size, but also because of a reddish sheen that made the doors glow even after all the thousands of years. Monica ran her hands over the stone, spat on a small spot and rubbed it in.

"This is red Aswan granite, one of the hardest granites on earth and definitely not from around here."

Matt shone his yellowing torch onto the spot Monica had just cleared. "You're right, it's not even from this side of the world. This rock only occurs in the Middle East; there was a sarcophagus inside the Great Pyramid of

Giza made from this type of stone and when it was discovered they said it shone like fire. To this day no one knows how the Egyptians managed to work it."

"How would it have got down here?" Aimee was running her hands over the stone as well.

"This was an advanced civilisation. I bet these guys visited all corners of the globe. I'll tell you one thing, this door was made to keep something in or out." Matt was shining his torch into a crack where the door didn't fit flush with the wall. "Hang on, I think it's open."

"OK, everyone push." Alex put both hands against the door and tensed his muscles in anticipation of the force that he expected was needed to move the stone monolith; however, the door swung open easily and in silence. After over 10,000 years the mechanism was still working smoothly. "They sure don't build them like this anymore."

"Not for thousands of years anymore." Matt was first through the door, quickly followed by Monica.

Beyond the doorway they found themselves in a large, domed room more than 150 feet in diameter. Blackened stone urns around the perimeter once probably held oil that when lit delivered light to the magnificent carved walls, some still bearing colouration that hinted at great architectural detail and ornate artwork. A smooth ramp led up to a higher doorway that also had a red granite stone door but this one had been smashed to pieces.

"It looks like a church." Monica stood just inside the door and hugged herself.

"Maybe, at least a place of worship, for sure," Matt responded, moving quickly in the dark, his torch beam darting from ceiling to wall and back again.

At the base of the ramp it looked like the building of a new wall had begun. The materials used were not the finely honed blocks from other parts of the room and looked more rough-hewn, with each piece about five feet cubed and weighing many tons. This newer wall was not for decoration; it looked hurriedly built and was more fortified than its predecessor.

There were also three stone pillars, each about eight feet in height that stood facing the door they had just passed through; heavily corroded metal rings hung from their front.

"This is a wonder of architecture. You know, everyone wondered where the Romans got the skill to build a giant domed building that defied analysis for centuries. But this . . . this is even bigger." Matt was twirling slowly in the centre of the room, trying to take it all in.

"It looks like some sort of arena." Aimee was scanning their surroundings and moved to the centre pillar for a better look. Around their bases the stones were darker, stained even after all the passing millennia.

Matt was moving busily around the walls, running his hands over the glyphs and moving his lips silently as he tried to draw out their meaning. "An arena? No, but close, more like an altar—and a sacrificial one at that. Most cultures had myths and stories about creatures from their own version of hell, and the Aztlan legends don't appear to be any different. They look like they had a rich mythology, filled with demons and gods of the netherworld. The only difference was, their monsters turned out to be real. They were offering up their slaves to *Qwotoan* to appease him. I'd say they came across each other when they were excavating their basements and regarded him as the ruler of the underworld—their very own devil made flesh."

Matt read from the wall. "OK, here we go 'Those who join with *Qwotoan* shall live with him forever and shall return as his servants.' I think we've seen what this refers to through the ability the creature has to mimic things it has devoured." Matt moved a bit further around the walls. "To keep him in check they tried to appease him with monthly offerings, but he became ever more demanding. That's the problem with some gods; they're never satisfied with just one virgin, are they?"

"Not funny, Matt, it's horrible." Monica hugged herself at the thought of being tied to one of the stone columns while giant tentacles came through the open doorway.

Matt reached out to touch her arm. "To us, yes. But to the Aztlan culture who saw the world as being upside down and this creature as being a god, definitely not. Heaven was below ground in an underworld of caves, guarded by fantastic beasts and gods. The caves themselves were very holy and would have been considered to be a portal of communication with their deities. I guess to them it was proof of their beliefs when they encountered this fantastic creature reaching up from the depths. It would have been a great honour to be chosen to 'join' with him. For all we know they may have volunteered."

"They didn't realise that they were creating a feeding pattern. To the orthocones they were just an easy and abundant food source." Aimee was examining the stains on the pillars.

Monica, Alex and Aimee sat down with their backs against one of the walls and followed Matt with their torch beams to give him extra light. They drank sparingly of the little remaining water, and finished the last dusty crumbs of their dark chocolate. Nothing had ever tasted so good.

"Look!" Matt pointed to some rings embedded up on the walls and a similar one high up on the giant stone door they had recently come through. "I bet they had some form of system rigged up so they could open and shut this door from up there, probably from behind the other broken door. They lashed their sacrificial victims to the pillars and then retreated behind their own door so they could open the gateway to the underworld in safety."

Monica brought her torch beam back down to the

crude half-built wall at the base of the ramp. "They were going to seal it off but never finished. Hmm, wonder why?" Monica posed the question and then answered it herself. "Oh, shit. It must have found another way in."

Alex pushed his hands up through his hair and expelled a long breath between his teeth. The implications of this were horrifying—they could be ambushed and now there was no going back. Best not to have them dwelling too much on it. "Perhaps. But even if that were true it was a long time ago. We're not home just yet, but we'll make it now."

"I agree with Alex. There haven't been people here for thousands and thousands of years. This would have disrupted the normal feeding patterns of the creatures and I doubt they could remember how to get into the city after all those centuries." Aimee was doing her best to support Alex and offer some good news to the exhausted group.

"But you said it yourself. We don't know how long these things live. What if it's the same creature or what if they have the ability to pass on their memories like, like . . ." Monica was trying to remember some Discovery Channel nature program she had seen in another life, when Aimee assisted.

"Flatworms."

"That's them. Could it remember, Aimee?"

"We just don't know. We don't know how long today's giant cephalopods live, let alone a creature that should have been extinct four hundred million years ago and may have caused the collapse of the first great human civilisation. However, I doubt very much it could live for tens of thousands of years. But the problem we have down here is that this is a very different world to ours with unique environmental effects resulting in very different natural laws. Could it find a way in? Sure, given enough time; it's certainly smart enough. Could it remember a way in? I just don't know, but there are studies now on cellular in-herited memory where transplant patients are recollect-ing tastes, smells and even images from the donor. I've read papers on memory inheritance that . . ." Aimee stopped talking. She had forgotten herself; the look on Monica's face told her the information wasn't helping.

Alex noticed that Aimee had omitted to share her theo-ries with Monica about the image of the girl and baby in the old-fashioned clothing. He got to his feet and walked back towards the giant stone doors. He removed his glove and placed his hand flat on the polished red stone. He felt for vibrations and more; he felt for the leviathan's presence—there was nothing. Aimee approached softly behind him and spoke quietly when she was close.

"Sorry, I don't think I was making things better back there."

"Don't worry about it; we're all exhausted. But I'll tell you one thing. I have no intention of donating my organs to this thing."

"Ha, is that what they call battlefield humour, Captain Hunter?" After all they had been through Aimee still man-aged to laugh gently at their predicament. Alex couldn't help resting his eyes on her beautiful upturned face, now dusty and streaked by the tracks of perspiration and tears. She made him feel at ease and comfortable; he liked that.

"So, Dr. Aimee Weir, how does a sensible, modern woman like you end up a paleobiologist working for the government?"

Aimee rested her back against the red granite and tilted her head up towards the dark domed ceiling. "Well, my father always said people with brains will rise to the top—boy, I'm glad he can't see me now, miles below the sur-face of the world. Fact is, I'm a science nerd. While all my friends were going to the beach to lie on the sand and im-prove their tans or rub lotion on their boyfriends' backs, I was over in the rock pools turning over stones to look at the tiny creatures. My grades were always good and after sailing through chemistry and biology, I got hooked on solving the world's energy problems by creating a biological synthetic fuel. Except I didn't know I was working for the U.S. Army until a week ago. Not sure it would have mattered; sure doesn't now. Now it seems such a small issue, as if it belongs to someone else while we're all hiding down here in the dark."

She smiled at Alex and moved a little closer. He noticed the set of her jaw was still strong. She's a brave woman, he thought. A strand of her hair had fallen out from under her helmet and hung across one of her blue eyes. He wanted to reach out and push it back behind her ear but stopped himself. His eyes saddened as he thought, she can never know me.

"We better start climbing again, we're nearly home." Alex walked away.

They climbed the ramp to the upper doorway, the silence broken only by their soft footfalls. Dust gently floated in the beam of their lights, making the rays stand out like wide lasers in the pitch darkness.

Aimee shivered—it was much colder here. "Look." She exhaled and her breath created a small fog in the light beam. "We must be closer to the surface now."

Alex pulled his stratigraphic sonar from his backpack and pointed it at the roof. After a few seconds the small screen lit up with the readings he was seeking. "Still says we're about a mile down, but I can't tell how deep we are in the catacombs, how much is rock or how much of that is ice."

Matt turned back to the group after reading the carved glyphs in the wall. "Could be a problem—the Aztlans seem to be similar to the Olmecs or Aztecs, who made extensive use of caves. Some of their artifacts and burials have been located many miles deep inside cave systems. My guess is they had been exploring and excavating the underground cave system for hundreds of years. They were obviously adept at stone cutting, so could easily have dug down many levels, perhaps miles. They could also have found the cave system and simply modified it for their use, which means this could be very deep indeed."

Aimee picked up the conversation. "Either an earth tremor opened the caves to the lake below, or they simply broke through on one of their daily digs. We know the creatures below are hunt-adapted for either full darkness and near dark environments, so vibrations from the digging would have been very attractive to them. They would have broken through and come face to face with one of their gods."

"Man, I'd pay a dollar to see the look on the face of that first guy." Matt laughed at his own joke and Monica couldn't help giggling as well; she elbowed him good-naturedly in the ribs.

From the doorway behind them came the sound of small rocks falling. The group froze and for a few seconds stood like statues, all focused on the large entrance they had only just come through.

"Probably just some of the debris settling," Monica said.

"I'm sure that's what it was. Let's go." Alex didn't believe their pursuer would give up. Though the man-made tunnels would give them better protection, he couldn't help thinking that it hadn't saved the Aztlans.

# Twenty-five

Having pulled back from the rock fall, the creature surged forward to test the boulders that barred its path. It pushed some out of the way, but encountered far too many for it to get much more access and the confined area didn't allow it to bring its enormous strength to bear. It laid its long clubs against the solid walls and grew still—it could sense the small vibrations of movement coming back from the warm bloods—they were still close by. It withdrew its tentacles and unfolded itself out of the rift crevice, back into the larger cave. Long-past images flashed into its brain. It knew there were other entrances it could use.

The bleeding from its ragged stump had slowed now to little more than a trickle and in a few hours it would be sealed over and the regeneration would commence. However, the bleeding had created a river of blood, not debilitating for a creature of its size but enough to create an irresistible blood scent trail that attracted all manner of carnivores from the lake cavern now far behind it. As the creature pursued the humans, it unknowingly drew behind it a silent, pulsating wave of teeth and claws.

"It doesn't look like it's been destroyed, more like it was just abandoned." Monica's observation seemed accurate as there was little sign of devastation or that the Aztlans had been pursued through the tunnels by a giant cephalopod. The corridor opened into a larger chamber perhaps 200 feet long with a high carved ceiling. Around the walls the glyphs were interspaced with carvings of pictorial scenes sculpted in splendid detail. The raised stone tableaus showed a level of craftsmanship that would have challenged some of the greatest artisans of today. Beautiful scenes of what the countryside must have been like, displaying heavily wooded forests or fields of low plants like grass. Many were of hunting parties capturing all manner of strange beasts of enormous proportions.

"Aimee, do you recognise these animals?" Matt was touching his hand to some magnificently carved images of great land creatures.

"Wow, they're perfect. *Diprotodon, dromornis, thylacinus*. This is a window to our past." Aimee pointed as she marvelled at the closest thing modern humans would ever get to a living representation of the long-extinct megafauna beasts.

"Say what? Dipdo who?" Monica smiled at their enthusiasm and encyclopaedic knowledge of the obscure as Aimee scrutinised another scene of a giant land-based lizard caught by the Aztlans in a sophisticated noose trap.

"And this reptile could be a *megalania*. These are all perfect images of extinct reptile and mammalian creatures—giant animals that died out tens of thousands of years ago. This one here, the *diprotodon* was the big brother of today's cute and cuddly wombat, but it stood as tall as a grizzly bear with claws to match. This here, the *dromornis*, was a thunderbird. Ten feet tall and over a thousand pounds, they were fearsome predators and voracious meat eaters."

Aimee stepped in closer to look at more of the fantastic images when Matt spoke. "It's not uncommon that we should find these. Many early civilisations depicted hunting in their religious and artistic carvings. It's the closest thing we archaeologists have to snapshots of the flora and fauna of the times."

"And what's this one?" Monica was pointing at a creature that looked to have a strong, four-legged body but instead of jaws it had a curving beak and two strong wings folded across its back.

Matt looked at it, looked at Aimee, who shrugged, and then shook his head. "A griffin? Nah, impossible. They obviously included some mythological creatures as well."

Matt looked again at the strange winged creature. The detail was perfect, right down to the tiger-like striping across its muscled back. He shook his head and moved on to the start of a series of more detailed and royal-looking glyphs. "OK, here we are; it's the story of Aztlan. Looks like it's set out in chronological order—now where does it start?" Matt's lips moved silently as he drew out the meanings from the stone story before him.

"Ah, and here is where we begin." Monica and Aimee followed Matt around the chamber's perimeter as he told the story of a civilisation now long dead for many millennia.

Meanwhile, Alex scanned the room, looking at the entrances, the debris size, and shape, and the ceilings above. He strained all his superhuman senses for any sound or sense of movement or life other than their own. For now they had time to look at the life and death of perhaps the first great civilisation the world had ever known. Maybe it could tell them how to fight the creature or, better yet, escape it.

"Bear with me as this'll be a subjective translation. I'll be filling in the gaps myself with what I think fits or looks right." Matt turned and shrugged, then went back to the glyphs. "The Aztlans believed they were raised by the gods from the very soil itself. The gods lifted, or maybe that's crafted them, from earth and stone and gave them the world as a gift. This symbol means they went forth over the waves and knew of many other lands. These lands were mainly populated by the 'hairy men' or 'hairy people.' This is incredible. This history could be around fifteen thousand years old—at that time some continents had creatures like saber-toothed tigers and mammoths roaming their plains. Most of the indigenous natives would have been little more than hunter-gatherers. To them, this advanced race must have been awe inspiring." Matt continued reading from the wall, pointing at one symbol, giving its meaning and then moving on to the next.

"Aztlan was a land of sunshine and abundance. The people were healthy, crops were plentiful and the gods cherished them. They believed of all the world's people they were the favourites of the gods. This looks interesting; this symbol could mean an earthquake. One day the earth started to shake and many of their buildings fell down. They were all thrown to the ground. They believed they had angered the mightiest god in Xibalba, the underworld, and he was coming to punish them himself. I bet this was when their digging broke through to the subterranean sea. Before then, it had probably been undisturbed for hundreds of millions of years."

Matt pointed to an image of small figures kneeling before a giant, tentacled creature. "Introducing *Qwotoan* himself," Matt read on. "The following pictures show more and more Aztlans kneeling before *Qwotoan*. Looks like they were upping the sacrifice ante each month, but all it was doing was feeding an ever-growing appetite."

"Feeding dependency, they created safari park lions. The creatures made humans their natural food source," Aimee said.

Matt nodded and continued, "*Qwotoan* was also coming up into the city and taking the people without waiting for the sacrifice ceremony."

"How? How was the creature getting into the city?" Alex stepped forward eagerly.

"Doesn't say, I'm afraid. He was haunting them with visions of their lost ones—this must be the mimicking we've seen before. The people were terrified, and with all the sacrifices they were making, I think they actually started to thin out their population." Matt was pointing at one of the images depicting hundreds of tiny figures kneeling before the waving tentacles.

"The people decided they had had enough and forced the king to act. The king assembled his army and put his two most trusted warriors in charge—this is the bit we know. It tells again of the brothers Hunahpu and Xbalanque who are sent into the underworld to, it looks like, negotiate with *Qwotoan*, with—and here's those number glyphs again—about two thousand warriors. Hard to tell whether their job was to fight or be sacrificed. Either way, the king hoped to attain some sort of peace for Aztlan."

Matt moved along the wall again. "Ah. Damn it, and here is our brave Hunahpu's reward." Matt's training had taught him to be dispassionate about events that occurred long in the past—they could not be changed, only learned from. Many cultures had very different concepts of mercy and sometimes an execution was actually an honour. However, he couldn't help feeling sad for the brave little warrior whose footsteps they had followed, who had survived one of the most dangerous and fantastic journeys in the history of his or any race, and who had unwittingly even guided them up from the depths.

"After Hunahpu had led the royal troops into the underworld, after he had lost his brother, after he had found and fought the great beast and managed to return alive, he was executed by the king for failing in his divine duty." Matt shone his torch on the pictoglyph. It showed a warrior figure being torn apart by several oxen-like creatures.

Matt seemed to be in a trance and his eyes watered, not just from the dust they had been kicking up. To bring him back Monica pointed at the next picture along.

"Even I can read this one. They're using fire to drive the creature off."

"Looks like it. They used fire, or Kinich Ahau's gift as they refer to it. I think they had their fires burning in the mouths of the caves for decades. It never drove it off, only slowed it down—the creature was always finding new ways to get to its food supply." Matt moved to the next pictoglyph and started to read, "Their winters were growing longer and colder, and because of the change in seasons there was less food. They believed that *Qwotoan* had cursed them and all their land. This could be the onset of the glaciation epoch when Antarctica was becoming frozen again. The timing tallies with our geological and meteorological evidence that puts it at about twelve thousand years ago."

Matt moved along again. "The new king commanded they build a giant fleet of boats and collect as many of their animals and seed crops as they could. He and his generals would command an expedition to sail in different directions and find a new Aztlan; he would take his bravest warriors, the alchemists, the priests and the healers. Looks like all the elite and intelligentsia had been chosen to get the hell out; the rest were to remain behind and wait for the boats to return so they could be transported when a new home was discovered."

The last pictoglyph was incomplete and Matt could tell the drawings and writing was of a slightly different style. Perhaps the previous artisans had departed in the boats. Matt read the last words from Aztlan, "The cold is always with us. There is no food and no wood for our fires." The last piece was more a lament of resignation and similar to the one they had seen in the upper caves at the beginning of their journey. "*Qwotoan* is angered and is always among us."

"Those poor people." Monica was shaking her head as if to blot out the image of the remaining Aztlans trapped in a city that was becoming iced over, with a giant hungry creature waiting for the fires to go out so it could rip them to pieces in the dark.

Aimee also couldn't help feeling pity for the small race of people who had loved the sun and were doomed never to see it again. "They would have been forced into the city because of the cold, and that's exactly where the orthocone wanted them."

"We don't know that for sure and probably never will— perhaps a few survived. What if some of them escaped down to the underground sea? There's certainly food, water and warmth. Who knows what was living on the far shores down there." Monica smiled weakly at Aimee, looking for some sort of confirmation that perhaps the small race didn't all perish.

Aimee nodded and turned to look at Alex who had been silent behind them; his eyes were half closed and he looked to be in a trance, listening intently to something only he could hear.

Alex was straining his senses to try and pick up any sound or impression that they were being followed or about to be ambushed. He couldn't feel the sliding vibrations or hear the wet slithering sound that told him that the creature was near but he could not help the feeling in the pit of his stomach that it was close and they were extremely vulnerable.

One by one they pulled themselves out of the sand on the black beach with a leathery, sliding sound. Each of the worms was roughly thirty feet in length and as thick around as a large horse. The blood-red segmented bodies were covered in short bristles that increased in length towards their feeding end, which was little more than a hole with hook-like teeth circling the entrance.

These creatures were the stuff of nightmares. Adapted to living beneath the wet, black sand, they had never existed in any fossil record.

The Antarctic worms hesitated at the mouth of the cave, their blunt heads raised and waving back and forth, tasting the air as their bodies pulsated greasily. In a quivering peristaltic motion they moved into the cave the humans had escaped into. However, it was not the scent of the small mammals that drew them out of the sand; it was the orthocone's blood that they followed. Even though the nightmarish creatures were blind, to them the blood trail was as wide and clear as a well-lit highway.

# Twenty-six

The large room ended in a doorway that was blocked, but not by a conventional stone door or a cave-in; the blockage was from a large, rounded, rough-hewn boulder of granite that had been purposely rolled in front of the door to seal it off. Matt watched Alex test the stone and, satisfied by something, called him over for assistance.

He looked at Alex incredulously; the stone looked to weigh several tons and the idea that just two men could shift it was to him at the very least a waste of time and at worst a lot crazy. Matt put his shoulder to the block and felt the huge mass of the boulder. However, when Alex put both his hands against the stone, braced his feet on the floor and began to apply all his strength, it moved. The grinding movement of the large stone made the very floor underneath them vibrate as it slid a few inches at first, then a few feet. Matt could see Alex had bared his teeth and the veins in his neck bulged; he decided he needed to push a little more himself—though he felt he might have been there for counterbalance purposes only.

A stone that large had to weigh many tons—movable with several draught horses, maybe, but not by a single human being. Matt looked at Alex and said, "How did . . ."

The opening was at a width they could now fit through. Alex turned to wink at Matt and slid through.

\* \* \*

Colder, much colder. Alex realised that although they might soon be free of the caves they would have another problem; none of them were dressed for the surface of the Antarctic. His own cave suit was ripped and punctured in many places and he'd noticed pieces missing from the others' suits as well.

Alex brought himself back to the present—no use getting ahead of the situation just yet. There were plenty more problems to be dealt with right now. He found himself in another large chamber and soon realised that what he had at first taken to be debris littering the floor was actually thousands of skeletal bone fragments. Given what they had already been through, Alex didn't think a few bones were going to make anyone squeamish anymore. He couldn't detect any imminent danger so called Aimee, Matt and Monica through.

The four of them looked at the sea of bones covering the floor in all directions. Aimee and Matt crouched down and were quickly sifting through them.

"Perfectly preserved; definitely human. Maybe it's some sort of burial chamber that was used because the ground had become too frozen for them to bury their dead?" Aimee said as she held a broken skull and jawbone in her hand while looking at the teeth. Most of them were missing and huge abscesses in the bone were plainly visible. She turned the skull over and could see a crack running right down the cranium area that had never healed. "Looks like this is what killed him or her though—some sort of accident." Aimee turned the small yellow skull over in her hands.

"I don't think so." Matt was holding some longer bones in his hands. "Look at this." He held out the bones for Aimee, Monica and Alex to see. "Notice those grooves on the thigh bone and again here on the rib? I've seen these marks before on bones recovered from mass graves during the great European famine of 1316. They're teeth marks, human teeth marks. These people were eating each other."

"Cannibals? They turned into cannibals? This is a nightmare; what would make them eat each other?" Monica was clearly shaken, her mouth trembling in both horror and disgust. Matt put his arm around her shoulders.

"Aztlan, the superpower of its time at the height of its scientific, architectural and artistic life cycle, perhaps the cradle of all civilisations, returns to barbarism within a few years. Maybe they were right; maybe their gods did abandon them. By now, even their harbours would have been iced over, making it impossible for any of the Aztlan fleet to return even if they wanted to. Forced below ground to escape the freezing conditions, running out of food to eat and wood to burn. Poor hygiene, malnutrition, did I forget anything? Oh yeah, a giant carnivorous beast was running amok in the caves below them. Man, I will never complain about having a bad day again, ever." Matt was surveying the room as he spoke. "Do you think the eaters are here among the eaten?"

Alex toed some of the bones aside with his foot. "It was the only resource they had left; each other. Humans have an enormous will to survive. Looks like these people were sealed in; can't tell whether they did it themselves to keep the creature or their captors out, or whether it was by the cannibals using this as their killing room."

"Perhaps they were still praying for the sun to return. They couldn't know that over ten thousand years later it would still all be frozen. Soon as that rock was rolled into place they were all as good as dead." As Monica was speaking her voice wavered and shrank, and her whole body trembled.

"This can't be all of them; there must have been hundreds and hundreds left behind. We don't know they were all abandoned, maybe some more were rescued or, as you said yourself, maybe they headed down to the underground sea," Aimee said. The odds were that the Aztlans had simply found more rooms like this one; she knew what could become of people who simply gave in to bleak depression. They tended to step off cliffs or just sit down and stop moving like a wound-down clock.

Matt rubbed Monica's shoulder as if to warm her and to his credit he held back with his silly humour to instead give her comfort and some whispered words.

"I'm OK, I'm OK. Let's just get out of here. I'd prefer that we not end up like these people and I certainly do not relish the idea of eating you guys—especially with the way that some of you smell by now." Monica managed a watery little smile.

"You heard the lady; let's keep going up." Alex led on.

Sliding, liquid sounds; Alex halted. He faced a three-way branching tunnel with all of the entrances sealed with heavy stone doors. Beyond the largest centre door he sensed movement, something waited. From its reaction to their footfalls, Alex was sure the creature knew they were on the other side. It was a cold intelligence that waited in ambush for them to come through the doorway. Alex knew he could move the stone if he wanted to and was pretty sure the creature would be able to do so as well. He moved to the door to his right. No sounds came from behind and nothing gave Alex the tingling feeling in his stomach; he pushed. The door slid with a gritty, grinding sound. If anything, the air in the new tunnel was even colder. The walls and roof were covered in more glyphs that showed men and women running, wrestling or throwing a ball-shaped object at a ring on the side of the wall.

"Looks like basketball to me," Alex said.

The others had squeezed through quickly; no one wanted to be left more than a body length behind. Matt now shone his torch around the walls and ceiling. "The early Mesoamericans used to play a game that was part basketball and part football nearly five thousand years ago. This might be one of their Great Ball Courts. If these Aztlans were the forefathers of the Olmecs, Aztecs and Mayans, then we should be able to assume that they had similar or in some cases identical cultures."

Matt stopped again to study one of the carvings. "The games look very similar. In most of these races the arenas were of significance to the people and their gods. The courts were considered to be portals to the Mayan underworld and were built in low-lying areas or at the foot of great vertical constructions. In fact, Mayan legend has it that the mythological Hunahpu and Xbalanque played a ball game with the lords of the underworld. I'd say that this tunnel will probably lead us to one of their open-air courts."

"Open air? I like the sound of that. Hey, be careful!" Monica grabbed Matt as he was about to put his foot in a hole cut into the floor.

"What is that? Is that for drainage?" Alex had noticed that the holes were cut in the floor near the wall every hundred feet or so.

"Probably, a culture this well established and advanced would have had some form of drainage and sewerage system constructed. Most likely it's gravity based, so it could be flushed downhill. There's probably all sorts of sewerage tunnels underneath us as well."

Alex groaned to himself. This was likely how the creature managed to get into the city after the Aztlans sealed the deep sacrificial chamber, and there was a good chance it was also how it planned to ambush them again now. "Let's move on, quickly now."

* * *

The tunnel was becoming more ornate and the architecture more magnificent. Large trapezoidal stones fitted together, forming a perfect seal. Jutting stone corbels of fierce creatures interspaced with large oval stone heads with benevolent stares looked out at the small group as it hurried along the tunnel. Smaller side doors gaped open and these offered little more than black holes into unknown passages of the Aztlan city. Their breath steamed in the torchlight and for the first time, ice crystals crunched under foot.

"We must be close to the outside, or at least where the outside used to be before it iced over." Alex felt they were in a race now, he mentally checked off his armoury—his rifle was gone but he still had his blades, and a single grenade. His propane cylinder was out and Aimee had lost her gun a long way back. Not much if it came to a stand and fight; but if it came to that in this enclosed space, he didn't think they would last very long no matter what armaments they had. Best if the lights went out before that happened.

The tunnel terminated in another stone door, this one also of the magnificent red granite and polished to a glass-like finish. At one time the door probably slid open as silently and smoothly as any modern-day palace door; now it was locked. Not by stone or steel, but by a rim of blue ice crystals surrounding the entire perimeter.

"This is it. At least we will be out from the stone and we can get a proper reading of depth. I might even be able to get a signal out to home base." Alex had reached around into his backpack and withdrew his small sonar device in readiness.

"How are we going to open it?" Monica was running her hand over the blue ice.

Alex could hear the suppressed excitement in Monica's

voice and took a step up to the door to test its weight and thickness and whether there was any give in the edges. It must have weighed several tons and without something to melt the surrounding ice was not going to move any time soon. Even combining his great strength with that of all the others he doubted they'd be able to do more than get red faces. The only option was to use his last grenade.

"Here're the options. One, we can find another way to the ice. Means we're going to have to double back, and we don't know how far. It's a pretty good bet to assume the creature hasn't given up yet so we may run into it again. Also, I reckon all the exits will be as iced up as this one. Second option is we use the last grenade to blow the door. It will get the door out of the way, but not the ice. Further, it will alert anything in these caves as to exactly where we are. It also means we will have exhausted our last major defensive ordnance."

Alex expected them to think over the option for a minute or two. However, Monica jumped right in.

"Blow it up. I'm not going to go back down into those black holes again."

Alex recognised the panic in her eyes. Even if they escaped, it might be a long time, if ever, before Monica wanted to go caving again.

Aimee looked across to Alex. "Blow it."

Matt nodded. "Yep, bombs away; blow it."

Alex smiled. "OK then, let's make some noise." He removed the small grenade from his belt pouch and wedged it into the corner of the door frame. Most of the explosion would be thrown back into their chamber, but there was nothing available for him to use to concentrate the blast towards the door—it had to work the first time as it was. Alex instructed them to move back down the chamber and take cover in the side tunnels, to brace themselves and cover their ears. Alex set the timer for thirty seconds and ran down the corridor, dived into a side tunnel and covered up.

The blast was deafening even with their hands over their ears. The hot whoosh rushed past them down the corridor, followed by the sound of bouncing debris of various sizes. Alex was the first back to the doorway—the grenade had worked spectacularly. The door was gone completely and their first sighting of the Aztlan city surface was before them.

# Twenty-seven

The smoke was clearing and all four of them stood bathed in a blue glow. In front of them the thick stone door had fallen away to reveal a solid wall of ice now barring the doorway. Its clarity was almost magical as it allowed them to see a blue world beyond and at least fifty feet out into the city courtyard.

"It's like being underwater." Aimee put her hand on the ice; it was slick from the heat of the explosion, but other than that untouched.

Monica was now also running her hand over the surface and shaking her head. "Oh, no. We should have expected this, it's prehistoric ice; extremely old and usually occurs when snow falls and is compressed over a long period of time. The more it's compressed the more the air is squeezed out and the larger the ice crystals become; then it becomes very transparent at depths." She stood back and looked like she was about to cry. Then, in a voice like a small child she said, "I thought for a moment it was the sky."

Matt put his arm around her again and asked, "Why is it blue?"

Aimee answered this time. "For two reasons. The ice is blue for the same reason water is blue. It's a form of reflection, but also at this depth it is the result of a molecular stretch in the water which absorbs light at the red end of the visible spectrum."

Alex looked at Aimee. "I'm no expert, but I've heard it's rock hard, is that right?"

It wasn't really a question. Alex knew the differing densities of ice as it related to his training for warfare in frozen oceans. A blue iceberg could tear a ship's steel hull like paper.

"Yes, like iron."

Alex pointed his sonar up at an angle from the bottom of the doorway, as close to vertical as he could get it. In a few seconds he was able to read his depth from the surface.

"Very good. Only about a hundred feet."

Alex removed a short, wicked-looking black blade from a hidden sheath on his thigh. The knife was one of several that he carried as standard equipment in the field. It was a modified K-bar, shortened and strengthened from its normal seven-inch length but still with the recognisable bowie features that U.S. Marines had carried into battle for generations.

He crouched down for a moment, looking up at an angle towards the outer rim of the door frame and then swung his arm. The blade connected with a squealing crunch and dug in about two inches. Alex could feel the juddering impact all the way up his arm. Hard as iron was right, he thought; a blow that powerful should have sunk the blade to the hilt. Like a machine he kept swinging his arm, occasionally changing hands to balance the impact and also share the fatigue across his shoulders. After twenty minutes he had a hole dug into the centre of the door frame ice approximately a foot in depth and diameter.

"How long to get us to the surface?" Aimee had her arms folded and was looking at him with a worried look on her face.

"Can I help?" Matt had also decided that one man, even one with superior strength, was going to take a very long time to get to the surface digging through a hundred feet of iron-hard blue ice.

Alex sat back for a moment and drew some deep breaths. He smiled at the three of them. "I estimate it would take me about twelve days to dig us up and out to the surface. If I had a dozen grenades it would definitely speed things up a bit. But no, I definitely do not plan to spend nearly the next two weeks digging through ice. I only need to get a hole dug so we are out from under the stone lintel. Then hopefully my comm unit headset can get a signal out. It doesn't have a very long range, but I'm betting my superiors won't have given up the search for us yet and if there are military choppers in the vicinity they will be carrying some armaments that can cut through the ice. And yes, Dr. Kerns, I would be delighted if you could take over for a few minutes."

Alex saw Monica slumped against the wall and Aimee resting her hands on her knees, watching him with a puzzled expression. She was at the point of collapsing from exhaustion and he could tell she wondered how he kept going.

"Phew, I'm tired," he said, more for her benefit. He didn't need the break but wanted to check down the tunnels as a feeling of disquiet had been growing within him. By now the creature would have an idea where they were and was probably working out how it could get to them. He needed to take a little walk back down into the dark and listen for a while.

The sudden explosion caused the creature to stop its forward movement. There was little it feared; however, without its shell it was vulnerable, and a cave-in could trap or crush it. After a few minutes when no further shaking occurred it continued sliding ahead, the rhythmic sound of the digging drawing it on. The tunnels were much smaller now and even compressing its boneless form to a third of its size it was impossible to use the tunnels as they were. The creature flexed its body and tested its enclosure—the roof above it lifted slightly. It paused. One of the small warm bloods approached; it was the dangerous one.

The creature coiled itself up and prepared for an almighty flex.

Alex walked back down the tunnel and began opening his senses to the stone, the walls and the floor. He could still hear Matt continuing with the digging, but knew he'd be lucky to be able to keep it up for more than a minute. Aimee and Monica stood on either side of him, either advising and commenting on his digging prowess or trying to take the knife off him so they could take a turn. Alex felt sorry for him; he knew how hard that ice was. Blue ice was not like normal ice where you could find a fault line or air bubble and cause a large chunk to crack and shear off. You literally had to dig it out chip by chip. It was a good thing Matt had a sense of humour.

A hundred feet farther down the tunnel, Alex stopped and stood silently in the dark. He blanked out the sounds of the digging and slowed his breathing until it almost seemed to stop. He was fully opening all of his extraordinary senses to his surroundings. He was listening, feeling, sensing for movement or a presence other than their own.

There. He felt it. It was close, too damn close. It was right here now. Like a bolt of electricity, Alex's body came alive once again as super-charged adrenaline surged through his body. He sprinted back down the tunnel.

Aimee felt the small tremor run through the floor and hoped it was nothing more than some minor geological activity. She was about to comment on it when Alex reappeared. Behind him the floor started to lift like a wave.

Giant stones that had been knitted in place for thousands of years were tossed aside like a small child's building blocks. The sound of crushing rock was ear-splitting.

Lieutenant Owen would wait another few hours. He wasn't surprised that he hadn't heard from the HAWCs yet and he hadn't expected to be kept in the loop. When those guys were involved, the brass knew the details and everyone else just did their job or got out of the way.

He kept the blades turning on the helicopter to keep the generators warm. Though it looked calm enough out on the snow he knew it was well below zero and while he trusted the SeaHawk-S in cold weather, there was nothing worse than lead in the feet when you had to lift a full load.

At last, he thought. Owen saw the large man come over the edge of the crater and unbuckle himself from the drop winch. He had his head down, his white parka suit straining across massive shoulders and arms and Owen couldn't remember the suits being so ill-fitting when he dropped the HAWCs off. He hoped he wasn't going to be asked to help them up out of the hole; he wasn't dressed for it.

The side door slid open and Owen turned in his seat. "Howd—" The sight that met him froze the greeting on his lips. A single eye burned from a blood-streaked veil of hate and fury. A meaty black hole where his other eye should have been and a beard matted with congealed gore completed the image of a Halloween mask. The man yelled something in a language he couldn't understand.

Owen reached for his sidearm as a fist like a pile-driver struck him in the face with enough force to knock out all his front teeth and flatten his nose. It would not be the last of his injuries that day.

Borshov dragged the American pilot out onto the snow. He needed more room to beat the man properly. His an-

ger from his defeat by Alex Hunter was now almost volcanic as he broke bones in the man's face and arms.

He carried the limp form to the edge of the deep chasm
and went to throw him over the edge a hundred feet to the
unforgiving rocks below. He looked at the man and hesitated. He spoke to him; shook him. The pilot opened his
eyes and groaned. Borshov shook him gently again, then
smiled.

With a mighty heave, the Russian threw him out into
the abyss. The pilot screamed as he fell. It was so much
better when they knew what was happening.

As Alex reached the group he did two things. He jammed
his communication squawk box into the shallow hole in
the ice. The hole was less than the depth Alex would have
liked but there was no other option now. He pressed send,
and the small device became a beacon sending out its
coded packet of information that contained the call signature for Captain Alex Hunter and his GPS position. The
second thing he did was yell a single word, "Move!"

They had no choice but to retreat back down the tunnel
towards the mayhem that was unfolding. The creature
had not yet breached the tunnel floor and was still pulling
its bulk up to where they were fleeing. The shock waves
were rippling out through their floor as it pushed and widened the hole it was making. They had several choices of
offshoot tunnels to choose from but stayed as close to
Alex as they could. Alex knew they trusted his instincts
and he hoped his choices led them away from the rising
horror.

Even Alex found it hard to stay upright as the creature
was literally shaking the entire floor as it pushed its way
up towards the surface. Monica was just skirting around a
large block of stone and had found herself on the other
side of the tunnel to the group when one of the creature's

deadly tentacle clubs burst through the floor and reared up between them. At that point the floor fell away; Alex, Aimee and Matt were on one side of the gulf, and Monica on the other. Alex could see Monica contemplating a leap across the abyss before quickly changing her mind. She took a last look at them; Alex could see the frustration and fear in her eyes. She looked at Matt, holding his eyes for a few seconds and then ducked quickly into one of the dark rooms on her side of the tunnel. Alex had to physically restrain Matt from trying to get back across to her as the beast hauled itself further onto their level.

"We'll find her later." Alex grabbed Matt by the arm and pulled him and Aimee into a tunnel directly behind them.

Monica kept running hard, the light of her helmet lamp jerking from the walls to the floor as she sprinted down the dark stone hallway. In no time her adrenaline levels dropped and she was out of breath, the recent exhausting days caught up with her and she had to slow her pace for a few minutes to get her strength back. She was slightly heartened to hear that the sounds of the creature were distant from her; unfortunately it also meant the sound of her friends had disappeared.

She didn't want to go too deep into the tunnels as she knew she would become hopelessly lost. The thought made her double over and she sucked in some deep breaths; she felt sick from the fear and for the first time in her life she felt the cold pressure of claustrophobia. Calm down, girl, you're better equipped than most to survive down here. She started to whisper to herself to try to draw back some of her old courage in the darkness; she'd give it a few more minutes of walking, then if the sounds grew more distant she'd double back. For now, though, she'd go on a bit further and see if there were other exits she could use.

\* \* \*

Alex and Aimee moved on at a jog.

"We've got to go back. Wait! Please, we have to go back." Matt had stopped dead and was gasping for breath.

Alex looked at Matt and shook his head wearily. Matt rushed at him and grabbed his arm, intending to drag him back down the tunnel the way they had just come. Matt might as well have tried to move a stone pillar. Alex gently reached out and took Matt by the upper arms. "We can't fight it in there. We have to stay ahead of it for now. She'll be OK as long as she keeps moving. We'll pick up her trail later on, I promise."

Matt sank to the ground and covered his face with his hands. "She was scared, so scared, and now she's alone in the dark." He lowered his hands and turned one over. There was a faint red chalk outline of a heart, now nearly erased.

Aimee sat next to him and put her arm around him. "We're all scared, Matt, but we've got to stay alive so we can find her."

Matt let out a long, exhausted and shuddering breath. "I can tell you one thing, I won't be going anywhere dark or cold for my next vacation."

"Why, a bit too quiet for you? Perhaps you can go caving with Monica on your honeymoon," said Aimee.

Matt smiled briefly and then looked towards the ceiling as though he was trying to see the blue sky above them. In his mind's eye he could see Monica by herself in the darkness; she called to him. He squeezed his eyes shut.

"Let's go." Alex moved them on again.

# Twenty-eight

Private First Class Dan Everson entered Major Jack Hammerson's office at a run. "Sir, we've received a coded call signature from the Arcadian."

The Hammer leapt to his feet. The pencil he had been writing with disintegrated into splinters in his large hand. His eyes bored into the young private. "Where and when," he said as he exploded around his desk.

Major Hammerson began walking quickly down the wide corridor, fists balled and chin jutting forward. His highly polished military-issue boots were beating out a quick drumbeat on the linoleum as his aides jogged to keep up. On his way to the command centre he barked questions and orders over each shoulder without drawing a breath.

"Exactly how far from the initial insertion point are they?"

Dan Everson shuffled the papers he had in his hands. There was one thing he had learned being assigned to the Hammer, and that was the information you provided better be up to the minute and accurate as hell.

"The message came in at 2109 hours, exactly seven point one miles from the insertion point. There's nothing visual on the surface, and the signal muffling indicates it is coming from just over one hundred feet below the ice."

"Who have we got in the proximity? What are they

packing? Who sent the message? How do we get down to them or them up to us? Have we responded yet? Organise a full briefing for me in ten minutes. Get me everything I asked for, and anything I haven't. Go."

Private Everson quickly peeled off to the operations room and the Hammer continued on his way to the command centre.

Borshov was hopping the helicopter along the ground in five-hundred-foot leaps; he was unfamiliar with the Sea-Hawk's controls and only needed to get it to the Leningradskaya base and out of sight.

The American message came in over his headset and lit up the computer screen in front of him—Captain Hunter had been found and the American station at Mc-Murdo was being ordered to respond. The coordinates displayed meant he was only a few miles away. He landed and thought for a few seconds, then touched the screen with a bloody finger. Borshov reached behind him and retrieved Benson's gas-powered M98 and slung it over his shoulder. He already had a little water and now both his and the pilot's communication devices; he had everything he needed.

He lifted off again and slow-hopped towards a ridge of broken ice. When he was a hundred feet out he opened the cabin door and leaped from the moving helicopter. As he hoped, it continued on its slow path, sliding to jam itself under one of the ice overhangs. The cabin collapsed and its broken rotor blades shattered like porcelain, catching the weak Antarctic sunlight as they flew to bury themselves beneath the snow and ice.

Borshov got to his feet and started to jog towards the last coordinates of Captain Alex Hunter.

Monica's tunnel abruptly ended in another large, round chamber as her helmet lamp was fading from yellow to a dull orange glow. She slowly examined the room, her heart thumping so hard she could actually feel it leaping in her chest as the nausea was rising in her throat again. Like most of the other rooms they had been in, it was largely featureless except for raised carvings of small figures on the walls but without Matt they were inaccessible to her. Anything of value had probably been removed and anything that could be used for fuel had long been burned. Towards the centre of the room there was a large hole roughly ten feet in diameter. She wished Matt was here to let her know whether it was a well or maybe a bathing recess where the bottom had fallen away into the chamber below. She whimpered to herself and couldn't help her bottom lip quivering as tears began to run down her cheeks. There was a familiar, acrid smell in the room that would have made her eyes water if not for her tears.

She almost completed her slow examination of the chamber's perimeter when she became aware of a figure standing silently in the doorway she had just come through. The figure glided smoothly and silently towards her.

She squeezed her eyes shut for an instant in the near total darkness and prayed for it to be Matt when she opened them.

"Matt, Alex? . . . No, not you . . . please, not you!" The image of Silex stared sightlessly back at her.

"We have to find Monica. What happens if we can't find her?" Matt was in a state of high agitation.

Aimee grabbed him by the arms and looked into his face. "We'll find her, don't worry."

She looked at Alex, and he met her gaze. Aimee could read his expression clearly; he didn't think the odds were in their or Monica's favour. "Of course we will," he said. "Let's go."

The sounds of the creature advancing had subsided a

while back. There were no more crushing-stone sounds and heavy vibrations under their feet. Alex, Aimee and Matt didn't think for a minute that it had given up; they just hoped that it didn't mean the creature had somehow managed to fully pull itself up into their level of the labyrinth.

The air in the tunnels was now a mist of falling dust from the shaking and rending. It caused the darkness to become more oppressive and their torch beams, now starting to burn a deep orange, were cut shorter and only illuminated about twenty feet in front of them. Alex didn't believe his senses would let him down and allow him to walk into an ambush, but with its enormous strength and bulk, if the creature was behind one of the walls and crashed through, it could easily crush them before they had a chance to flee.

Alex's mind worked furiously at calculating the odds of his signal being picked up. He expected the Hammer would have floating birds looking for them, and the Australians had a close base at Casey, but since the SINCGARS had gone offline there was no chance of any transmission relay via the more powerful unit. If the transmission sweeps missed them or there was a storm in the ionosphere, then they were as good as dead.

Alex sensed the giant presence close by and looked over his shoulder into the darkness. The atmosphere in the tunnel carried a familiar chemical smell and a sensation of enormous power, and more alarming for Alex, a primordial aggression that made the skin on his neck prickle. They would have no second chance.

# Twenty-nine

The military personnel assembled by Major Hammerson were in the darkened command centre looking at an image of a field of snow broken only by the black dots of men moving over its blinding whiteness. The live feed was coming from one of the reconnaissance choppers they had in the area from the McMurdo base but the images gave no clue as to the whereabouts of the missing team. Since they had lost communication with the group, Hammerson had authorised both surveillance and attack birds to be on constant rotation until further notice. He knew it was asking for too much to expect that they would find some way out already cut or open for them. This was going to be an ass-and-elbows free-for-all.

"Either way, if we want to reach them or bring them up we need to cut through that ice. We can dig through it, blast it or melt it. My guess is that they are sheltering in some sort of cave below that ice and snow layer." Captain Hicks gave a summary of the pros and cons of each option. "Digging is by far the safest option, but also the slowest. Even if we bring in large-scale boring equipment it would take four days—and add to that another two days just to fly it down there. Blasting could fracture the ice and the impact shock wave could bring the tunnels down. Our engineers believe they can mitigate this through layer blasting, but it's slow and the risk is still there." Captain

Hicks handed Major Hammerson pages of statistics and continued talking. "However, my choice would be to melt it. We could burn a hole in the ice fifty feet in diameter and one hundred feet straight down in minutes. We also have the ordnance on site right now."

Hammerson looked up at Hicks and raised his eyebrows. "Thermite?"

"Yes, sir."

Hammerson knew that thermite was messy, dangerous stuff but their choices were limited. Thermite wasn't used in battle anymore, however its high burn temperature meant it was excellent for stealth missions where the enemy armaments needed to be neutralised quickly. Its high temperature and low visual flaming, depending on the barium/sulfur mix, meant that the molten thermite would permanently weld the breech of an artillery piece shut, making it impossible to open and load the weapon. Dirty, portable, and very useful.

Hammerson also knew when it came down to brass tacks they were running out of time, and the U.S. military wasn't even supposed to be down there; any long-term digging operations and explosions had to be kept to a minimum.

"Talk me through it, Captain."

Hicks gave Major Hammerson some more notes and continued with the briefing. "We recommend thermite as it contains its own supply of oxygen and does not require any external source of air. Meaning it won't be smothered by the snow and will even continue burning while wet—it can't be extinguished with water. That's a good thing as we expect the melting ice will create a lot of water. Even underwater the molten iron produced from the burning thermite will extract oxygen from water and generate hydrogen gas in a single-replacement reaction." Hicks flipped a page.

Hammerson interrupted, "TH3 or Standard?"

"Standard, sir; it's hotter than thermite-TH3. Standard iron-thermite burns with little flame, but enormous heat. It's a lot dirtier, but it will be a more effective incendiary composition for our purposes."

"Risks?"

"Computer models recommend three iron-thermite blasts with seven-second intervals between each—the first two containing twenty-seven units of thermite, and the last blast containing just twenty-five. This should take us down between ninety-eight and one hundred feet and leave little residual water. The risks are that if our team under the ice is too close to the burn zone and we are out by just a few feet we'll cook them. They must be under cover before ignition."

Hicks paused for a few seconds and rubbed his chin.

"Go on, Captain."

"There is one more thing. If there are any shallow deposits of petroleum in the vicinity we could light up the whole area. If there's a big deposit, it could either go off like Hiroshima or create a burn hole that could continue to combust until it is capped or exhausted. Either way, it isn't going to be a very well kept secret for long."

"Better make sure you just burn the ice then, Captain."

"Yes sir, we can do that."


Alfred Beadman, the Chairman of GBR, was ushered into the room. Hammerson nodded to the chairman and then turned to Private Everson and glared. "Any contact yet?"

Hammerson already knew the answer to his own question, as he asked it just as low-level background noise emanated from the speaker in the centre of the enormous command room's oak desk. He just wanted to keep the pressure up on the communication team.

"Nothing yet, sir."

Everson was listening in as the communication team did everything they could to boost the signal and raise a response. The good news was that it wasn't plain white noise which meant no communication. There was just the soft hiss of non-contact; someone was there, they just weren't answering yet.

The Russian president looked at the security brief containing the transcript of an intercepted message from the Vostok base at the Antarctic. The Russian base contained some of the most sophisticated electronic surveillance equipment in the Southern Hemisphere, and anything outside of a frequency hopper could be trapped, decoded and digested by the Russians at about the same time as the legitimate receiving party.

The Americans were preparing an extraction from the ice; their mission must have succeeded. That idiot Petrov had failed him one too many times.

Volkov squeezed the briefing paper in his fist, compressing it ever smaller as he mentally sifted through his options.

He spoke to the officer without turning. "I need an extraction from the southern ice. There is a man I want brought back here within twenty-four hours." Volkov turned his watery stare on the young man. "See to it."

The Russian president watched the officer leave then opened a desk drawer and removed a small black phone. He dialled a long number and waited as the signal was coded and bounced to the other side of the globe. He spoke softly when the connection was made.

"Comrade Borshov, your job there is finished. I have another for you. Priority."

On the other side of Moscow, Viktor Petrov jumped into a large black Mercedes and headed for the airport. Several large diplomatic bags nestled safely beside him on the soft leather seat. Upstairs in his large drawing room the ashes of a copied security brief still smouldered.

Borshov heard the call disconnect and let his hand drop to his side. A priority assignment from the Little Wolf meant other missions were to be immediately abandoned. He reached up and touched the frozen blood around the ragged hole in his face. He ached, not from the raw wound, but for vengeance.

Alex Hunter would die by his hand, this day, next or whenever he got close enough. Borshov had his own priorities; Volkov would never know.

*Ping.* Alex's headset stopped everyone dead.

Aimee bent over and rested her hands on her knees, drawing in deep breaths through clenched teeth to try to filter the dusty air. She tried to spit out the dirt but realised there was no saliva in her dry mouth. She saw Matt stifle a cough, both of them not wishing to make any noise in the suffocating darkness. Their torch beams were nothing but a dull brown now and the reduced peripheral light made her feel the colossal stone blocks in the walls were getting closer and heavier around them. A wave of fatigue and nausea passed through her and she looked up at Alex to see him place the unit over his head, close his eyes and press the receive button. She crossed her fingers.

"Arcadian receiving, over."

When Alex's voice came over the speaker in the command centre, everyone stopped what they were doing and then cheered loudly. Though the Hammer felt like leaping to his feet and punching the air, he needed to stay cool and clear-headed as the mission was a long way from being over.

"Good to hear your voice, Arcadian, what is your immediate operational status?" Hammerson smiled to himself; he only just stopped himself from calling Alex "son." Captain Alex Hunter, the Arcadian, was a HAWC field agent. In dispassionate military terms he was an "asset," a weapon to be deployed and expended without emotion. However, the Hammer couldn't help taking pride in the way Alex had grown to be the leader and ultimate professional he was.

There was another crackle of background noise and then: "Are we ever glad to hear you, sir. HAWC unit is down to one member; there are three remaining scientific personnel; two with me, one missing. Plane crash survivors, if there were any, and Hendsen party look to have encountered large indigenous biological. There are no remains and no survivors."

Hammerson placed large fingers on his forehead and rubbed. His HAWCs, all those men and women, dead. Another bloody mission paid for in flesh, he thought.

Alfred Beadman was shaking his head and muttering to himself. "Who's missing and what does he mean by indigenous biological? They're a hundred feet below solid ice." He stepped towards the conference unit. "Captain Hunter, Alfred Beadman here. Dr. Aimee Weir: is she OK?"

"She's right here, sir." Alex removed his comm unit and placed it over Aimee's head.

Everyone held their breath in the command centre, the silence broken only by a hiss and crackle coming from the speaker in the centre of the large oak table. Then smooth complete silence as a signal was engaged.

"Hello?"

"Aimee! You're safe, thank God. I was so worried." Alfred Beadman rocked back on his heels and folded his arms about himself as though to give himself a big hug.

"Alfred, I'm better for hearing your voice." Aimee

couldn't help smiling as she spoke to the avuncular chairman.

"Is Adrian there? Is he okay too?" Beadman asked.

Aimee paused for a second, deciding what to tell him, then thought it best to keep it brief. "I'm sorry, Alfred, Dr. Silex didn't make it. He's dead."

"Oh, my dear, you must be shocked. Adrian was a good man; one of the best." Alfred's voice was full of pain.

"Yes, Alfred, Dr. Silex really surprised us all." She turned to Alex and rolled her eyes before changing the subject. "I've got bad news on the petroleum signatures, I'm afraid. They were false positives given off from a gigantic body of deep-crustal warm water with a biomass reading that's off the scale. There are also signs of ongoing geological activity, so I doubt there is anything of interest for GBR in the vicinity."

"My dear, all I care about is getting you home. Now, what's this about indigenous biologicals?"

Major Hammerson nodded to Alfred Beadman and leaned forward as a sign that he needed to take control once again. Though he was over the moon about hearing that Aimee Weir was alive, there was a lot to do if they were going to be safely extracted anytime soon.

"Dr. Weir, I'm delighted you're still with us and I look forward to having you here again in person. Now, though, we have to plan to get you out of there. Can I speak to Captain Hunter again, please?" Aimee passed the headset back to Alex.

"Here, sir."

"OK, Captain, continue with your update."

"Sir, as Dr. Weir mentioned, there was no petroleum, but a deep body of warm water. The heat is probably from some geothermic activity. This body of water contains many large non-surface-dwelling aggressive life forms. We are currently being pursued by one of these biological hostiles that were most likely responsible for the removal of the previous plane crash personnel and termination of the Hendsen party."

Hammerson leaned back in his chair and exhaled.

"OK, Arcadian. What is your current physical location and operational capabilities?"

"We are currently in the tunnels of an abandoned city that is structurally sound, but we estimate it is buried approximately one hundred feet below high-density ice. Our defensive capabilities are near exhausted. We're caught between creature and ice and our backs are against the wall. One last thing, sir; we weren't the only ones under the ice. We encountered several Krofskoya agents, headed by Uli Borshov. They have since been neutralised."

In the command centre, Hammerson's jaw worked beneath his cheeks at the thought of the Russian interference. This was Cold War stuff. He knew a few Russian generals and this was off-key. Someone was exceeding orders; someone would pay.

"Captain, Alfred Beadman again. Can you barricade yourself in somewhere until we can reach you?"

"Mr. Beadman, this thing is bigger than a blue whale and is coming through the walls like they are paper. Our plan is to stay ahead of it if we can. However, this strategy will only be successful for a short while until we end up cornered. Major Hammerson, I can't dig us out from here, can you reach us?"

"We believe so. We're going to cut a hole using standard thermite. It'll be approximately fifty feet in diameter and will overlap your beacon signal. You're correct on your estimation on the ice depth; it's exactly a hundred and one feet deep. We're planning a series of detonations that will vaporise approximately one hundred feet of ice. You'll need to bust through that last foot or so yourself. Any more burn and we'll flood your chamber with scalding water and steam; any less and you won't be able to punch through. Comments, Captain?"

"Works for me, sir. How long until you're ready?"

Major Hammerson turned and looked at Hicks who put down the phone he was speaking into. "Ten minutes until all charges are calibrated. First charge ready to drop in eleven minutes."

"Ready, Arcadian, ten minutes on my mark." Hammerson and Alex counted down from twenty and synchronised their watches. "OK, you need to be away from that transmission device you planted, but in ten minutes twenty-one seconds you need to be back there knocking a hole through. We estimate in another five minutes after the blast, runoff from the walls will start to refreeze at about six inches every twenty seconds. Good luck, soldier."

"Thank you, sir, we'll see you soon." Alex pressed the small stud on his earpiece and drew in a deep breath. Just give us a few more minutes, he thought.

# Thirty

"They're coming to get us. In less than ten minutes there'll be three staged thermite blasts that'll hopefully burn a hole right down to our door. The blast and burn will be all over in twenty-one seconds and then we need to be back at that door breaking through any remaining ice before the runoff refreezes. We're nearly there, guys."

Alex looked at Aimee who gave a wearied smile showing teeth darkened by grit. Matt, however, exploded.

"Ten minutes? That's not enough time; we'll never find her in ten minutes. Can they hold off for a while? What if they drop down and send in some more soldiers to help with the search? Ask them, please ask them."

Alex felt for the young man. They would need to pass close to where Monica disappeared on their return to the door, but the odds of finding her now were small. The tunnels were silent now, and he should have been able to pick up her soft breaths or even her racing heartbeat; but there was nothing. How could he tell Matt that he couldn't find her; she had either travelled well away from her initial position, or she was dead. Alex knew he didn't have the time to negotiate; if Matt tried to slow them down, Alex was prepared to carry him, conscious or not.

"Sorry, Matt; we can look out for her on our way back, but that's all. If we don't make that opening before the refreeze, we'll all die down here."

Aimee put her hand on his shoulder. "Please, Matt."

Matt turned to Alex with red-rimmed eyes as if he was going to say something before changing his mind. He took off his helmet and threw it hard into the dark, then ran dusty fingers through sweat-slicked hair. He took a deep breath and nodded.

Thank God, looks like he's still with us, thought Alex.

They moved cautiously, Matt and Aimee straining to hear and see past the weak beams of their light. From time to time they stopped still to listen—the only sounds came from their own breathing. Alex checked his watch—six minutes remaining. This was not good, time was running out too quickly.

They had made their way back to where they became separated from Monica. No longer was there a large ancient tunnel splitting into sub-tunnels; now it was a yawning chasm falling away into inky blackness. Alex could not see or sense anything in the pit in front of them, but getting across to the side tunnel on the left where Monica had disappeared was going to be impossible. Over to the right was the way back to the original tunnel that led to the ice door and the coming blast zone. That way offered a hazardous but small chance of passing, but at least it was a chance. There was a line of single stones still attached to the wall, jutting out about a foot and acting as a narrow shelf—they could make it back if they held their breath and acted quickly. Alex was conscious of the fact that they needed to be away from the blast zone, but close enough to punch through before it refroze. If they looked for Monica, they'd never make it. His choice was simple: lose one, or lose all three.

"How are we going to get across?" Matt looked at both Aimee and Alex waiting for an impossible plan to cross the black pit and rescue Monica. He must have known that the chasm was impassable, but by now he had come to believe Alex was capable of anything. Given enough time, perhaps Alex could have managed to scale his way across. However, time was not something they had now. Aimee looked down at her feet so she didn't have to meet his eyes.

"We need to get back to the ice door, now. We don't have much time." Alex spoke quickly while keeping his eyes on the gaping pit in front of them.

"What about Monica? She's just over there."

"Once we're in the main chamber, we'll see what we can do." Alex hated misleading Matt, but he needed to get them on firm ground and into the main chamber. The last thing he needed was to end up having to wrestle with Matt on the edge of a near bottomless pit.

Alex quickly checked the remnants of his equipment, then turned to Aimee and looked to see if there were any loose straps or equipment hanging off her that could snag on the wall or trip her up. He turned to Matt next, but he was brushed away as Matt moved in close to Aimee and asked her to check his suit.

"You'll help me find her, won't you? She must be petrified in the dark by herself." Matt was keeping his voice low and looking into Aimee's eyes with an intense gaze that was bordering on mania.

"Help's coming, Matt."

Aimee began fiddling with her belt webbing so she didn't have to look into his face and tell a lie. She also didn't think that Monica could be alive now that the creature was almost among them. It had stopped chasing them, but she knew it hadn't given up so she figured that meant only one thing—it had gone after Monica.

"Aimee, you're going first. Matt, you after me."

Aimee knew this way Alex could keep them both in arm's reach. They edged along the precipice with the stone holding firm under their feet. From the pit below there was an odour of ammonia and ancient decay. Thankfully, no sound rose from the darkness.

"Very good, Aimee, keep moving and looking ahead, just a few more feet."

With one hand Alex held on to Matt's shoulder; Aimee bet he would drag Matt if he had to keep him moving forward. Matt's eyes were fixed on the empty tunnel across from them; Aimee knew why. If Alex let him go and he could manage it, he would disappear into that tunnel, charging blindly into its depths and calling Monica's name. Part of Aimee wanted to do the same, but she knew deep inside herself that to leave Alex now meant certain death. She remembered the emaciated skulls in the lower tunnels and shivered; she wanted to see the sun again.

Aimee stepped off the ledge onto the main tunnel floor and knelt down to draw in breaths; the strain on her already fatigued calf muscles had been enormous. Alex was next, followed by a still reluctant Matt.

*Ping.* Alex's comm unit signalled an incoming message.

"Arcadian, this is Lieutenant O'Riordan in *Blackbird One* overhead, we will be commencing drop in three minutes and counting down from two. Expect communications to be down from ignition and for approximately five seconds afterwards. Good luck, sir."

Alex knew he didn't expect a response; things were in motion now. The size of the chemical blast would scramble communications as the incendiary coupled with an already magnetic environment.

"We've got three minutes till they begin the burn. Let's go."

"No, wait. I thought I heard her. Monica! Monica, it's us!" Matt stepped back to the edge of the pit and screamed at the top of his voice towards the side tunnel. Her name bounced off down into the chamber and was echoed back again and again.

"Monica! We're here. Can you hear us?"

All that came back after the echoes died down was the sound of small rocks falling; then of something large shifting.

"That's her." Matt's eyes were bulging out of his head and he strained to see inside the far tunnel.

"I don't think that's Ms. Jennings, Dr. Kerns. We need to leave here, right now."

Alex reached out to get hold of Matt so he could drag him away from the edge of the pit. The smell of ammonia was now growing and Alex could perceive massive movement below them; his senses were making him tingle all over. Pushing a bow wave of air pressure before it, the creature exuded a sense of power, hunger and deadly intent.

More rocks bounced to the tunnel floor and fell away into the pit's darkness and dust once again started to rain down on them. Noises were coming now from both the pit in front of them and Monica's side tunnel.

*Ping.* "Two minutes, mark." The countdown had begun. They needed to be closer when those blasts started to occur—they were still much too far away.

"We need to go now. That is an order. Dr. Kerns, that is not Ms. Jennings."

Alex started forcibly dragging Matt backwards when a figure appeared in the mouth of the side tunnel.

"Monica!" Matt looked like he was about to leap across twenty feet of gaping blackness to reach her. Even Aimee broke out in a smile.

"She's alive!"

Monica stood there, just out of reach of their fading torch lights. She stared ahead and remained unresponsive to all Matt's shouting.

Alex's unique senses were going into overdrive, even without his infrared equipment he could tell that the figure of Monica was even colder than its surroundings. A normal human figure generated a slight orange to yellow warmth aura, however, Monica appeared totally blue-black—as cold as a fish, or a corpse.

Alex's whole body was screaming to run and he reached for Matt just as Aimee happened to look down into the pit before them. At first it looked like the floor of the pit was rising to meet them until the torchlight brought detail to a single emotionless eye, as large as a Buick, that swivelled to focus on them. Aimee screamed.

It all happened very fast from there, the orthocone's giant feeding tentacles burst from the pit and slammed down onto the tunnel floor. They lifted huge blocks of the stonework out from in front of them, creating a deadly shower of massive debris. Alex lifted Matt and Aimee and pushed them forward up the tunnel towards the ice door. His movement triggered activity in the figure of Monica and it flew forward as if fired from a cannon; its mimicry fell away and turned back into a lethal, hooked and sticky tentacle club. It struck with unnerving accuracy—onto the centre of Alex's back.

The pain was unbelievable. Alex's backpack and armoured suit protected him from the full extent of the lethal, dagger-like talons that erupted from their sheaths to impale him. However, he was stuck fast in the biological adhesive that the creature used to ensnare its prey.

"Run! Get back to the ice door and take cover." In one fluid movement, Alex removed his full-sized blackened ka-bar blade and slammed it down with enough force to spike four inches into the ground between two of the ancient flagstones. He needed to anchor himself, for even

with his superhuman strength he was no match for a creature that was hundreds of times his size and bulk.

*Ping.* "Sixty seconds to first drop." The final minute
countdown had begun.

The creature, sensing that its prey was somehow caught,
moved up closer to use more of its bulk and bring its feeding tentacles into play. Another two elephantine tentacles
slammed down just short of Alex's feet. He knew that if
the creature got more than one of its tentacles on him he
would simply be torn apart like an overcooked chicken.
The six-inch talons were working their way through
Alex's armour and his knife was starting to bend. Its
toughened blade would hold against an enormous amount
of torque but eventually it would shatter like glass, leaving him holding nothing more than a handle; he needed a
Plan B now.

With his other hand he reached into his belt and removed a small curved folding blade. It was a modified
Spyderco Manix, one of the few folding blades in the world
that could be easily opened with one hand and locked se-
curely. Alex flicked it open and ran the razor-sharp blade
with as much force as he could muster from his wrist up
his arm and across his chest just below his neck. He could
only get as far as his other shoulder before mobility stopped
him going any further. Blood welled up along the cut
marks, he needed to cut hard enough to slice open the
hardened caving suit without slicing any veins or tendons.
All this fast and delicate work while some monster from
a sailor's worst drunken nightmare was trying to tear him
apart.

It did the trick. With a sudden ripping noise the top half
of his suit was ripped away from the tentacle club and disappeared into the pit. There was a brief spray of blood as
the talons raked his back before they lost their shallow

grip on his flesh; but he was free. In the blink of an eye he was on his feet and sprinting down the tunnel. It was like a bomb went off behind him as the creature realised its prize was escaping.

The colossus hauled itself up from the abyss, tossing large rocks out of its way like pebbles. Its rage could be heard above the smashing of stone in an ear-splitting squeal.

*Ping.* "Five-four-three-two-one . . ."

There was no sound. Or at least nothing that could be heard over the maelstrom behind him. Alex was only a minute from the ice door and he increased his speed. He could easily out-sprint the creature as it could only move so fast in tunnels that were never meant for something its size. Alex mentally counted off the seconds to the next blast—three-two-one. This time there was a slight tremor and blue light flared in front of him, only fading after a few seconds. The ice door had lit up like a homing beacon. At least the charges were going off in the right place, he thought.

Alex could now see Aimee and Matt standing in front of the door. He reached them and in one fluid motion picked them both up, one under each arm and kept moving quickly into the side alcove.

"Three-two-one" . . . this time there was an audible *whump*, and dust and grit poured down on their heads with some larger stones also dislodged from the walls. Once again, the tunnels lit up. However, this time it was a yellow light that hurt the eyes and stayed bright as the thermite continued to burn even under the ice and water. It was doing its job and continued to vaporise the ice down towards them.

# Thirty-one

The Aztlan ruins returned to silence. Even the massive creature in the tunnels below had stopped its crushing forward movement as it waited to see if the explosions heralded an earthquake. After a few more seconds the blinding light from the doorway faded. But not to a soft blue glow; this time it faded to something that Aztlan hadn't seen for thousands of years. Sunlight.

Matt and Aimee were on the ground where Alex had dropped them. He stood immobile, half turned away from them, looking back the way they had come. Even his breathing was imperceptible. Aimee thought he looked like a statue; hewn from dirt and blood and iron. As she watched, one of the wounds on his back stopped bleeding and started to knit over. A thought flashed briefly through her mind—he's not human—and was gone just as quickly.

They didn't need their torches as light now shone through the opening, and as the tunnels weren't filled with boiling steam or water Alex made a decision: back to the doorway—pronto.

It was still filled with ice. However, now it was like being in shallow water as the sunlight reflected down onto the remaining ice layer, perhaps for the first time in more than 10,000 years, giving them a view over the Aztlan court of almost crystal clarity. The ceremonial courtyard was filled with beautiful murals and intricate stone carvings made from polished granite. The colours, the finish on the stone, and all the fine detail had been preserved perfectly.

Matt and Aimee pressed themselves up against the ice and stared at the vista before them—at what was perhaps the cradle of all human civilisation. Almost hypnotised by the wondrous sights, their reverie was quickly interrupted by a deafening shriek from the tunnels behind them.

Alex had to act quickly; he only had minutes before the ice started to refreeze—though by the sound of the creature's advance he'd be lucky to have half that time. He stepped closer to the wall and looked upwards. The doorway was six feet high and he could see that the ice looked to be about two feet over and above this. He needed to dig a hole wide enough for them to get through and up at an angle of about forty-five degrees. If he started at the top of the doorway, that was only about three and half feet of ice—four max. He stepped back and reached to his hip; nothing. He had nothing left on him he could use.

"Can we help?" Aimee asked. She looked at him standing there in thought. Alex turned around and looked at her, and then over her shoulder at the cave floor and smiled. "Yes, you can. You and Matt can take cover."

Alex walked over to the wall where several large pieces of the black granite had been dislodged. Alex knew that the granite the Aztlans used was as hard and tough as steel; it was the best tool he could find. He lifted a piece the size of a fruit crate and walked back to the doorway. When he got within ten feet he lifted it above his head. The stone must have weighed in excess of 700 pounds. Alex charged.

Using the force built up from his momentum, he launched the stone up at an angle at the ice doorway. It struck the top of the ice with an explosive crash. Vein-like cracks appeared right throughout the ice door and the impact mark he had made was a frosted crater. About twenty pounds worth of ice was dislodged; Alex brushed away some of the looser ice and had a quick look at the job at hand. Making a mental recalibration he picked up the rock again and walked back to his starting position.

Matt had moved behind him and was determined to help, perhaps trying to keep busy so he didn't have to think about Monica. He had found a stone about one tenth the size of Alex's but found he had trouble lifting it above his knees. He saw Aimee looking at him and remarked, "I think I'll stick to doing the thinking."

*Good idea*, Aimee mouthed back. She appreciated his attempt at humour, but his voice didn't sound right and his face looked slack.

Alex walked back a few paces, looked towards the doorway then charged. This time Alex aimed the large stone into the hole he had previously created. The granite boulder shattered in two and half the stone stayed embedded in the ice. Alex pulled it out and used a shard of stone like a shovel to clear away the loose ice debris. The hole was now two feet in diameter and intruded into the ice a little more than that. The impacts had created numerous faults in the once dense blue ice and each one made the next throw more effective. The beautiful vista of Aztlan was now gone as the ice doorway was a craze of shattered and splintered ice.

An unearthly howl came from beneath their feet. It was so close they could feel as well as hear it. Matt and Aimee forgot about Alex's instruction to stay clear and inched closer to him. Alex was looking down at the tunnel floor with his head slightly turned.

"OK, nearly there. Another couple should do it." Alex still wasn't even breathing hard; he walked back down the tunnel to select another stone. This time he selected one a little bigger than a football. He hefted it in one hand, then took another run at the ice door. In a long arm throw any

football coach would have been proud of, he launched the
stone at the hole with even more of an upward angle. It
left Alex's arm so fast Aimee and Matt could barely see it
travel through the air. It struck the upper centre of the ice
hole like a cannonball. On this launch it didn't bounce back
or become lodged in the ice; it punched its way through
and let a streaming ray of white sunshine into the tunnel,
followed by a gush of warm water.

Aimee watched the muscles in Alex's back ripple as he let
loose the stone. She realised that all the wounds on his
back had ceased to bleed and most now were even starting
to knit. Who was he? What was he? Why did he call himself the "Arcadian?" She knew from school that Arcadia
was the legendary birthplace of one of Zeus's sons. But it
didn't make sense. Ever since she had watched him defeat
the giant Russian and then, by himself, shift stones that
must have weighed tons, she had questions. Aimee knew
about stress-related adrenaline bursts that gave normal
men short but explosive strength to perform superhuman
acts. But those capabilities disappeared immediately after
the act or stress event was removed. But this man, Alex
Hunter, could summon those strengths and extra abilities
at will.

   He must be some sort of military experiment, she
thought. Aimee drew in a cold draught of fresh air and
smiled. As a spotlight of real sunlight hit the tunnel floor,
she realised it didn't matter. It was enough for her to know
he was special. He had risked his life for all of them, dozens of times. He had saved them.

Lieutenant O'Riordan was the first to spot the dark debris
appear out on the ice.
   The three helicopters hovered over the almost circular
bowl-shaped hole in the ice. Just under forty feet across at

the top, it widened at the bottom to a belly of approximately fifty feet. This was due to the heat effect of the thermite being concentrated downwards and sideways the further it sank into the ice. The edges were glass smooth as if the hole had been polished by a thousand jewellers, and now that the surface snow was removed the outline of the city could be seen under the ice. The only blemish was a football-sized piece of dark rock and its exit crater towards one side of the ice hole.

The helicopters landed back from the edge and immediately disgorged men carrying an array of climbing equipment. Drop winches were pinned to the upper ice lip and the men quickly rappelled down into the crater.

Water was just starting to run down the sides of the large bowl and the air at the bottom was balmy and very humid. It wouldn't be like that for long; the bottom of the pit would fast fill with warm water and once that cooled to slush it would block the hole. From then it would set like stone.

O'Riordan and his men charged towards the hole with ice axes and a single portable pneumatic jackhammer.

The initial flush of water never abated and quickly became a torrent as the melted ice poured through the hole Alex had opened. The good news was that the liquid was still warm and it was smoothing and ever so slightly widening the edges of the hole. The light flooding down into the tunnel suddenly darkened as objects could be seen moving around on top of their prison and then came the sweetest sound they could ever have heard—another human voice.

"Captain Hunter? Lieutenant O'Riordan at your service." O'Riordan lay down on the ice and extended his arm into the hole. Alex could just reach the hand and he grasped it firmly.

"Glad to see you, O'Riordan. It's getting a bit boring down here, mind if we come up?"

As Alex finished speaking a petrifying screech sounded from all around him. It finished with a grinding squeal as though rocks were being moved and pulverised under their feet.

"What the hell was that?" O'Riordan's face, peering down into the hole, had paled and he quickly withdrew his arm.

"Just a little motivation, Lieutenant. We need to leave, right now."

"You got it, sir," O'Riordan said and asked Alex to stay back a few feet from the hole while they widened it. They only had a few more minutes before everything started to re-ice. Alex gave the OK and called for one thing—the biggest gun they had.

# Thirty-two

The most powerful ordnance they had on hand was an army-issue M16 assault rifle. Primitive compared to what the HAWCs used as standard operating equipment, but better than throwing large rocks, which was all Alex had left.

Alex grabbed the weapon and stepped back from the ice hole. The sound of the jackhammer was not loud, just a grinding pump followed by chunks of ice coming through the hole. He ran down the tunnel; he knew their pursuer would not have given up and he could sense its presence all around him. The smell of ammonia was strong but not overpowering, meaning the creature was near, perhaps just behind one of the walls. Alex knelt on the ground and put his hand flat to the cold stone surface; he could feel the vibrations. Below the freezing blocks he could now hear the liquid sliding sound as if a river of flesh was moving quickly along just below them. He could sense a massive gathering of strength.

Alex picked up the rifle and sprinted back to the ice door. They were about to be ambushed.

The creature could sense them just ahead and above. It compressed its boneless body into a long elongated pipe and moved along the large drainage tunnels, gently widening the old stone walls as it went. It was being driven mad by hunger as the pumping of the jackhammer gave off vibrations similar to a creature in distress, and that meant easy prey. It would get below them and launch its final attack.

"We've got company." Alex ran back to Matt and Aimee just as the jackhammer stopped and a rope dropped through the hole. The water had stopped flowing and was now solidifying into an icy sludge. The new hole itself was large enough for a body to be pulled through. Alex grabbed Aimee and lifted her towards the opening.

"Aimee, go."

Aimee turned around and quickly kissed Alex on the side of his mouth and then said, "Don't you dare be long." With that she grabbed the rope and disappeared up through the hole as if by a conjuror's rope trick. In a few seconds the rope came back down and Matt wasted no time in grabbing hold; he turned briefly and gave Alex the thumbs-up and he too disappeared up through the hole. Matt looked older. Alex remembered when he first saw Matt and how young he seemed. Now he looked hollow, weary with loss. Alex turned back into the darkness. Monica, Tank, Johnson; all of them gone. He felt little sorrow. As a HAWC he was trained to ignore physical and emotional trauma. But he was still human; there should have been more. What else was changing inside him?

Alex shook his head to clear his mind and opened his senses to the underground. He could feel the enormous malicious presence lurking nearby. He could sense hunger, strength, anger and an eons-old intelligence. This was not a creature that deserved to roam the earth today; it was a thing of myths and nightmares—a creature of darkness and brutality.

The rope dropped back down. Alex seized it as the ground shook beneath his feet.

* * *

It was a tight squeeze and Alex was thankful the water had smoothed the edges and made them slippery—though his tolerance of pain was much greater than an ordinary person's, he didn't relish the idea of being dragged over iron-hard jagged ice with a naked upper body. It took four men to haul Alex out of the ice hole. The glare from the light on the ice and snow brought tears of irritation to his eyes but the air was cool and clear even with the faint odour of thermite. As well as Lieutenant O'Riordan and the other soldiers who pulled him out, there were six other military men on the ice loosely cradling either ice axes or M16s. Aimee and Matt stood off to the side, covered in army-issue blankets. They had refused to be winched back to the surface until Alex was out and safe.

The ice was thickening up again now, and was already another few feet higher than when the rescue team had started to widen Alex's hole. The mist of humidity had dropped to the ice; the refreeze had begun.

O'Riordan walked quickly up to Alex and shook his hand. "Good to see you, sir. Incoming transmission for you." O'Riordan handed Alex his radio.

"Arcadian, I knew you'd make it."

At the edge of the melted pit a mound broke open and the muzzle of the M98 lifted out of the snow.

Borshov blinked his remaining eye and focused on the large man that had just been pulled from the ice hole. There was a lot of distance between them and he had no sniper scope—it would be a long shot, but he had the high ground and there was nowhere for Alex Hunter to hide. If he missed on the first round, he would get another, and another.

He had plenty of time before Volkov's men picked him up. He steadied his breathing and lined up on the HAWC leader's head.

* * *

Seeing Alex now free, Aimee and Matt consented to be winched towards the rim of the large pit. Looking down, the surface of the ice was still remarkably clear and as Aimee rose she could make out the beautiful Aztlan court in all its fantastic detail. However, while Aimee watched, she could see something that refused to make sense to her already tired mind. The structures below the ice seemed to be falling away. The open courtyard that had been just outside the doorway looked to drop into a black pit and something mottled and sickly greenish seemed to now boil below its surface—a giant stain was spreading to cover the city once again, but this time not of ice, but of muscle and flesh. The roiling motion slowed and Aimee could make out what it was she was looking at.

A huge eye was rolling under the ice and Aimee felt it stop to fix first her, then Alex and the other marines with its cold stare. She screamed a warning as all hell broke loose down in the pit.

Alex was the first to sense the movement—a deep shuddering beneath their feet. Something grazed his temple and he ignored it to yell to the men in the ice pit.

"Everyone clear the area, out of the hole. Now!"

Alex's warning got most of the marines moving to the ropes, however, some who were unfamiliar with the danger or Alex's rank looked instead to O'Riordan—it was their fatal mistake.

The first two marines had buckled themselves onto the guidelines and depressed the lift studs when the ice in the centre of the pit exploded upwards.

A fury of mottled, grey-green giant tentacles burst out of the ice. Now in the raw daylight, the true colour and size of the creature could be appreciated. It was a monstrosity. Something that had been hidden away from natural selection for millions of years and grown to be the ruler of its domain once again entered the world of man. In a sweep of one of the tentacles it latched onto two of the marines who had failed to move quickly enough. They were held fast by the suckers and the deadly talons embedded themselves into their flesh with ease. The struggling men were pulled into the pit below the ice and Alex could see that the creature wasted no time in stuffing the tiny morsels directly into its cruel, jagged mouth.

The other marines were hooked onto their lines and slowly ascending. Alex and O'Riordan shared a rope and this made their ascent slower than the rest. One of the hovering helicopters banked and positioned itself above the pit so it could provide cover for the retreating soldiers now that they were out of the line of fire. It poured hundreds of deadly rounds from its big M60 machine cannon into the hellish leviathan, bringing forth waves of a greenish ichor from the punctured tentacles before one of the long clubs shot upwards like a rocket and stuck to the bottom of the helicopter. The 1,662-horsepower engines were no match for the strength and weight of the creature, and it easily drew the helicopter down almost gently onto the ice so it could tear open its canopy and pluck out the still belted-in solders as if they were sardines from a newly opened tin.

The giant cephalopod gave a heave and pulled more of its bulk up from under the ice. It fully filled the pit now and from above it looked like some horrid hell-borne blooming flower. Alex and O'Riordan made it over the lip of the ice pit and sprinted to the last helicopter. Matt and Aimee waving them on, they launched themselves into the remaining seats and the pilot lifted off immediately.

"Got any thermite left?" Alex looked at O'Riordan who was ashen-faced.

"My thoughts exactly. Prepare an immediate drop canister with detonation on impact."

"Hold that order; something's happening."

The helicopters hovered hundreds of feet overhead, well out of range of the orthocone's deadly tentacles, but Alex noticed that the creature was starting to thrash uncontrollably. Blood began to spread out below and now above the ice line.

Borshov had fired several shots and only grazed his target. What kind of *chush' sobách'ya* gun was this? He had only been stopped by the rock and ice beneath him pulsing like an earthquake, cracking the continent from below. Then before his ruined eye, a great creature was growing up out of the pit. *Dragan Zmey Gorynych!* To Borshov, it was an ancient dragon from Russian mythology, the *Gorynych*, the devourer of men.

Borshov feared no man, but this monstrosity liquefied his bowels and broke his nerve. He burst from his snow cover and sprinted away to his rendezvous; his white suit and the chaos behind him masking his escape.

The jackhammer and its vibrations had excited more than just the orthocone; the inexorable climb of the giant blood worms had at last brought them to the base of the ice roof. They could sense and taste the blood in the air and it was filled with the scent of the orthocone. The blood that splashed down to the ice from the helicopter attack spurred them on.

The orthocone had traded its armour-plated shell for speed and manoeuvrability, but in doing so had left itself vulnerable to the worms. The first worm reached the body of the massive cephalopod as it was occupied with trying to launch itself at the buzzing helicopters above it. At first the leviathan felt nothing as the worm burrowed its head deep into the unprotected flesh. Then as more and more of the worms attached themselves to the cephalopod's hide so they could saw into the skin and suck the flesh from the body, the giant nightmare beast finally realised the danger it was in.

It turned over and tried to drag its body against the stones and edges of the ice, hoping to dislodge the giant parasites. But by now, the bodies of the worms were burrowing into the flesh, their tough bristled shapes impossible to dislodge.

"What the hell are those things?"

O'Riordan and all the crew could see the orthocone as it turned over to fight the parasites, exposing the thistly red bodies of the worms. The squid managed to pull some free with its powerful tentacles and crush them, however, more simply inched their way on towards it with a blind hunger.

"Hell is the right word." Matt was shivering in the back of the helicopter as they watched the battle. By now some of the worms had actually disappeared into the body of the orthocone—the giant beast now carried its own death within it.

The eldritch screams and thrashing of the gargantuan creature with its tentacles waving madly about and its mottled body now covered in either manhole-sized wounds or the disappearing bodies of the blood worms created an unreal vision for the men in their helicopters. For Major Hammerson and his men back in the command centre watching over the live video feed, it was an image straight from the mind of Lovecraft. With the tail ends of the giant bristling worms still protruding from the cephalopod's body, it started to withdraw back into the pit where it either thought it had a better chance of fighting the parasites or could die in the darkness of its netherworld.

"My holy Christ." Alfred Beadman collapsed back into his chair and looked to have passed out.

Major Jack Hammerson, who had seen things throughout his long brutal career that would freeze a normal man's
blood, was stunned to silence. The images that had been
streamed to the command centre were of a battle that had
no place in this modern, sane world. At last Hammerson
spoke. "Tell me you're recording this, Private."

Private Everson who had been in a trance leapt for the
console.


"We need to seal that hole over, Lieutenant." Alex was
damn sure that not a single one of these creatures should
ever be allowed to escape from their deep world, as much
for the creatures in the world below the ice as for the world
above.

"Roger that, sir." O'Riordan spoke some clinical orders into his microphone and the remaining helicopters
took strategic positions around the rim of the ice pit. On
command, each fired multiple AGM-114 Hellfire missiles
into the ice and snow about twenty feet back from the rim.
At first all that was thrown up were large sprays of snow
and some large ice boulders. But by the third explosion
large sections of the walls started to collapse inwards, pour-
ing thousands of tons of snow and hardened ice down
over the bloody, hellish scene below. In just three minutes
all that was left was a slight, smoking depression in the
ice. The leviathan's doorway had been closed, hopefully
forever.

Alex sank back into his seat and closed his eyes. Aimee
leaned over and pulled the rough green blanket tighter
around his shoulders. He opened his eyes and smiled at
her. "Afraid I'll catch a cold?"

She laughed and shook her head. "You? Impossible."
She looked down at the ice and said, "Think that'll hold
them, Arcadian?"

Alex raised an eyebrow at her and smiled; he knew she

had a lot of questions. He turned to look down at the endless sea of ice and spoke without emotion. "The Antarctic ice is melting faster now than at any time in recorded history. Those things are chained by geology and ice, not by us. No, Aimee, I don't think that will hold them—if it ever did."

Aimee reached across and placed her fingers flat on the back of his hand, a small sigh-like yawn escaping her lips. Alex looked down at her and turned his hand over to grasp her tiny one in his, his thumb stroking her skin.

Aimee rested her head on his shoulder and closed her eyes, her lips turning up contentedly at the corners. Even with the noise of the helicopter, Alex knew in a moment she had fallen asleep. He lifted his arm and carefully folded Aimee into the blanket, kissing the top of her head as she relaxed in closer.

Alex let a long breath escape his lips, leaned back against the cabin wall and after a few more seconds he too closed his eyes; already the dark and the ice seemed a long way away.

# Epilogue

One Week Later—A World Away

Viktor Petrov climbed out of his four-poster bed, not caring whether he disturbed the sleeping thirteen-year-old prostitute or not. He smiled to himself as he pulled on his shimmering red silk robe and poured two fingers of L'Esprit de Courvoisier. From a burnished oak box inlaid with pearl, he withdrew a large Cohiba cigar—Castro's favourite, when he was well enough to smoke them.

Petrov took a large swallow of the golden liquid and chuckled. The forged documents he had purchased were the best money could buy. He had told no one of his plans, left no trail, paid by cash. "Out of your reach forever, Volkov, you little puppy."

Viktor pushed open the double doors to his balcony and listened to the sounds of a Pattayan early morning. Thailand hadn't been his first choice, but better to live like a king here than die trying to live like a prince somewhere else. He held his cigar at arm's length and breathed in all the beautiful Asian aromas—spices, dried shrimp, rotting vegetation and sex. The little Thai *dek lek* girls were plentiful here and didn't mind that he smelled or his large, hairy belly almost hid his penis.

There was a small breath on the back of his neck and Viktor half turned. Standing behind Petrov was an apparition from his worst nightmare. A giant figure clad all in black with no features but a single red lens jutting out of a full face mask.

A massive hand wrapped around Viktor's neck as the giant pulled the mask off his head. Viktor wet the front of his silk robe and his legs would have given way if not for being held in place like a puppet, his feet barely touching the floor. He whimpered as he stared into a brutal, disfigured face with a dark red hole where one eye should have been. The Beast's deep voice spoke in close to his ear, "Greetings from the president, comrade."

"I can pay more," was all Viktor could squeak out before he saw out of the corner of his eye a twelve-inch spike, thinner than a knitting needle, being raised towards his face. He heard the Russian assassin's voice once again. "An eye for an eye, *da*?"

The last living thought he had as the pick was being forced in beside his eye was that the Little Wolf had long teeth after all.

Two Weeks Later

The SS *Titan* was moving at a leisurely ten knots—well within its top speed of seventeen, even when fully laden. Like most modern tankers, the *Titan* was highly automated and computerisation meant everything ran as smoothly as a Swiss watch. The eighteen-foot single-propeller was tooled so perfectly that its rotations were just a gentle and pleasant vibration beneath their feet.

Olaf Jorgenson was a fifty-three-year-old Dutchman by birth but regarded himself as a citizen of the world's oceans. He cultivated an Ernest Hemingway look with a neatly trimmed beard and small white hat tilted back on his whitened hair. He'd heard that his crew thought he looked more like the Skipper from the old TV comedy *Gilligan's Island*, but they would never say that to his face.

They were halfway through their homeward voyage and as the ship had delivered its load the *Titan* rode high in the water. Olaf was delighted with their progress as the Southern Ocean could be a real bitch if she wanted to be. Forget about the water-level icebergs or the recent seabed tremors they had been warned about, it was the cyclonic storms that could howl around the continent that frightened the crew. The Antarctic Circle had the strongest average winds found anywhere on earth and could be a very dangerous stretch of water indeed. The *Titan* was just passing over the southernmost tip of the South Sandwich Trench; deep water, deeper than normal, at nearly 24,000 feet it was beyond the abyssal zone and descending right down to the hadal zone—cold, cold and black water.

Today the weather was calm with a steady, misty rain reducing visibility to a few hundred yards. It didn't matter; their sonar and radar were state of the art—he could have guided the ship on the darkest of nights and avoided the smallest of fishing boats.

He wasn't alone on the bridge; two of his senior officers were with him, continually checking charts in between a game of slow-motion chess. Suddenly, the sonar alarm flashed red, signalling imminent contact.

"Report, please."

"Large body contact, five-thousand-foot depth and rising at speed," his officer replied as he raced from illuminated screen to screen. Olaf knew they were over very deep water; the Southern Ocean averaged 15,000 feet—it had to be whales.

His other officer's fingers were flying over buttons and he placed some headphones over his ears. He spoke after a few seconds. "No whale song . . . and not multiple sig-natures but a single mass, a big mass. Very, very big." He typed some more commands into the computer. "Solid contact, but non-metallic. High-density materials present, but they aren't metal or any ferrous materials, more biologi-cal." His brow was furrowed.

"Three thousand feet, speed increasing. Now at fifty knots." The first officer's eyes widened as though trying to take in all the screens and images at once.

Olaf now came out of his chair. "Fifty knots, that's bullshit. Nothing travels at that speed." Olaf knew his na-val armaments and even the most sophisticated U.S. aquatic missiles, such as the Mark-50 advanced lightweight tor-pedo, could only muster forty-seven knots.

Olaf's thoughts were that there must be an error in the system and it was probably nothing more than a giant school of deep-water mackerel. However, he had been at sea long enough to know that there were many things that could never be explained away, things that only ever got whis-pered over a few drinks.

"Increase speed to full ahead. Sound general alarm and rig for impact."

The collision alarm continued wailing as the crew braced themselves at their stations. Everyone held their breath . . . waited . . . nothing. Two of the forward cameras went black.

"We're slowing." It was true, the mighty ship that mea-sured its stopping distance in nautical miles was easing down as though they had been caught in a gigantic fishing net. "Are we tangled?" Olaf asked. He turned to his first officer. "I'm going up on the foredeck to get a visual."

Olaf jogged up to the foredeck. After the warmth of the bridge, the raw cold made his ears redden and cheeks sting, and a numbing rain was heavy enough to create a fog-like effect that made any visual difficult. An acrid, burning smell assaulted his nostrils. Through the rain sheets he thought he could see a figure by the rail.

"Hello?" he called.

The figure moved towards him. He could see her clearly now.

His last conscious thought was to wonder how a young woman holding her baby had come to be on his tanker.

Read on for an excerpt from
Greig Beck's next book

# Dark Rising

Coming soon from St. Martin's Paperbacks

Red winds, the disfiguration of faces and people being swallowed into the ground. The moon is buried
in darkness and the world is folded.

Signs of the Yawm al-Qiyamah,
the Day of Judgment,
Mohammed ibn Ismail al-Bukhari (810–870)

# One

"Are you ready to witness history being written, my friend?" Mahmud Shihab appeared from the back of the canvas tent like a ghost. "*Salem Agha-ye*, Hakim," he said softly and kissed the military man on each cheek before grasping his upper arms and looking earnestly into his face. "History being written in this, the very cradle of Persian antiquity—it is fitting, yes?"

"*Salem mamnoon*, Shihab. Yes, *inshallah*, God willing." The soldier nodded and parted his dry lips in a yellow smile, showing rows of teeth stained by decades of smoking the pungent local Marlleak cigarettes.

Mahmud Shihab led Hakim to the back of the tent, where a modern metal door was embedded incongruously in the ancient stone wall. He entered a code into the recessed keypad and the heavy door swung inwards soundlessly. As Shihab escorted the military man down a dimly lit corridor carved into the interior of the ancient Persepolis ruins, a proud smile curved his lips at the thought of the design and engineering feat he had mastered beneath this once great city of the kings. Above them, its mighty stone skeleton still dominated the landscape and had survived twenty-five centuries of rain and rock-cracking heat—a powerful symbol of a time when Persia had commanded the world.

And now Shihab had been chosen to oversee a project so important that its success would shape Iran's place in the world for the next century, or perhaps even forever. The operation was codenamed Zirzamin Jamshid, The Basement of the Kings. Shihab liked the name—Jamshid was a mythical king who, legend had it, had buried his amassed treasures throughout his mighty empire. The president had chosen the name himself, and had told Shihab that there was no more valuable treasure than the capability to produce nuclear weaponry beneath the scorching earth of the Iranian desert. Shihab recalled that first meeting with the great man, his intense countenance and his softly spoken command. "Bring me success and you will bathe in riches in this life and the next." He had been too nervous to reply and had only nodded and bowed.

Hakim sneezed, interrupting Shihab's thoughts. Beneath the ruins, the temperature was pleasantly cool, but the atmosphere was dry and filled with fine powdery dust that sparkled in the cones of light thrown down from the low-wattage ceiling lamps.

Shihab smiled. "Ah, Hakim, it is impossible to keep the dust out at this level. But just think—those very particles could be all that remains of a former king or prince of Persia."

Hakim blew his nose—Persian king or not—on a dirty brown handkerchief. He had just pushed it back into his pocket when they came to a steel miner's cage floored with thick rubberised matting. They entered the cage and Shihab pushed the single smooth lever to the downward position. The cage dropped silently into the darkness. Shihab smiled with pride, counting the passing layers of toughened concrete and lead shielding. The facility was all his own design, built to give off as small an energy signature as was possible. He knew full well the capabilities of the U.S. spy satellites—high-resolution digital images were only one of their talents. These days they could sniff out heat, power and radiation signatures to fifty feet below the surface. So the Iranians needed to be careful, needed to go deeper.

After many minutes, the cage slowed with a hiss and stopped at a darkened corridor and a fortified steel door, considerably stronger than the one they had come through at the surface. Shihab entered another code and hidden rollers pulled the large metal slab out of the way. He closed his eyes briefly as a blast of negative air pressure rushed past him, only opening them when he perceived strong light on his eyelids. Before them was a chamber of almost surgical whiteness.

Shihab and Hakim knew what was expected, having performed this ritual many times. They both sat on the benches provided and removed their shoes. From a recessed cupboard they drew out particle-free garments, donned lightweight polymer all-over suits, pulled rubber-soled shoes over their feet, and used a small towel lightly moistened with demineralised water to wipe their faces, neck and hands.

When Hakim had finished, Shihab clipped a small radiation badge to the soldier's breast pocket. "They're the latest—each one contains a small sheet of radiation-sensitive aluminum oxide. When it's exposed to radiation, the tag shines with a visible blue glow. We all have to wear them now. Let's hope they don't shine for us today, yes?"

The two men moved to the facility's final access stage: a glass booth with another metal door beyond. The entry requirements here were far more stringent—as well as keying in a numeric code, Shihab had to lick his thumb and place it over a small mesh circle on the entry pad. Fingerprints and DNA were obtained, scanned and verified before the curved glass door slid back. Anyone trying to access the facility without proper authorisation would find himself locked in the chamber as it rapidly filled with lethal tabun gas. Clear and odourless, the gas immediately shut down the human nervous system, and then just as quickly dissipated, allowing safe removal of any bodies.

Red lights turned green and the metal door hissed open. Shihab entered first, then stood aside, allowing his companion to see the progress achieved since his last visit to the Jamshid I facility.

They were in a round, gleaming laboratory, 500 feet from one end to the other with a ceiling height of at least another 100 feet. The walls were covered in banks of computers and monitors, all online and glowing gold or green. The entire area was a sea of electronic chattering and blinking lights, save for one large window overseeing the chamber.

Shihab gestured towards the centre of the circular laboratory. "This is it, my friend, the sphere. This day will mark the first steps in the rise of the new Persian caliphate. *Allahu Akbar.*"

"*Allahu Akbar,*" Hakim repeated automatically.

Shihab watched Hakim's face as he stared at the giant silver orb that looked like the planet Saturn. It was fifty feet around and circled by a waist-thick polished cylinder.

"It is magnificent, Mahmud, you are to be praised," Hakim said as he slowly moved his eyes over the strange device, and then around the chamber.

Dozens of Iranian, German and North Korean scientists buzzed around the banks of computer monitors and the sphere itself, preparing for the first live test of the device. One of the Germans, a tall, bespectacled man with a blond toothbrush moustache, gave Hakim the thumbs-up. Rudolf Hoeckler was being paid a Persian fortune to bring the laser-enrichment technology models to working status. Shihab knew that Hakim disapproved of mountains of Iranian money being paid to anyone from the West, but it was difficult not to like the tall German. Hoeckler was in a constant good humour and had made amusing attempts to learn Farsi.

"Blue hair eels in the morning, Herr Hakim," Hoeckler said now with a grin, obviously pleased with himself for mastering yet another phrase in their language.

Shihab chuckled and took Hakim by the arm to lead him towards a small set of steel steps. "We're just about ready," he said. "Let's go up to the observation room and have some tea. We have been requested to call the president the moment we have the results."

Shihab handed Hakim a small, gold-rimmed glass of the steaming local tea. He knew that after the dry of the desert, the soldier's mouth would be watering in anticipation. "You know, my friend, a successful production run today will be good for both of us, *inshallah*."

Shihab hoped the test run's success would not benefit the soldier *too* much. He liked Hakim's quiet presence and his stay-out-of-the-way approach to managing the security of the site. A big promotion would mean reassignment, and the facility may end up with a more intrusive guard. Shihab would take one Hakim over a hundred of those psychopathic Revolutionary Guard any day.

He put down his cup and wiped his hands down his sides; it was nearly time. On the computer screen nearby, a single line of ten glowing circles were all green except for one—and then this too changed to green, indicating a positive *all systems go* sequence. Shihab started the image recording of the laboratory floor and commenced the data transfer program to distribute the information back to their sister facility. The second site was a few months behind Jamshid I, so if anything went catastrophically wrong with this test they would learn from those mistakes. *Please, oh merciful Allah, don't let there be any mistakes*, Shihab prayed.

He keyed in a few commands and the overhead lights in the laboratory dimmed. The technicians and scientists pulled protective visors over their eyes and the observation window darkened to deflect any laser scattering. Shihab pressed the microphone switch down and his voice echoed over the floor of the chamber. "Is everyone ready?"

He scanned the floor for any dissent, and licked dry, nervous lips. Hoeckler turned and smiled. Shihab felt a bead of perspiration run down beside his left ear. He drew in a deep breath, feeling his heart thump sickeningly in his chest.

"*Allahu Akbar*," he whispered as he entered the final codes and made a single stroke on the keyboard.

An infernal shriek tore through the laboratory and permeated the thickened glass as if it were paper. In the centre of the laboratory, where the sphere had stood, there was now a blackness darker than night. At its core was a pinprick of nothingness that hurt Shihab's eyes. He felt as if he were caught in a thick mucus that trapped his limbs. Time slowed, or perhaps stretched and a cold darkness spread out into the laboratory. It was the only thing moving; everyone else seemed frozen in time too. As Shihab watched, he realised to his horror that the growing mass of darkness was absorbing everything in its path. He watched helplessly as the bodies of his colleagues elongated and then began to tear as they were pulled towards that dark curtain of space.

His eyes briefly met those of Herr Hoeckler for a second—or perhaps it was for an eternity—before the large man was engulfed, his body stretched into a plume of flesh-coloured streamers.

*We all died when I pressed that final key*, he thought, *and now we are in hell*.

From the corner of his frozen vision, Mahmud Shihab saw his friend Hakim become a long white streak as he was dragged mercilessly into the void. And then his sanity left him as he saw his own tongue and the lining of his throat distend from his body and rush towards hellish oblivion.

# Two

"What the fu—" Corporal Marcs scooted his office chair
across the floor of his horseshoe-shaped booth to replay
what he had just seen on one of his screens. "Holy shit.
Major, you gotta see this! VELA just picked up a whale
of a radiation spike from the Middle East."

Offutt Air Force Base was one of the most strategi-
cally placed and defensible military bases in the world,
home to the Strategic Air Command, the 55th Wing and
also the primary hub of the United States military network-
centric space command. Its role was to manage the con-
stellation of military hardware orbiting the planet and
oversee the billions of bits of information received from
their flock of extremely attentive high-orbit birds. Normally
the command centre was a place of professional calm. Today all hell was about to break loose.

"What the hell are they doing?" Marcs went on. "This is
strong gamma—just gamma—where's the rest of the radiation package? Is this a detonation?"

Major Gerry Harris was instantly at the corporal's
shoulder. A brilliant military specialist, Harris had been
heading up the space command centre for the past eighteen months. His background in physics and information

technology were the perfect credentials needed to understand and manage the complex information received by the satellites and translated by the sophisticated computer applications. But these signatures defied logic; they refused to make sense even to his analytical mind. The advanced VELA satellites used radio-frequency sensors to detect electromagnetic pulse prints and could measure the strength of high-intensity ionising radiation even from high orbit. If there was a higher than naturally occurring radiation signature across the X-ray, alpha- or beta-particle, neutron or gamma-ray spectrum, a VELA would see and taste it. But these pulses? Their sudden appearance and strength made them seem almost non-terrestrial.

"Can't be a detonation," Harris said. "These guys shouldn't even have fission capability yet. And if it's some sort of subsurface nuclear test, why aren't there any seismic signatures—and why are we seeing this single particle in such concentrations?"

Harris paced for a moment, then started yelling commands across the floor to his technicians. "I need all our birds with digital, thermal and ground-penetrating imaging capabilities looking at these coordinates now!"

Then he reached for the phone on Corporal Marcs' desk. "Get me General Chilton," he said. "ASAP."

Frank and Lorraine Beckett had been driving in stony silence for the past hour. They had left the Interstate at the Limon hub after sharing soggy, coffee-flavoured peanut butter sandwiches and disintegrating donuts—apparently Lorraine had left the top loose on the goddamn thermos, yet again.

Both in their mid-fifties and comfortably stout after years of double-portion dinners and chocolate candy in front of the TV, the Becketts were making a once-in-a-lifetime road trip, from their home in Knoxville weaving all the way to Santa Barbara on the West Coast. It was a joint gift to each other to celebrate their twenty-fifth wedding anniversary, but what had seemed like a magical and exciting idea when they planned it was turning out to be days on end of featureless highways, frightening-looking hitchhikers and roadside motels with orange and brown décor that should have been put out of its misery in the mid-seventies. To really ice the cake, Lorraine's stomach was acting up again and Frank was threatening that if she let loose one more fart in the car he was going to leave her at the next bus stop.

*Praise the Lord*, he thought. Just one more hour on Highway 24 and they'd be in Colorado Springs—which meant warm showers, a nap before dinner and maybe even some plain, home-style food that would help slay the dragon making war in the pit of that damn woman's stomach.

The flat purple-grey highway cut through the dry and scrubby landscape like a new zipper down an old canvas sheet. Frank was starting to get his good mood back, and was about to break the silence by telling his wife a bad joke when the car died. Everything just stopped at once. Frank coasted the car to a halt, frantically pushing buttons and stamping on pedals.

"Did you see that, Frank?" Lorraine said, pointing through the front windscreen. "The sky seemed to shimmer slightly, like we were driving through a curtain of oil." She touched her fingers to her face and they came away slick and bright red. "Frank, I'm bleeding."

Frank noticed that his nose was streaming blood too. "Outta the freakin' car!" he said. He didn't want them soiling the beautiful leather seats with bloodstains. There would be a nasty amount to fork out on the insurance if there was even minor interior damage.

The dry prairie air assaulted their senses and made

them grimace after the Suburban's air conditioning. Lorraine staggered and her face looked slick and waxy with shock.

As Frank went round to swing the car hood open, he spotted something lying on the road ahead. "What the hell's that? That weren't there before."

"Is it a deer?" burbled Lorraine through a handful of blood-stained tissues.

The clouds were moving rapidly across the flat land all around, and as they slowly approached the mass, a long shaft of yellow sunshine illuminated the lump on the road. It looked meaty and slightly moist. Frank had to will himself to take a step forward; his animal instincts were screaming at him to get the hell out of there.

Lorraine held Frank's arm and remained slightly behind his left shoulder as they neared the strange organic mess. "Oh my god, Frank, what is that?" she whispered.

Slight tics and squeaks emanated from the lump, and as they got closer they realised that the sounds were caused by the mass thawing in the sun—a sparkling coat of frost dripped, twinkling onto the road surface. Frank knitted his brows; the thing seemed to be sprouting up from the hard black tarmac. Not pushing up through it exactly, just . . . stuck.

"This can't be real," he said. "It's some kind of sick joke."

Half of the mass looked like a man wearing a white laboratory coat, but the other half was stretched out like elongated taffy. It looked like plastic that had been heated and then frozen solid again. The face was wet-raw, like the skin under a blister, and where the eyes should have been were just hollow, ragged sockets. The mouth was intact, and above it a blond toothbrush moustache twinkled with ice crystals. But what really made Frank's stomach lurch was the pink organic matter that protruded between the bared teeth like a veined, deflated bag. It had to be the guy's lungs—pulled or blown out.

Lorraine staggered to the side of the road and vomited. "Frank, I'm bleeding inside!" she screamed. The mess of digested bread and donuts was streaked with blood.

Frank went to her, blinking rapidly to clear his stinging eyes. But it wasn't tears running down his cheeks, it was blood. When Lorraine saw him, she started to cry.

Frank sat down heavily next to his wife. "I don't feel well, Lainey."

He looked over at the creature again and noticed something he hadn't seen when he was standing above it. On the pocket of the lab coat was a small badge that was pulsing with a soft blue light.

# Three

Major Jack "Hammer" Hammerson shouldered open the
heavy panelled door of his office and headed straight for
a hulking oak desk near the back wall. The impressive
piece had once stood in front of the enormous set of double
windows that dominated the room, but old warrior habits
die hard and the Hammer never liked to have his back to a
door or window. The desk, like most things the Hammer
bumped up against, had to give way.

Major Hammerson was one of the hard men of the military. His face could never be called friendly; its deep clefts
and creases hinted at too much outdoor living and quite a
bit of blunt-force trauma. You didn't need to read the major's background files to know he could incapacitate an enemy in less than seven seconds. Hammerson headed up the
elite Hotzone All-Forces Warfare Commandos—HAWCs,
for short. His uniform, except for rank, was insignia free.
His only identification was a plastic card with a barcode and
the lightning bolts and fisted gauntlet of the U.S. Strategic
Command.

Major Hammerson and his special unit had been reas-
signed to USSTRATCOM eighteen months ago, and it

seemed a good fit. The United States Strategic Command was one of the ten unified combatant commands of the United States Department of Defense. They controlled the nuclear weapons assets of the U.S. military and were a globally focused command charged with the missions of Space Operations, Integrated Missile Defence, Combating Weapons of Mass Destruction, and Other Special Operations. The "Other Special Operations" was where Hammer and his HAWCs came in.

Normally a blunt and brusque man, today the major was in a great mood. In just over three weeks, and for the first time in five years, he would be fly-fishing in the land of the midnight sun. He was taking two weeks off to camp out in a little place he knew up high on the Kenai River bend in Alaska, where the tides from Cook Inlet washed in the biggest king salmon found anywhere in the world. Biting cold air that made the breath fog, and water so clear you could see the pebbles on the bottom at near any depth. Hammerson sighed and rubbed his large hands together. Just a few curious grizzlies for company and the odd bald eagle watching suspiciously from overhead. He knew that a record ninety-seven-pounder had been caught in those parts, and he reckoned there was a hundred-pounder with his name on it.

The Hammer was practising long, slow casting motions across his desk when the phone rang. He hit the receive button on the console and barked a curt "Hammerson" while still jerking on an imaginary rod. When he heard the deep voice on the line, he sat forward immediately and picked up the handset.

"Sir."

He listened with the intensity he always gave the highest-level mission briefings. His face was like stone, the only movement his eyes narrowing slightly.

"I agree, that size pulse could signify weaponability," he said. "Yes, something a little more surgically precise would be best. We can be ready in twenty-four hours, sir."

There was a click as the connection was severed. Hammerson held the phone in the air for a second before replacing it softly in its cradle. Time to reactivate the Arcadian.